THE EVENTS IN THIS BOOK ARE REAL.

NAMES AND PLACES HAVE BEEN CHANGED
TO PROTECT THE LORIEN,
WHO REMAIN IN HIDING.

OTHER CIVILIZATIONS DO EXIST.

SOME OF THEM SEEK TO DESTROY YOU.

THE LORIEN ▭ LEGACIES

BY PITTACUS LORE

Novels

I AM NUMBER FOUR

THE POWER OF SIX

THE RISE OF NINE

THE FALL OF FIVE

THE REVENGE OF SEVEN

THE FATE OF TEN

The Lost Files Novellas

#1: SIX'S LEGACY

#2: NINE'S LEGACY

#3: THE FALLEN LEGACIES

#4: THE SEARCH FOR SAM

#5: THE LAST DAYS OF LORIEN

#6: THE FORGOTTEN ONES

#7: FIVE'S LEGACY

#8: RETURN TO PARADISE

#9: FIVE'S BETRAYAL

#10: THE FUGITIVE

#11: THE NAVIGATOR

#12: THE GUARD

#13: LEGACIES REBORN

The Lost Files Novella Collections

THE LEGACIES
(Contains novellas #1–#3)

SECRET HISTORIES
(Contains novellas #4–#6)

HIDDEN ENEMY
(Contains novellas #7–#9)

REBEL ALLIES
(Contains novellas #10–#12)

I AM NUMBER FOUR
THE LOST FILES
REBEL ALLIES

PITTACUS LORE

HARPER
An Imprint of HarperCollinsPublishers

I Am Number Four: The Lost Files: Rebel Allies

I Am Number Four: The Lost Files: The Fugitive © 2015 by Pittacus Lore

I Am Number Four: The Lost Files: The Navigator © 2015 by Pittacus Lore

I Am Number Four: The Lost Files: The Guard © 2015 by Pittacus Lore

www.epicreads.com

ISBN 978-0-06-236404-3

Typography by Ray Shappell

15 16 17 18 19   CG/RRDH   10 9 8 7 6 5 4 3 2 1

❖

First Edition

CONTENTS

I AM NUMBER FOUR

NUMBER

FOUR THE LOST FILES

THE FUGITIVE

CHAPTER ONE

YOU'RE AN IDIOT, MARK JAMES.

This is the thought that screams through my head every one hundred miles or so on the road when I have a moment of self-doubt. Or maybe it's a moment of clarity? I don't really know which. But when I face the facts—that I've stolen an FBI agent's laptop, pissed off some evil aliens and am now driving across the country in order to try to find my missing ex-girlfriend, Sarah, who happens to be dating a *good* alien—I can't help but think it's true. I'm an idiot. Or I'm crazy. Or both.

Whatever I am, it's too late to go back to being who I was before aliens blew up my school and took over my town. Not too long ago I was hot shit at Paradise High, with a bright future ahead of me. Now I'm the dude who's wanted by government agencies and bad ETs from the planet Shark-Face.

I down an energy drink and crush the can in my

fist, tossing it to the passenger seat floorboard, where it finds a home with a bunch of its empty brothers. I've been on the road for about nineteen hours, and I didn't exactly start on a full night's sleep. The only thing keeping me going is a mixture of adrenaline, worrying about Sarah and what are probably enough energy drinks to kill an elephant. One glance in the rearview mirror tells me I'm way overdue for sleep, my eyes all bloodshot and dark looking, but I don't have time to take things easy. Sarah's in Dulce—or at least, that's what the email I read on the stolen FBI laptop said. Before I tried to access a file called "MogPro," and the whole computer shut down. Now, the computer won't even turn on. It's just sitting on my back floorboard, wrapped in my letter jacket.

I try not to think about what the FBI or the Mogs might be doing to Sarah. I can hardly even wrap my head around the fact that the FBI—or at least the agents in Paradise—are working with the aliens. Instead, I focus on the fact that I'm on my way to bust her out . . . somehow. After a few more hours of empty roads on my fifteen-hundred-miles-in-one-day journey from Ohio to New Mexico, I'll be there to try to save her. Me. Alone. Against a bunch of pale-ass aliens and probably the FBI, NSA and the Illuminati or whatever.

My phone dings—a burner, one I bought at a truck stop an hour outside of Paradise. The sound reminds me that I'm not *technically* alone on my mission to save Sarah. There's someone helping me. He's the only person who has this number.

I look at the text.

GUARD: Getting close to the NM border?

I glance up to see a sign on the side of the road telling me that Colorado State Highway 17 will turn into New Mexico State Highway 17 in ten miles. GUARD has been weirdly good at guessing where I'm at since I've been on the road.

I text him back, saying I'm about ten minutes out. Almost as soon as the message goes through, I get another ding.

GUARD: Gas station on the NM side of the border. On the right. Pull off there: I've got some stuff for you.

My brain basically explodes when I read this. I'm actually going to be face-to-face with GUARD: head conspiracy theorist at the They Walk Among Us website, hacker extraordinaire and kind of my only friend now that Sarah's gone. Even though I've never met him. Even though I've never even talked to him on the phone because he's as obsessed with his own privacy as he is with the Mogadorians and Loric.

Okay, so maybe we aren't friends, exactly. I guess we're more like partners in all this alien shit. He's the computer brains, and I'm the good-looking brawn who's going to save the girl and then figure out a way to keep what happened in Paradise from going down anywhere else.

The idea of being face-to-face with GUARD sends my thoughts into overdrive as I start imagining us pulling some badass action-movie moves while we storm the alien base in Dulce. Liberating anyone who's been taken hostage by the Mogs in a montage of explosions. Then the pounding in my chest starts to drum faster, and I remember that this is real life, no matter how strange it all seems. I think of the huge Mog dude I saw while I was acting like a spy at the police station in Paradise. He was a black-eyed giant, built like a professional linebacker. He easily had two hundred pounds on me and was probably packing all kinds of alien weapons. Then I think back to all the gross-as-shit Mogs we faced at the school. I mean, I managed to fight my way out of that whole mess and protected Sarah in the process, but the idea of going up against those guys again makes me want to turn around and head back home.

I crank up the radio and tell myself it'll all work out.

I'll be okay. I'll save Sarah. GUARD and I will do it together. He'll know what to do.

It's two in the morning when I cross the border from Colorado into New Mexico. Sure enough, there's an old-looking gas station at the first exit. This time of night, the place looks deserted.

It's only as I turn into the station that my head throbs and I wonder if I'm in danger for some reason. But that's impossible. I've been supercareful, and God knows GUARD isn't going to screw up on his end when it comes to flying under the radar. I still feel uneasy, though.

I blame the sudden paranoia on my lack of sleep.

I park at one of the pumps because it's the only place that's lit up, loud industrial lights buzzing overhead. Being under the light makes everything else seem that much darker, so I flash my headlights twice, half to get a better look at the area around me and half because I've seen enough movies about gangs and secret meetings to know this is sometimes a sign. No one appears, though, so I jump out and start to gas up since I'm already stopped, keeping my eyes on the lookout for any movement.

I'm five gallons in when a tall figure emerges from the darkness of the side of the station.

"GUARD?" I call out.

The figure doesn't answer, which isn't exactly a good sign.

I suddenly wish I had a weapon other than my

throwing arm—a perfect pass isn't going to protect me if this dude's a Mog. My heart beats so loud I'm guessing the other person can hear it over the buzzing lights. I clutch my fingers around the gas pump. If things go bad for me, maybe I can hose the dude down and throw him off balance long enough to make a break for it.

Fortunately, I luck out. It's obvious from the moment the person steps into the light that she's no Mog. First off, I don't even know if there *are* Mog women. Secondly, she's dark skinned, unlike any Mog I've seen. She doesn't exactly scream FBI either. She's got on a motorcycle helmet that leaves just her face exposed. Between that and the form-fitting leather jacket, I'm guessing she's got a bike stashed on the other side of the gas station. I can't get too relieved, though, because she looks like she's pissed off as she approaches. That's when I notice there's a box under one of her arms. I keep my hand on the gas pump.

I don't realize she's taller than me—by about a head—until she's a few yards away. I don't think I've ever met a girl who's made me feel so short. Actually, she's not really a *girl*. I'm guessing she's in her midthirties, but with the crappy light and her helmet, it's hard to tell exactly.

"Uh . . . ," I murmur. I don't really know what to say. "I'm not sure . . ."

"Jolly Roger?" she asks.

It takes me a second to answer because no one's ever called me that in real life. Hell, I don't think I've ever even said the words out loud. Technically I *am* JOLLY-ROGER182, at least when I'm blogging on They Walk Among Us.

"Yeah?" I ask, as if it's a question.

I'm still trying to wrap my head around what's happening when she pushes the box into my chest.

"Sign here," she says, holding a pen out to me with one hand and pointing to a sheet of paper on top of the box with another.

I do as I'm told, only halfway registering the courier service listed at the top of the page. Sure enough, the package is intended for Jolly Roger. This must be GUARD's way of keeping my real name out of the equation, which is smart, I guess. Still, I can't help but be bummed that he sent a courier instead of coming to the station himself.

I thought I was finally going to meet GUARD. I thought we were going to team up.

The woman keeps her eyes focused on me. Not blinking. Her intensity creeps me out a little bit, keeping me from wallowing too much in the fact that GUARD's not here.

She takes the page back after I've signed for the package but keeps staring at me, like her dark-brown eyes are trying to read my mind. Finally she speaks.

"You should get off the road and get some sleep." Her voice is stern, more of a command than a suggestion. "You look like shit."

And then she walks back off into the darkness.

I fling open my truck door and get in, tearing into the box. I pull out all kinds of stuff I don't recognize: computer equipment, maps, little electronic gadgets. There's a smartphone in the box, along with a stack of cash that's got to be at least a grand. There's even a black, padded messenger bag—I'm guessing to carry all this stuff around in.

What is going on?

Suddenly, the phone's screen comes to life, powering on. After a few seconds, a text message pops up.

GUARD: Thought you could use some supplies. Instructions are on the phone. Careful: they'll self-delete after you've read them. Good luck. -G

GUARD sent me a care package.

There's no return address on the box. I jump out of the truck cab, but it's too late—I can already hear the whine of the courier's bike fading away somewhere down the highway.

The gas pump clicks. I'm about to pack everything back into the box when I notice one last item at the bottom of it. I pick it up: a metal cylinder about half an inch wide and four inches tall that's covered in weird markings I've never seen before. Near the top is what appears to be a button. There's a Post-it note attached that has "do not press me" written on it. I'm suddenly afraid I'm holding some sort of next-gen bomb.

Looking back and forth between the possible weapon and the stack of cash, one big question is louder than all the others going through my head: Who the *fuck* is GUARD?

CHAPTER
TWO

I PACK EVERYTHING UP AND GET BACK ON THE highway—I'm only a few hours from Dulce, and now that I have a bunch of weird gadgets and cash, the last place I want to be is parked out in the open under the lights of a gas station. So I drive, fighting the urge to go over all the notes on the smartphone. Once I get close to where the secret Dulce base is supposed to be located, I give in and pull off to the side of the road to get my shit together. I can't exactly charge into a secret government base and demand to talk to Sarah Hart. I start by taking a full inventory of the stuff GUARD sent me, carefully reading the notes on the new phone, which I'm supposed to use to communicate with my unseen partner now.

Most of the stuff in the box seems to be computer related. There's a little netbook that's got a stealthy Wi-Fi hotspot installed inside that will bounce my location to satellites around the world, making anything I do impossible to track. That way I'll be able to communicate with people and upload stuff to They Walk Among Us without worrying about a bunch of black helicopters swooping in on me. There's also a USB drive that's supposed to help get the FBI computer I swiped up and running again—GUARD thinks that the files I saw disappearing before the screen went black may still be hidden somewhere on the hard drive. The trigger-looking thing covered in weird symbols *is* some kind of cutting-edge grenade. GUARD says it should only be used in a life-or-death situation. All I have to do is press the button on top and throw. There's no explanation as to what it actually *does* or what the symbols mean. They don't look like any alphabet I've ever seen, and I can't help but wonder if GUARD somehow managed to snag an alien weapon.

I kind of wish he'd also sent along a laser pistol or something.

The cash is self-explanatory. Well, not really. The fact that GUARD would just up and send fifteen hundred dollars—I counted—to someone he *sorta* knows makes me wonder if he's actually some kind of hacker billionaire operating out of a secret lair that looks like something out of *The Matrix*.

I shove everything into the messenger bag, including my old burner phone. As cool as all the gadgets are, the most helpful thing in the box for me right now is the stack of satellite images and blueprints of the Dulce base. All the maps I found online showed nothing but desert where it should have been, but the stuff GUARD sent is comprehensive, laying out the big-ass complex and giving me a good idea of the size of the thing and where I might be able to sneak in. There are even blueprints of what the underground levels of the place might look like.

It's intimidating as hell.

Flipping through the maps, I don't know how I'm going to be able to find Sarah in this mess. She could be anywhere. She might not even *be* there anymore. My body feels like it's sinking in on itself as I consider how impossible this mission is. How stupid I am for thinking I can just waltz in and rescue her.

I crack open another energy drink, guzzling it.

Man up, Mark.

I put my truck into gear and get back on the road. I'll have a better idea of what my plan should be once I get there. Surely.

After about fifteen minutes of driving, I take an unmarked side road that's circled on the maps GUARD sent. The base shouldn't be that far now. I turn off my lights and drive slowly. There's just enough moonlight for me to sort of be able to see. For a few minutes, I see nothing but hilly desert in front of me, but then I finally spot a tall chain-link fence in the distance that's topped in razor wire.

That's got to be it.

There doesn't appear to be any gate or path leading to the base perimeter, so I say a quick prayer, blow a kiss to the dashboard of my truck and off-road through the desert, trying my best to avoid any big shrubs or rocks and pretending not to worry about the fact that, for all I know, there could be mines and stuff all around out here.

But there aren't any. Or at least I don't hit any of them. Instead, I get within a few yards of the fence and park. Just in case there are hidden cameras around, I fish a baseball cap out of the back of my truck and pull it down low, trying to hide my face as much as I can.

The fence is at least three times as tall as I am, and I can't see most of the base because of a mesa or hill or whatever that hides it. There aren't any lights on—or at least not outside. I wish I'd thought to buy night-vision goggles or that GUARD had sent some along. I squint, trying to make out what all the dark shapes are in the moonlight. It looks like there are burned-out Humvees and other kinds of military vehicles littering the desert around the base. From what I can tell, something crazy definitely went down here recently. Something *epic*.

It reminds me of Paradise and the way my school looked after John, Henri, Six—after we'd *all* fought and escaped from the Mogs. This is the kind of shit that happens when good aliens and bad aliens collide. Were the Garde here? Was John Smith here? Maybe Sarah doesn't even need saving anymore.

But she would have contacted me if she were free, right? And what if dumbass John and his other ET friends *did* try to save Sarah but got captured?

What if I'm the only person left to bail *them* out?

I have to get in there. Now.

"Okay, Mark," I say. "Time to save the day."

I walk beside the fence for a few minutes, trying to see more of the base while at the same time wondering if I've got anything in my truck that might be able to snip a hole in the chain length. But I luck out, because I get to a section of the fence that's been knocked down— maybe even blown apart, judging by the mangled little pieces of metal littering the ground.

That's my entrance.

I think about going back to the truck to grab the grenade thing GUARD sent with me, but I'm kind of scared that it'd go off in my pocket accidentally since its trigger is apparently just a *button*. Probably the lamest possible outcome of the night would be me trying to be a hero and blowing myself up instead, leaving Sarah all alone in a cell.

So instead, I take a deep breath and step through the hole in the fence.

Once I'm inside the perimeter of the base, I jog towards some of the wreckage dotting the desert hills and look for a way to access the main facility, which, according to GUARD's maps, is mostly located underground. I try to stay low and out of sight, hiding behind half-crumbled walls and wishing I'd thought to buy darker clothes since my white T-shirt probably makes me stand out in the darkness. But I keep moving, eventually crouching behind what looks like a collapsed watchtower.

What the hell happened here?

Some of the buildings and vehicles around the main facility look like they've exploded—all scorched and burned-out—while others appear to have been blown apart by some other force. Maybe telekinesis? Maybe John or the other Garde really were here? The place looks completely vacant. Decommissioned. Half of my brain says I should just forget about trying to find a way inside and go back to my truck since it looks like there's no way a major FBI or Mog operation could still be working out of this broken-down base. But I can't do that. I've come too far. And if there's any chance that Sarah is still inside . . .

I think I see a shadow move out of the corner of my eye. I hold my breath and stand frozen for what feels like a long time, trying to figure out if there's anyone around—squinting in the moonlight. But there's nothing. The wind whistles, and I exhale.

I run to one of the charred Humvees, staying close to the ground, and roll behind it. In movies, spies and badass cops are always rolling behind cover, but all this does is get sand all over me and in my eyes. I try not to cough as I blink for half a minute, telling myself not to be a douche bag and try to pull any fancy moves anymore. I just have to get in, find Sarah and get out.

I spot my entry point. There's a bunch of debris lying around a pit about twenty yards away from me where it looks like the ground has collapsed into some kind of sinkhole. I can just make out a few walls and stuff below—the hole must lead straight down into the facility. All I have to do is jump down and I'm in, no locks to try to get past or anything.

Whatever battle took place here has given me a perfect way into the facility.

I start for the hole, keeping my eyes peeled for any movement. I'm halfway between it and the Humvee when a blinding light appears from somewhere to my right.

Shit.

My eyes burn, and I can barely see as I try to run back to the Humvee to take cover. But then there's another light that looks like it's coming from on top of the wreckage. And then there are lights everywhere, stunning me, making it impossible for me to even know which direction I'm facing anymore. I'm not sure if this is some kind of defense system or if I'm about to be beamed up to a Mog ship or something. My head spins, and I start to hyperventilate, completely regretting not bringing the grenade with me.

A figure emerges from the light, silhouetted. I can't make out a face or anything. Can't tell if it's even a human or a Mog. I plant my feet and clench my fists.

If this is my last stand, I have to make it count for something. I shout the first thing that comes to my mind.

"I've come for Sa—"

But before I can finish the sentence, someone attacks me from behind, and there's fabric over my head. Everything goes dark. I swing around, flailing wildly, but I'm struggling against a bunch of people, and before I know it, my hands are cuffed in front of me.

I've made a big mistake.

I'm dragged through the sand until I'm inside some kind of building, my feet kicking against a hard floor. I struggle and shout the whole time, but no one says anything to me. It's like they can't even hear me. Not until they start pushing me down some stairs and one of them threatens to Tase me if I don't shut up. So I do.

The bag over my head is scratchy against my face, and the air inside is thick with my rapid breathing. The more I think about what's happening, the faster and deeper my breath gets, until I'm sucking a bunch of fabric into my mouth every time I inhale.

I'm afraid I'm going to die here. I'm going to be Mog food. Or I'm going to end up a human lab rat. My parents will never know what happened to me. I'm going to become an unsolved case, just some good-looking dude with an all-American past as Ohio's greatest quarterback that ends up on a bunch of MISSING posters for a while.

You're an idiot, Mark.

Someone forces me into a chair and rips the bag off my head. The lights are way too bright, and I wince. I try to cover my eyes with my cuffed hands when I realize they've been chained to the center of a metal desk in front of me. I pull against them with all my strength, but there's no way I'm breaking free.

I am in way over my head.

I look around frantically. The room is small and looks empty except for the high-powered lamp shining right in my face. There's nothing in here but me, the desk and the light.

And a voice.

"Mark James," a woman says.

It's a voice I sort of recognize but can't really place. I hear a few footsteps from somewhere behind the light and squint as the woman comes into view.

And then I realize why I know her. She has red hair

pulled back in a severe ponytail. One of her arms is in a sling, peeking out from underneath her black jacket. She couldn't look more pissed off.

"Agent Walker?" I ask.

She sighs and raises her good arm to her face. She closes her eyes and rubs one temple.

"You're a real pain in the ass, kid," she says, shaking her head.

CHAPTER THREE

IT'S ODDLY COMFORTING TO SEE AGENT WALKER instead of a Mog, but I'm not sure how much of a lucky break it is since she's sneering at me. After being dragged into the base with a bag over my head, I can't stop my hands from shaking. The chains around my wrists keep jingling.

It's some kind of cosmic joke that she's the one here, like I've traveled all this way but ended up exactly where I started. I try to think back to the last time I saw her, when she came to my grandmother's house asking about Sarah—the morning I found out she was missing. Walker had been her steely self, but there'd been a moment or two in our conversation when it had actually seemed like she was letting her hard-ass persona slip and was acting like a real human. Someone who cared about the fact that the girl she'd been keeping a "protective watch" over had disappeared. She seemed . . . sympathetic.

But I have no idea how much of the Mog Kool-Aid she's been drinking since then, and I know I can't count on her to cut me any slack. I'm in trouble for trespassing, but there's a chance that she doesn't know anything about the computer I swiped yet. There's still a chance I can talk my way out of this.

Maybe.

"Uh, hi," I say. I raise my hands to wave, but all that does is remind both of us that I'm chained to the table.

"What the hell are you doing here?" she asks. Her voice sounds like she's equally pissed and impressed, so at least I have that last bit going for me.

"I'm on vacation," I say. I'm painfully aware of how lame of an excuse this is, so I keep talking. "Well, not vacation, really. The University of Arizona offered me a football scholarship, so I'm on my way down there and figured I'd stop and check out this base I'd heard about on *Ancient ETs* or one of those shows and—"

"Don't try to bullshit me, Mark," she says. "You're terrible at it."

I try to laugh.

"No, no. I'm just a little on edge because of all the black bags and stuff, you know? This place looked abandoned from the outside. I didn't think anyone was here."

Her smile comes back. The one she always had in

Paradise. The fake one that says, *No matter what you may think, I'm the one in charge here.*

"Right," she says. "I'm sure your nervousness has nothing to do with, oh, I don't know—a stolen FBI computer?"

Well, so much for trying to charm my way out of this. I'm screwed. I'm in so far over my head that I can barely breathe. This fact must register on my face, because she keeps talking.

"Do you have any idea what the punishment for stealing classified intel like that is?"

"I don't know what you're talking about," I mutter. My voice actually cracks a little, like I'm a damned thirteen-year-old. I clear my throat and try to regroup.

She shakes her head.

"Why did you come here?"

"I told you, Arizona State—"

"Earlier you said University of Arizona. We both know that's not true."

I try to remain calm.

"I should probably call someone to let them know I'm here," I say, trying to remember all the rules of due process I learned from my dad over the years. "If you're arresting me for trespassing, I still get a phone call, right? And shouldn't I have a lawyer or something here too?"

At this, she starts to laugh. It starts out genuine, like

I've just told the best joke she's ever heard, but by the time it dies down, the laughter is sad.

"Start talking," she finally says, "or I'm going to have to bring in someone less understanding than me to interrogate you."

We stare at each other. At this point, I figure there's no harm in telling her the truth. Or at least some of it. I have nothing else to lose.

"I'm here for Sarah," I say. "I know you took her."

Walker purses her lips. She keeps her eyes trained on me. I swear she hasn't blinked since I sat down.

"And you think Sarah is here because of something you read on the computer you stole?"

"You were supposed to be protecting her," I say, raising my voice. All I can think of now is how much Walker and her fellow agents lied to us in Paradise. How they watched us, worked with the Mogs—how they took my dad's job away from him and kidnapped the only person who was keeping me sane. "Isn't that the bullshit you told me and Sarah? That you were going to make sure nothing bad happened to us? I should have known you were all working for the damned Mogs and—"

Walker slams her fist down on the table between us. I shut up. She lets out a long breath and then starts to pace around the room.

"I didn't know Sarah Hart was going to be taken," she says. "When I came to your house looking for her, it's because I really was concerned."

"Concerned about her, or that you'd lost a potential lead on John Smith?" I spit.

"Both," she says, turning back to me. "If you're here, that means you know a lot more about what's going on in the world than most. At least enough to know how bad things could get for all of us. Hell, you probably know more than *me* at this point after stealing that computer."

I shrug. "The laptop basically self-destructed. I don't know anything important." I'm so obviously out of my league here, and there's nothing I can do but apologize and try to convince this woman that I'm a dumb jock. Maybe they haven't found my truck and searched it yet. "I don't have it with me. But if you let me go, I can get it and send it back to the guy I took it from. What's his name? Agent . . ."

"Purdy," Walker says. There's weight to her voice when she says his name. Something in her face changes.

"Yeah," I say. "The piggish-looking dude."

She shoots me a look that reminds me of one my grandmother only saved for the worst offenses.

"He doesn't need it anymore," she says slowly. "He's dead."

She's quiet for a few seconds, as if she's trying to work something out in her head. Maybe I'm just desperate to not be thrown into FBI prison, but Agent Walker actually looks upset about Purdy being gone.

"I'm sorry," I say, because it's the only thing I can think of.

She nods but remains quiet.

"Was there some kind of attack or something?" I ask. This sounds like a question about Purdy, but what I really want to know is anything about Sarah. To gather info.

"A lot has changed around here in the last few days," she finally says. "I'm not sure anything will be the same from now on. For the Bureau. For us. Hell, even for Earth. The things I've seen . . ." Her mind wanders off for a moment.

"Like what?" I ask.

She shakes her head.

"What am I going to do with you? I have much bigger things to take care of and incredibly limited resources." She adjusts her sling and grimaces a little. "We should have already left this place. It's only a matter of time before they realize what we're doing."

I don't know who "they" is exactly, but I see my opening.

"Well . . . ," I start reluctantly. "You could always pretend I was never here and let me and Sarah go."

She starts circling the table, ignoring my proposition.

"I read your files in Paradise, Mark. You were an athlete. Not the best in school academically, but you excelled at what interested you."

"Thanks?"

"We never really thought you were involved in any of this. But then you went and stole Purdy's computer. You've gotten yourself into quite a predicament. There are other agents from the Bureau out there trying to hunt you down as we speak." She stops beside me.

"I only took that computer because I was trying to find Sarah," I say. Which is true, but also leaves out the part about me being an editor for They Walk Among Us and someone who's trying to dig up any information he can about the Mogs and leak it to the public. The last thing I want is for her or the government to realize that I'm also JOLLYROGER182. As a teenager trying to track down his ex, I'm kind of excusable, but as a rebel blogger, I'm probably a big, fat target.

"I figured as much," she says. "But I don't really think most of our agents—or the people they're now working for—really care. If I thought it would actually ensure your safety, I'd put you into protective custody immediately. As things are, though, I think that would be on par with throwing you to the wolves. And I don't exactly have men to spare here. . . ." She seems like she's talking more to herself now, hardly looking at me.

I try to comprehend all the things she's just told me.

"You . . . aren't working with the Mogs, then?"

She twists her lips a little bit into a small frown.

"I work for the American people," she says firmly. "For a while, that meant working with the Mogadorians. Now I'm not so sure."

The door behind me opens, and another agent comes in. One I remember as being Walker's flunky in Paradise. I think his name was Noto. He whispers something to Walker. Her posture goes rigid.

"We'll move at oh-eight-hundred hours," she says. "I want every asset we can strip from this base loaded up before then. We can't be caught unprepared if things go south."

"What about the agents still loyal to the Mogadorians?" Noto asks. "Should we release them?"

"The Mogs or the Bureau will send a team when they realize this base has gone dark. The agents will be fine. Let them sit and think about where their loyalties lie."

"And him?"

Walker turns back to me, pursing her lips a little.

"I'll deal with him," Walker says.

Noto nods and hurries out of the room.

I take a deep breath and try my luck again.

"Take me to Sarah and let us go," I plead, leaning forward onto the desk. "Please. I just want to make sure she's all right. If you can't protect us here, let us protect ourselves. We'll disappear."

Agent Walker looks at me for a few seconds before nodding.

"Sarah's fine," she says, and I breathe out a long sigh of relief. "Or she was when they broke her out of here and destroyed most of this facility."

"They?" I ask.

She snorts a little bit.

"Who do you think? Your old friends who caused such a scene at Paradise High."

John. Sarah's with John.

CHAPTER
FOUR

WALKER TELLS ME TO LAY LOW AND THAT IF SHE sees me again, she'll personally make sure that I'm shipped back to Paradise. Luckily, whatever she and the agents loyal to her are about to do must be more important than keeping tabs on me. Before I can try to pry any info about what's happening out of Walker, two agents are shoving me through the half-ruined top level of the facility. I want to ask them a million questions about what's going on and where they're going, but the fact that I'm being released at all has stunned me into silence, as if one question might send me straight into another interrogation room.

The agents are just black specks in my rearview mirror silhouetted against the rising sun by the time I finally breathe. And then I'm screaming and shaking my steering wheel and trying to calm down about the fact that I, in all seriousness, could be being tortured in a secret prison instead of driving away. I pull GUARD's messenger bag out from under the backseat, happy to see that Walker's agents either didn't care if I still had Purdy's computer or simply didn't have time to look through my stuff. I'm so relieved that I got out of there that I'm a good fifteen miles away by the time I start to realize what all this means. Sarah's been rescued by John, but that doesn't really mean she's safe, since her boyfriend is a walking target. What are the Garde doing now? There are still a bunch of evil aliens gunning for them, not to mention the idiotic humans who've decided to work with the bad guys.

What the hell am I supposed to do now?

I turn to the one person who might have a clue. I text GUARD.

Me: Dulce's a bust. FBI is abandoning it. Sarah's gone. I think John and others got her out.

He gets back to me almost immediately.

GUARD: You got in and out and no one saw you? I'm impressed.

Me: Nah. Ran in2 agent Walker from Paradise. She let me go. I think she's turned against the Mogs.

GUARD: That could be helpful. Where are you going now?

Me: No damn clue. Can't go home. Bad FBI are still looking for me.

This whole time I've been so focused on trying to get Sarah out that I only really saw two possible outcomes: me getting locked up with her, or me rescuing her, then going on an anti-Mog campaign to help save the world. Now that she's gone, my only real option is to try to find her. Again. I promised John when all this started that I'd keep her safe, but I'm doing this for me, not him. *I* want to make sure she's okay. Plus, if she's with the Garde, she's the best link I have to everything that's going on. Whatever she knows can be used on They Walk Among Us to help warn everyone about what's happening with the Mogs and Garde. Hell, maybe I could even show photos or videos of John and his other alien friends doing crazy shit to convince people that these damned aliens I keep posting about are real.

But first I have to find Sarah.

And I don't even know where to begin. She could be anywhere, and I have nothing to go off of.

My new phone chirps.

GUARD: If you're still serious about fighting the Mogs, head towards Alabama. I can set up a base for you to work out of. You may have an easier time finding Sarah and John

if you're not on the road so much spending half your time driving.

GUARD: Just take the long way there and stay out of sight for a few days so I have some time to work everything out.

And there he is again: a Hail Mary pass keeping me from feeling like a completely useless human being. Giving me my next task.

I text him back.

Me: Thx man.

I stare back at the text, having one of those weird moments of clarity when I realize that I'm traveling across the country at the suggestion of some dude I've never met in order to help stop an alien invasion. I fire off another message.

Me: Will I meet u in Alabama?

It's a few minutes before I get a response this time.

GUARD: I'm not certain. I have some personal business to take care of. In the meantime, you might look into switching cars if you can. The FBI will have all your info.

Sure, I'll just drive up to the next dealership I see and buy a new one. Because that's exactly how the world works.

I shake my head.

I drive until I find a big-looking road that goes east and take it. After a while, I'm heading more south than anything, but I don't mind—I just want to get away before Walker decides that I really *would* be safer under her protection and sends some black-clad henchmen out to get me. Plus, it sounds like GUARD needs some time to get our new base or whatever set up.

After a few hours of driving, I start to feel really strange and kind of like I'm dreaming, even though I'm making it a point to keep my eyes open as wide as possible to stay awake. I finally accept the fact that I've got to get off the road and start to weigh the pros and cons of sleeping on the side of the highway when I see a sign that tells me I'm only twenty miles outside of Santa Fe, which, honestly, I thought was in Nevada or Arizona and not New Mexico. Geography was never one of those subjects I took much interest in. On the upside, Santa Fe's a city I've actually heard of, which means that it's got to be pretty big.

Or at least, big enough for me to stay anonymous and find a place to sleep.

Before I hit the city line, I see the sign for thirty-nine-dollar rooms and pull into a place called Desert Oasis, which is a single story of motel rooms that look like they've seen better days. It's a sort of pinkish-brown stucco building with crumbling corners and long rows of flower beds outside the rooms that are filled with sticks and brown bushes that look like they'd disintegrate if I touched them.

Considering I'm a person of interest to the FBI, it seems like the perfect place to hunker down for some z's.

The inside office is just a little waiting room with some ripped green vinyl chairs. There's a guy with a big, brown mustache, a bad comb-over and inch-thick glasses reading a torn-up paperback at the counter.

"I'd, uh, like a room," I say.

"Sure," the guy responds, hardly glancing up from his book. "Name?"

"Um," I say, because I'm feeling a little out of my mind and apparently want to make it completely obvious that I'm trying to be incognito. I think of the name the courier called me—my *other* identity. "Roger."

The guy looks at me a second and then shakes his head, motioning to the book on the table in front of him. "I mean, you need to sign in there," he says. "I'll also need a credit card on file for incidentals and an ID to go with it."

"What if I don't have one?" I try to say casually as I

sign in with the name "Jolly Roger," writing in cursive like I don't normally do.

He shrugs, finally putting his book down. "Then you'd better have some other kind of collateral."

I thumb through my wallet, keeping it below the counter so the front-desk guy can't see it. Then I pull out a hundred and fifty dollars—over a hundred dollars more than what the room costs. I slide the bills over the counter. The guy looks back and forth between me and the cash. Then, finally, he tosses me a key.

"Room number four," he says.

Of course.

"Thanks," I mutter.

On my way out, he calls after me, "If you make too much noise, I'll call the police. Damn kids come out here to drink and always end up—"

But I slam the door behind me, and I don't hear the end of what he has to say. Besides, I'm not going to make any noise, and even if I did, I have serious doubts that the guy actually *would* call the police. More likely, he'd just demand another hundred bucks from me.

The room is just a bed, table and a square-tube TV with fake wood on the sides like the one Nana kept in my grandfather's office. The place is dingy, and the faded brown bedspread is scratchy, but I'm just happy to not be sitting in my truck, or a detention cell. I'm exhausted but am still wound up by everything that's happened in the last few hours, so after making sure the curtains are completely covering the windows and the door is bolted and chained, I fire up GUARD's untraceable netbook. It's fancier than any computer I've ever seen. There's even a little fingerprint scanner on it. I follow instructions that pop up when the system is fully booted and set the computer to respond only to my thumbprint, then I log into my personal email account. I'm looking for something from Sarah, telling me she's safe. That she got out and wants to make contact again because she knows *I* know what's happening and that I'd be worried about her.

But there's nothing from her. There are some spam emails, a few chains of messages from my old teammates and friends in Paradise and half a dozen from my family, all of which get filled with more and more capital letters and question marks the longer I've been away. I shake my head and sigh. I knew I'd be making them worry when I left Paradise in the middle of the night, but I was hoping I might be back sometime soon. Or at least that I'd be able to let them know that I was with Sarah and that we were *both* safe—maybe even make up a story about how we'd run away together.

But now, I don't know what to tell them. All my earlier hopes seem stupid, like they never could have really worked out. How do I try to explain to people back in my hometown that I'm half a country away trying to track down my ex-girlfriend and a bunch of people from another planet? I start to reply to a message from my dad to tell him about the Mogs and how he needs to watch his back and probably just leave Paradise completely. But I know that if I tell him evil aliens and corrupt government officials are snooping around his town—taking up residence in his *office* even—he'll look into it. He'll start poking around and trying to play hero. And that's dangerous. I don't want him to get involved. And if the Mogs or FBI are intercepting my emails or something like that, one mention of them to Dad and they'll be all over him.

I don't want him to end up getting hurt because of something stupid I've done.

And so I send back a reply that's not exactly a lie but not really the whole truth.

Dad,

Chasing after Sarah to try to bring her back to Paradise where she belongs. Lost my phone. Sorry if I scared you guys. Be home soon. Don't worry, I'm okay.

Mark

It's not much, but it'll have to do. I send it off and open up a new email, one I address to Sarah. And then I just start typing. Everything that's happened. Everything I'm worried about. In the end, after a thousand words, I tell her that if she gets this, to write back. *Please.*

I send that email off too, unsure if it will ever make it to her. Scared that there's no Sarah for it to go to at all anymore. And that in the end, I'm going to be alone trying to warn people about the shark-faced aliens that might show up and destroy their lives. That I'll just be some crazy guy who no one believes.

I know that if I just sit around waiting for a response, I'll go insane. I need to keep my mind occupied. And so I open up the JOLLYROGER182 email account that's connected to They Walk Among Us. This is something I can focus on. Something to occupy my time and energy when I'm not driving or trying to figure out how to contact Sarah. Plus, if I can help get the word out about the Loric and Mogs, in a way I might actually be helping. Making a difference.

There are about two hundred unread messages, tips and comments in my in-box. I make it through about fifteen—mostly crackpot tips but one about a weird-looking community in a super-rich suburb in Maryland I want to follow up on—before I pass out on the bed.

I sleep for the rest of the day and night, completely crashed. I wake up a little before noon, take a much-needed shower and then spend an hour or two trying to make sense of the electronics GUARD sent me. I plug the jump drive into Purdy's computer and hit the power button. The computer actually starts to make noise for the first time since it died in the diner, and my pulse starts to race.

Yes, GUARD, you genius mother—

But the only thing that appears on the computer is a command screen full of what looks like a foreign language mixed with big lists of numbers. I'm scared that poking around too much will end up causing the thing to crash again, so I follow GUARD's instructions carefully, running a series of tests or something on the machine using the jump drive. But nothing happens, just gibberish that I can't figure out.

In the meantime, I go back to the netbook and type up the blog post I've been thinking about since I saw the Mog in my dad's office and discovered that the FBI were working with the wrong aliens. I don't have any hard proof—just a story—but I can lay out for TWAU readers all the stuff that *I* know is true.

The second after I post the blog, there's a knock on the door. I jump to my feet, searching for the weird grenade GUARD sent along, when I hear a voice from outside.

"Hey, Roger," the motel guy says. "Checkout's in ten minutes. Unless you want to spend another night— same fee."

I gather my shit and hit the road.

CHAPTER
FIVE

I TRAVEL FOR A FEW DAYS, FORMING A SORT OF routine. In El Paso, I swap my license plates out for a pair of Texas ones when I see a truck similar to mine in a McDonald's parking lot. I pick up supplies—a toothbrush, a case of energy drinks, some dark clothes in case I end up sneaking around at night again—at a drugstore in some Podunk town near the border. Motels become my new home, because the people there don't ask questions or seem to care that I sometimes check in at weird hours. Also, cash has been pretty good at buying my anonymity with them. I drive towards Alabama, trying to avoid going into big cities or anywhere that I think FBI agents might be posted. I keep my radio tuned to twenty-four-hour news stations, listening for anything that could possibly be Mog related. When I'm not driving, I try to get info off Purdy's computer, but none of the systems running on GUARD's jump drive have been able to get the damned thing functional yet. Every night before I go to sleep, I email Sarah.

She hasn't responded.

When I'm on the road, I've got one eye in my rear-view mirror, because no matter how stealthy I think I'm being or how good I know GUARD's gadgets are, I can't help but feel like I'm being followed. I spend a lot of time telling myself that I'm being delusional. Sometimes I miss just being a dumb quarterback who had no idea what was going on in the rest of the world, or even my own backyard. At least then I wasn't holding my breath every time anyone passed me on the highway for fear that they were Mogs or FBI agents trying to run me off the road.

I spend a lot of time wandering around Texas, texting GUARD on occasion to update him on where I am. He arranges for another care package to get sent to me—or to Jolly Roger, more specifically—and I retrieve it from the front desk of a motel outside of Abilene. Enough to keep me fed and sheltered for a little while longer. Other than that, he's pretty much been on radio silence, responding to texts or emails at odd times, if at all. Whatever he's got going on, his life must be pretty hectic. I just hope he can get the base set up soon so we can start doing some real work.

And so I can learn who he is.

It sucks being stuck in my truck or a musty motel room all the time, so I hop between coffee shops and diners for a few hours in the afternoons so I can pretend to have some sort of a normal life, and even then I'll only stop at places that are empty and have secluded tables open in the back. Half a week or so after starting my trek towards Alabama, I camp out at a truck stop an hour outside of Dallas—the kind of place with barstools up against a counter and a dozen different types of pie on display. In a corner booth, I multitask by watching the muted TV mounted over the counter and tuned to a news station, responding to TWAU emails on my netbook and keeping an eye on one of GUARD's systems running on Purdy's laptop. I'm not sure what all GUARD had installed on the USB drive he sent me, but the stolen laptop screen keeps blinking with lines of code that mean nothing to me. Hopefully that means the programs are working and I'll be able to use the computer again soon so I can mine it for info.

The waitress comes by.

"Can I get you anything else?" she asks.

"I'll take a refill," I say, nodding towards my cup of coffee but keeping my eyes on the screen.

"You sure about that?" she asks.

I pause and look up at her. She's old enough to be my mom, and her eyebrows are scrunched together.

"It's just, that's your fifth cup and . . ." She trails off, but her eyes land on my fingers. They rest on my keyboard, but they're twitching from the caffeine. I can feel my blood pulse behind my eyeballs.

"I have a lot of work to do," I say. "I'll take another."

She shrugs and leaves, and I rub my eyes. I probably look like a crazy person, or some kind of junkie who's wandered in off the streets. I've been staying up at night until I literally can't keep my eyes open any longer, then waking up to dreams of Mogs and FBI agents raiding my motel room after only a few hours of sleep.

I start to go back to the computer when I notice a breaking news report on the TV. Some building in Chicago called the John Hancock Center is on fire. I almost ignore the whole thing to keep working on TWAU blog stuff. And then I see it, in the bottom corner of the frame. Sitting on the roof of the burning building as plain as day to anyone who's seen one before: a Mogadorian gun. The kind that looks like a cannon and wreaks havoc on an Ohio high school.

This is no accidental fire. The Mogs are responsible for whatever's happening in Chicago.

That can only mean one of two things: either the Mogs were using the building as a base, or their enemies were. Meaning, the *Garde* were. Meaning Sarah could have been there.

"Turn that up," I say to no one in particular. When

nobody responds, I talk again, louder. "Can someone turn this up?"

The handful of people sitting at the counter look at me like I'm some kind of idiot.

"This is an emergency!"

"Hey, kid," a big guy wearing a trucker hat says. He looks like a stand-in for Larry the Cable Guy. He nods to my booth. "Why don't you just read about it on one of your computers over there and let us enjoy our afternoons."

Anger surges through me, and for the briefest second, I think about jumping out of my booth and yelling at the guy, but there are more important things going on now.

And besides, he's got a good point.

My fingers fly over the keys as I scan developing news stories about what's happening in Chicago. There's little actual info, though. Eventually, I find a live stream and plug in my headphones in the hope that some of the talking heads will have more details about the situation. The stream shows helicopter footage of smoke billowing out of the building again, and I wish I knew how to record video from my screen. What I *do* know how to do is take a screen grab, so when the Mog weapon comes into view again, I save a bunch of photos before the video cuts back to some woman in a studio talking about how initial reports suggest the fire is the result of an electrical issue.

Right. That definitely explains why there's an alien gun on the roof.

I have to tell my readers the truth. The world needs to know. If the Mogs are ballsy enough to attack a building in the middle of Chicago, who knows what they might have in store for us next?

I log on to They Walk Among Us, and I write up what is probably a completely typo-riddled post about what's going on in Chicago—or at least what I can gather based on what the media is saying and the footage I've seen. I include a few screen grabs of the Mog gun, pointing out that it's obvious this whole thing was more than just an electrical malfunction or something. At the end of the post, I ask anyone who's reading to be careful and to start looking for suspicious activity in their own towns and cities. Because this could be the beginning of a full-scale invasion for all I know. Then I upload the post with a title that I hope will get people's attention: "Mog Attack in Chicago: Is This the Zero Hour?"

The second after I hit Publish, someone taps on my shoulder. I'm so in the zone that I didn't even realize anyone was beside me, and I jump so much that my legs bang against the table. My coffee cup rattles, and some silverware falls to the floor. The waitress takes a few steps away from me before slowly setting my check down.

I realize that a few other people in the diner are looking at me. Maybe because I just jumped. Maybe because I was shouting for people to turn up the TV volume earlier.

Jesus, Mark, chill and get the hell out of here before you cause a scene.

I take a deep breath and start to gather up my things, throwing some cash down on the table. As I leave the diner, I text GUARD, telling him to check out what I've just posted—that shit's going down. It's only after I've sent him the message that my adrenaline starts to die down and is replaced by a different feeling—the fear that Sarah may have been in Chicago. She may have even been in that battle.

Back in my truck, I open up my netbook again and send off a quick email.

Sarah, please, just find some way to let me know you're safe.

CHAPTER
SIX

THE CHICAGO STORY GETS BIG OVER THE COURSE
of a few hours. The Comments section explodes. Some
guy out in Oregon posts side-by-side screen grabs of
the original news footage and the more recent airings
that have the Mog weapon digitally removed, as if no
one would notice that they edited the footage. But the
followers of TWAU noticed. And as view counts on the
article continue to rise, the word gets out. The word
"cover-up" start getting thrown around, and people
start questioning *why* the media would edit the footage. All because of the blog post.

I did some good.

No one on the news mentions that the footage has
been altered. Obviously. I'm guessing the Mogs have
probably already infiltrated the media too. All the talking heads keep saying there were no casualties, but I
don't believe them. I worry that the Garde, our only real

hope against the Mogs, are gone and that Sarah's been dragged down with them. And when I think of that, all the excitement I have about the blog post going a little viral disappears. It's just a single shot in an intergalactic fight. Child's play.

I've managed to get in touch with GUARD. He thinks the Chicago story is great and tells me to keep up the good work.

My luck continues later in the night after spending the evening driving from the truck stop near Dallas to the middle of Louisiana. At a motel outside of a suburb of Shreveport, there's a breakthrough with the FBI computer. The blinking, running codes disappear, and suddenly the computer boots up to the normal desktop. The MogPro file is still missing, but the computer itself is up and running and unlocked so I can read all the emails the late Agent Purdy had downloaded to his computer—the stuff that led me to Sarah to begin with. Only, I never had time to actually go through most of the emails before I got shut out of the laptop.

This is some real-life hacker sort of badassery that can actually make a difference.

I compile as much data as I can. Over and over again Purdy keeps talking about some secretary, and for the first twenty emails or so, I'm pretty convinced he's banging his office assistant or something. Then I hit gold with a chain between Purdy and someone I've never heard of who signs their emails simply as "D." D writes:

Secretary Sanderson's body is reacting remarkably to the procedures. Intel suggests that many high-profile targets will join the cause when they see the results.

Uh, what?

I search for Secretary Sanderson online and feel like a total dumbass when I realize that it wasn't a "secretary" that Purdy kept referencing in his emails, but a capital-*S* "Secretary." As in Secretary of Defense Bud Sanderson.

The Mog corruption goes higher up in the government than we thought.

I speed-read the other emails, which reference more weird injections that Sanderson had to look younger. At first I can't figure out why everyone is so worried about his plastic surgery, until I read enough emails that it dawns on me that these procedures must involve the Mogs. Sanderson is filling himself up with alien shit that apparently makes him look, like, twenty years younger than he actually is. I pull Sanderson up on an internet image search but can't find any pictures of him from the past year or two. In the most recent one I can track down, he's an ancient-looking dude who looks like he hasn't seen the inside of a gym since the '50s.

I try to make sense of what this means. If someone that high up on the government food chain is involved, it makes me wonder if the president could be in on it. Or even leaders from other countries. Could the Mogs be working over other nations just like they are the United States?

I text GUARD about this, wondering if he's got any way to hack into the secretary's computer, even though I'm guessing it's hidden away behind a million government firewalls or whatever. Maybe he'll be able to track down a recent picture of the secretary for the sake of comparison. GUARD hasn't been the best at getting back to me lately, but this could be *huge*. I start to get a little worried that GUARD's somehow been caught, and without him . . . what would I even begin to do? I'd be screwed, broke, without guidance—not to mention the fact that if they found GUARD, they will sure as hell find me.

And then there's Sarah. My only other friend in this mess. Despite being afraid that she might have been caught up in whatever went down in Chicago, I hope for the best and write my daily email to her, telling her about the secretary. I hope she's getting these messages. I hope she's somewhere safe and that she's using the info I send her to help the Garde. To help *Earth*. Even if she can't get back to me.

After writing her, I start reading more of Purdy's

email until I fall asleep with my netbook sitting on my chest. Then, in the middle of the night, I'm jolted awake by an electronic chirping sound. At first I think it's coming from the computer on top of me, but I tap on the keys a few times and realize that it's dead because I never plugged it in to charge. Then I recognize the noise: it's the text message alert on my old burner phone, the one that's been floating around in the bottom of my messenger bag ever since GUARD sent me the new one. I dig it out and breathe a sigh of relief.

GUARD's finally written me back.

GUARD: Hey.

Me: DUDE. Where have u been? Why are u txting this phone?

GUARD: Long story. Lost some of my contacts. Where are you?

Me: Outside Shreveport

GUARD: Perfect. I'm not far. Meet with me.

Me: K. When?

GUARD: ASAP

And then the next text comes in: an address. It's a place on the other side of Shreveport, just off the highway.

It's three in the morning, but I'm suddenly wide-awake with relief that GUARD's okay, and *stoked* that

I'm finally going to meet the man himself. I get all my shit together, head out to my truck and then speed towards the other side of the city. As always, I keep an eye out for anyone who might be following me, and take a few extra turns and sidetracks before eventually stopping in front of the place GUARD sent me to. The building looks like an abandoned warehouse, the windows mostly boarded up or barred. The outside is a light-colored brick covered with layer after layer of graffiti.

This is so badass, I think. *I bet he has a hi-tech safe house in here or something.*

I park, slip my messenger bag over my shoulder and get out. I'm a few steps towards the building when my pocket starts to ring. It's my new phone—the one GUARD sent me. The call is coming in as blocked— which, considering who must be calling me, is not surprising.

I hit the Talk button as I jog up the steps of the warehouse.

"Yo, man!" I say. I pull open the big metal door at the entrance. It makes a loud, wrenching sound that echoes through the dark building. "Where are you at?"

"Our communications have been compromised," a voice says. It's electronic, computerized. GUARD must be masking his identity, or else the phone's speaker has completely crapped out. The voice is so weird that it takes me a second to even register what he's saying.

"Dude, what are you talking about?" I take a few steps into the warehouse, using the old burner phone as a flashlight. It only lights up the space a few feet ahead of me. I'm getting total flashback vibes to the haunted houses and dark cornfield hayrides of Halloween in Paradise. "Are you here yet? Is there a light switch or something? I'm here to . . ."

"Listen to me: someone's linked you to your old phone," the electronic voice says. "I never texted you. It's a trap. You need to leave. Now!"

I freeze. Not just because my brain is trying to process GUARD's words, but because the light from the other burner has lit up a pair of black boots. Someone standing just a few yards away from me. As the phone against my ear goes silent, I raise the one in my hand until I'm staring down the barrel of a hand canon. The same kind of Mog firearm I spotted on the roof of the building in Chicago. A man in a black suit holds it. His finger hits something on the side of the weapon, and the gun lights up with a deep-purple color. Around me, half a dozen identical lights power on.

I'm fucked.

Everything happens really fast. Suddenly there are giant overhead lights on throughout the warehouse. Seven agents stand around me in a circle. I'm guessing they must be FBI—that, or the Mogs have gotten really good at playing human.

"Drop what's in your hands," someone shouts. I hesitate, but then I feel something cold and metallic butting up against the back of my head, and I open my fingers, letting both my phones fall to the ground.

"Mark James," one of them—a man—says as he steps forward, keeping his weapon trained on me. "You are in deep shit."

My head starts to spin, a million thoughts and questions and fears all exploding at once. How did they find me? What do they know I know?

"You look surprised," the man says. "But you've been sloppy, kid. We found video of you buying your disposable cell. Those burners are handy, but they can easily be compromised and tracked once we've got the model and phone number figured out."

"The texts . . . ," I murmur.

"You think the FBI can't fake a few text messages? For someone wanted for stealing top secret materials, we figured you'd be smarter."

Dammit. I should have thrown my burner out. How could I have been so stupid?

I wonder if they've read all my old texts on that phone. I try to think back on my conversations with GUARD. Shit—they must know I'm also JOLLYROGER182.

I never should have responded to those texts from the burner.

"I don't know what you're—" I start.

"Save it for the interrogation," the man says. His lips curl up in a satisfied grin.

The word "interrogation" sparks something in my brain, and I start a desperate attempt to get out of this thing. I sigh loudly, shaking my head.

"Do you have any idea what's really going on here?" I ask, taking a step towards the man talking to me. I can see his finger tighten around the trigger, and I swallow hard and try not to shit my pants. "I'm working undercover for Agent Walker's team. She recruited me in Paradise. I'm tracking a . . . cyberterrorist. The whole thing with the computer was to prove I'm *not* working with you guys. You're going to blow my damned cover."

I can see something in his eyes that tells me he's actually entertaining this idea as possibly being true. Still, he doesn't lower his weapon.

"Agent Walker has been out of contact with the Bureau for days. She's being labeled as a traitor to—"

"You have no idea what happened in Dulce," I say, cutting him off. "Purdy's dead. Walker's taken her team underground to do some . . ."—I struggle—"dark-black ops work."

I pray that "dark-black ops" is a real thing.

The agent's smile fades, and I can see some of the others looking back and forth at each other in my peripheral vision. The thing is, it would probably only take, like, one phone call to find out that I'm totally bullshitting them. I need to get out of here as fast as I can.

Still, acting like a total badass around these guys pumps me up. I'm starting to feel a little bit like my old self again. Like when I was hassling freshmen or tripping new kids at Paradise High. When no one would dare mess with me.

"Where's Walker now?" the agent asks.

There's a hint of a smile on his face, and I crumble as I realize that even if he *is* buying my story, if the government thinks Walker's a traitor, this agent is probably imagining all the awards and honors that'd be handed to him for hauling her in.

"That's classified information," I say, trying not to let my voice waver.

"That's fine. I have a feeling you'll *de*classify it very soon." The agent nods to one of the others. "Get him out of here."

That's when I see the big, black van parked at the other end of the warehouse, near a metal loading-bay door.

"Wait!" I practically scream as two of the agents grab my arms. I try to shake them off, but one of them digs a gun into my back. The other pulls my messenger bag off my shoulder and hands it over to someone else. I can't believe they're going to get their hands on my computers, my notes, that weird grenade. . . .

"Save it, kid," someone says.

"No," I say. My mind is racing. Even if I wrestle free from the agents holding me, there are too many here. There's no way I'm making it back to my truck. Not without something crazy happening.

So I get a little crazy.

"There's a homing beacon," I say. "In my bag. An emergency signal in case I got pinned down. All you have to do is press it, and Walker will be here within the hour. She'll back my story up."

The leader looks at me, then at some of the other agents. After a few seconds, he walks over and grabs my bag from another suit.

"It's, uh, Mog tech, so it looks kind of weird," I say as he starts rummaging through my stuff. I note that he doesn't look confused at all when I say "Mog." Of course not. He's using their guns, after all. I wonder if he hasn't realized that they're the real bad guys yet, or if he just doesn't care.

Finally, he pulls out the little cylinder covered in the weird symbols.

"You just have to click the top of it," I add.

He stares down at the object in his hands for a few seconds and then motions towards the van.

"Take him back to headquarters," he says. "Call in reinforcements. I want a strong perimeter. We're taking

Agent Walker in for questioning."

The two agents at my sides start to drag me towards the van.

"No!" I shout. If I get in that van, I'm never seeing the outside world again. "You can't do this! Let me stay here and wait for—"

Something hard hits the back of my head and shuts me up. My vision goes a little starry.

I shake my head and look back at the agent who took the grenade. He's still eyeing it curiously. And then he does it—he pushes the button. I hear a click, followed by a few electronic beeps. He stares down at the grenade in confusion.

"What the—" he starts.

I muster all the strength inside me—every weight lifted and drill run and tackle practiced—and break free from the agents' grips.

I hit the cement floor just as the grenade goes off.

CHAPTER
SEVEN

THE CONCUSSIVE WAVE PASSES OVER ME AND presses me into the concrete floor so hard I'm afraid my ribs are going to snap. There's no fire, just pressure, like some telekinetic force pushing anything and everything away from the detonation site. Agents fly through the air. The lights go out almost immediately. All around me there's the sound of breaking glass as the force of the weapon shatters the windows of the building and van.

And then it's over. I'd probably think the whole thing was pretty awesome if I wasn't in the middle of it.

I get to my feet as fast as I can and run towards the rectangle of moonlight where the front doors had been earlier—the blast must have blown them out. My head is all fuzzy, like I've just stuck it inside a subwoofer. I can hear people groaning and moving about in the rest of the building, but I can't tell where any of them are or how hurt they might be. All I can do is run.

I'm almost to the door when I realize I can't leave without my bag. It's got my computers and my notes—everything, really—in it.

Including my keys.

Luckily, the blast blew out all the dirty windows and the boards that'd been covering half of them, so there's at least *some* moonlight, and it only takes me a minute to locate the messenger bag. I find it piled up with a bunch of debris. But this detour is enough time for a few of the agents to get back to their feet—I can hear their boots pounding against the concrete floor. Which is great, because it means that I didn't accidentally kill anybody, but also means I'm one step closer to getting shot, arrested or both. I sprint towards the door. I just have to make it outside and into my truck.

The lead agent steps in front of the doorway when I'm just a few yards away. He holds his gun up directly at my chest.

"You smug little asshole," he says. "Didn't you know stealing classified intel is considered treason?"

He lowers the gun to my legs and pulls the trigger. I brace for impact, ready for my knee to be destroyed. It's all over now.

Only, nothing happens. I see him pull the trigger again and again, but there's no bullet or laser or even wisp of smoke. Just a little click each time he tries to shoot me. It's only then that I realize the gun's not lit up anymore. I take a quick glance around and don't see any of the purple lights anywhere. Whatever that grenade did must have screwed with the Mog weapons.

Which means the only thing standing between me and freedom is an unarmed man.

The lead agent is still trying to pull the trigger when I lunge forward. I may not be the best spy or computer geek or liar, but I do throw a hell of a right hook. All the fights I got into back in Paradise taught me that. And while John Smith may have been able to kick my ass with his alien kung fu, this guy is very much a human. He tries to move too late, and my fist connects with the bottom of his jaw. He drops like a stone, and by the time he actually hits the floor, I'm jumping over his legs and then running down the stairs, digging through my bag with one hand as I make a beeline for my truck.

I'm starting the engine when the first shot is fired— the other agents must have realized the Mog weapons weren't working and dug out their normal guns. I hear the bullet bounce off the metal of my hood. Then there's another one, and my back windshield shatters.

"Shit!" I shout, crouching down as much as I can. I shift into gear and slam my right foot down on the gas, peeling out as I hear more shots go whizzing through my tailgate. I think I'm out of harm's way when suddenly I feel a burning pain in my left arm, causing me to swerve and almost crash into a cement pylon. I look down and see blood pouring through my shirtsleeve.

Oh my God. You just got shot, Mark. Holy shit.

I think the bullet just grazed me, but it still hurts like hell, and there's a lot of blood. As I barrel onto the highway, keeping one eye on my rearview mirror, I find a dirty T-shirt from the back cab and wrap it around the wound to try to stop the bleeding. I'm just glad that the sun hasn't come up yet. This early in the morning, there's hardly anyone on the road to notice my terrible driving as I try to figure out how injured I am while the wind roars through my truck thanks to the shattered back windshield.

After ten minutes or so, I take an exit at random and enter a neighborhood. I figure if the FBI called in reinforcements or police or anything, the highway is the first place they'd look, and a bullet-ridden truck missing a back windshield isn't exactly the kind of thing you can easily hide from a police chopper on a deserted highway. I buzz through dark streets, just trying to get as far away from the city center as I can.

I drive, and try not to completely freak out. My heart pounds in my chest so hard I'm afraid I'm going to have a heart attack, which would be the biggest joke ever—I survived fights with the FBI and alien invaders; but in the end, the excitement was all too

much for me, and my heart exploded in some godforsaken little town in Louisiana.

I want to text GUARD, to tell him I'm okay, but I've
just realized I left both my phones back at the warehouse. Plus, my netbook is dead.

I am completely alone right now.

The T-shirt around my arm at least seems to have
stopped the bleeding for now, so I keep driving and try
to make sense of what just happened and not vomit,
which feels like something I might do at any moment.
Walker was right: not everyone in the FBI is as smart
as she is. There's fighting within the Bureau. And if
the FBI is breaking into factions, it might be like that
in other government agencies across the country, right?
Maybe even the world. At first this thought gets me
excited, to know that people aren't just following along
blindly with the Mogs. But then I realize that if we're
fighting each other, it'll make Earth that much easier
for them to take over when they're done with the Loric.
What we need is a strong defense. A united human
front.

We need to support the Garde.

Sarah. Where are you?

Somewhere on the outskirts of a suburb, I notice the
first hint of smoke coming out from under the hood of
my truck. I tell myself it's probably just dust or something, but after a few more miles, there's more smoke

or steam pouring out of the bullet holes. The fact that I even *have* bullet holes in my hood is a pretty good indicator that something is screwed up inside.

"No, no, no, no," I say. It starts in a whisper, but each word gets louder, until I'm shouting at my truck.

When the engine starts to make a clicking noise, I pull into a strip mall parking lot and get all the way behind a liquor store before the truck just up and dies. I have enough momentum to sort of hide it behind a wall of Dumpsters. When I lift the hood up, smoke billows out.

There's no way I'm going to be able to fix this.

I'm completely overwhelmed. Lost. No phone. No computer. A gunshot wound.

And no one in the world knows where I am.

I let the hood fall back down. Anger, fear, confusion—my blood is *boiling*. I bring my right fist down onto the hood, denting it a little. It feels good to do so. And then suddenly I'm kicking at the headlights and slamming my knuckles into the side of the truck over and over again. The wound in my arm hurts with each impact, but I'm so overcome with rage that I keep on beating the crap out of this vehicle, this thing that has let me down and stranded me in the middle of nowhere. I don't even care about the noise I'm making, all the grunting and shouting and banging.

Finally, I stop, exhausted. I let my head rest against

the driver's-side door. My breathing is fast and shallow, making me a little lightheaded. The knuckles on my right hand are bloody, and my skin feels clammy.

Calm down, Mark. Get your shit together.

I take a deep breath. In the distance, I see a sign for a hotel. That at least gives me a destination. I can't exactly walk in with a bloody arm, so I fish my letter jacket out of the backseat, grimacing as I slide my injured limb through it. I gather all my important belongings and shove them into the messenger bag, then start out on foot, walking the half a dozen blocks to the hotel. Before I go in, I tiptoe through the side gate where there's a pool and dunk my hands into the cool water to wash them off. A dark-red cloud drifts away from my fingers as I rub them together, and I wonder how the hell I ended up in this situation.

Inside, I feed the front-desk girl a story about how I was mugged and just left the police station and don't have any ID but, luckily, still have a stack of cash I'd hidden in my shoe that can pay for the night. She seems hesitant at first, but I put on my best pouting face and practically beg her to get me a room. This must work, because she relents, and then suddenly I'm inside a decent hotel room that looks like heaven after some of the shit-box motels I've been staying in lately. I've got an exterior room, meaning the front door opens up to the parking lot and a window in the bathroom leads to a wooded area out back. After the last hour of my life, it's good to know I have multiple escape routes if I need them.

On the bed, I take stock of everything in my bag. The computers are a little scuffed up but don't look too damaged. I plug the little netbook in, fire it up, and then log on to TWAU's secure chat client. GUARD messages me right away.

GUARD: I thought you were a goner.

Me: How do I kno this is the real u?

GUARD: I come from the planet Schlongda.

I actually laugh. I can't help it. The planet Schlongda appeared in one of the first issues of *They Walk Among Us*—the old print version I took from Sam Goode's house—and was supposed to be the home of a bunch of krakens or something. When I'd read the name of the planet, I'd immediately forwarded a scan of the article to GUARD and laughed about the fact that someone had obviously made it up to screw with the editors there.

This is the real GUARD.

I give him the short story of what happened, being sure to point out the fact that I just faced half a dozen evil FBI agents and survived while he was hiding behind a computer somewhere. Eventually, I get to the real issue: I'm kind of stuck here now, and as soon as someone finds my truck, they'll start looking for me in this area.

> GUARD: Stay there for the night. I'll have directions for you in the morning. I'll work something out.

> Me: What the hell was that grenade?

> GUARD: Combination specialized EMP and concussion blast.

I stare at the computer, wondering yet again who it is that's on the other end of this chat. All I know about GUARD is his screen name and that he's someone who can deliver a bunch of cash and military-grade weapons at a moment's notice.

GUARD notices that I haven't responded.

> GUARD: Are we cool?

> Me: Yeah. Sure.

I close the netbook and carefully peel off my jacket. The left sleeve is stained with blood. Ruined, I'm guessing. But that's okay. It's not like Paradise High even exists anymore.

In the bathroom, I inspect the wound on my arm, cleaning it off using some cold water and a plastic hotel cup. There's a two-inch gash just under my delt. A little higher and it would have totally screwed up my shoulder. It probably needs stitches, but the last thing I can do is go to a hospital right now. Not here, where the FBI is surely looking for me. So I tie a hotel towel around it and hope for the best.

At least it's not your passing arm, a voice inside me says, as if that even matters now.

I sit on the bed. I should sleep. I need to get as much rest as possible. But all I can do is stare at the door, listening for the sounds of people who've tracked me down and have come to drag me away to some hell I'll never be able to escape from.

CHAPTER EIGHT

I WAKE UP TO SOMEONE POUNDING ON MY HOTEL room door and am on my feet and throwing clothes on in record time, ready to fly out the bathroom window and disappear into the woods. I forget that I have a damned gunshot wound on my arm until I pull my bag over my shoulder and end up wincing in pain, grinding my teeth together to keep from shouting. I'm just about to make a dash towards the window in the bathroom when I notice that I'm still logged onto the blog's chat client—I remembered to keep the computer plugged in this time—and that GUARD has sent me like a dozen messages telling me to expect someone, and to answer when they come knocking and to not use my real name or info when they ask for it.

Reluctantly, I look through the door's peephole. There's a man with a clipboard. He's wearing the kind of shirt that has his name sewed onto a patch on his chest. I slowly open the door, keeping it chained.

"Hey," I say through the few inches of space.

"You expecting a big delivery?" he asks. He smells like a cigar and is sweaty, even though it can't be very hot outside.

"Uh . . . yeah?" This must be another one of GUARD's care packages.

He holds the clipboard out in front of himself, obviously waiting for me to open up the door so that he can hand it to me. Instead, I squeeze my right hand out and grab it, sliding it in through the crack. The man sighs loudly and mutters something about what a pain in the ass this job has been today.

"I need you to sign the top one and fill out the one underneath," he says.

"Okay. Give me a second."

The top form on the clipboard is from some towing-and-cargo service that wants a signature as proof of delivery. The other page has something to do with a title, and wants my name and home address.

GUARD's message suddenly makes sense.

Still trying to wrap my brain around what's happening, I rely on the name GUARD used in his first package delivery and that I've been using at motels. I sign "Jolly Roger" on the forms. As for my address, I think of the dogs waiting for me at home: 182 Abby St. in Dozer, OH, with a random assortment of numbers as a zip code.

When I hand back the forms, I actually open the door. The man takes a look at the pages.

"Interesting name," he says.

"It's, uh, a family thing." I shrug.

I'm expecting him to hand me a box, but instead he holds out a pair of keys.

"It's gassed up," he says as I take the keys and stare at them dumbly. "Per the instructions we received."

"Instructions?" I ask, but the man's already halfway to a big tow truck parked right in front of my room.

"Make sure you get her insured," he calls back to me. "They're not supposed to let you drive off without proof of insurance, but . . . hell, whatever you said on the phone to the boss at the dealership must have been pretty convincing to drag me out of bed so early."

He starts to walk away as I stand dumbfounded in the doorway to my hotel room. I click the Unlock button on the keys in my hand, and a shiny, blue, extended-cab truck honks in the parking lot.

I run back inside to the computer.

Me: You're kidding me with this right?

GUARD: It should get you to where you need to go.

Me: This is crazy.

GUARD: As crazy as invaders from Mogadore?

**GUARD: I figured I might owe you after
everything you've been through.**

Me: What about my other truck?

**GUARD: A separate towing company is picking
it up in an hour and taking it to a secure
location. Get anything you need out of it now.**

Something clicks in my brain, even over the rush of
the fact that *I have a new truck.*

Me: Wait. How did u kno where I am?

**GUARD: I've been monitoring the netbook I
sent you. I can track it, even when it's powered
down. Once I knew the place you were staying,
I just had to nudge the front desk for your
room number.**

A weird feeling overtakes me—something I haven't
felt since Sarah started dating John. A particular sort of
anger that can only come from realizing that I've been
betrayed by someone I thought was looking out for me.

GUARD has been keeping tabs on me this whole

time. Why? I start to worry that this whole "drive towards Alabama" thing is just a prank.

Me: What the hell man?

GUARD: Apologies. I had to make sure we were working towards the same goal. There's a lot of double-crossing going on in the world right now.

GUARD: If it makes any difference, I trust you.

Before I can respond, he messages me an address in Alabama.

Me: Is this where you're at?

GUARD: It's what I've gotten set up for you. Home sweet home. I'll be stopping by to see you soon.

GUARD: Now if I were you, I'd get the hell out of Louisiana.

I sign off. I'm about to pack up my netbook when I realize that I didn't write to Sarah yesterday, so I sit back on the bed and open up my email.

Sarah—

**I don't even know what to say about the last twenty-four
hours. You know what's funny? When we were both still
in Paradise, I actually thought that maybe we'd go to
prom together. Not dating or anything, just together. I was
worried about prom. Getting a tux and corsage and crap.
Yesterday I got shot at by a bunch of FBI agents. Sarah, I
hope you're okay. . . .**

I'm not saying my old truck was a piece of crap or anything, but this new one is kind of the shit. I'm still
pissed that GUARD's been secretly tracking me this
whole time, but my new wheels help make up for that.

I plug the address GUARD sent me into the truck's
GPS system and head towards Alabama. My destination is about eight hours away. I can make it to my new
home base by the late afternoon. That leaves me with
plenty of time to figure out what the hell has happened
in the last few days. Time to digest—just me, an energy
drink and eight hours of open road and news radio.

Some of the FBI is working with the Mogs. I don't
know how many agents, or what percentage. Actually,
if the FBI is working with them, then there are probably
other agencies on their side as well. And some of the
government is in on it too. Sanderson is proof enough
of that. There are some people rebelling, but again,
it could be just Walker and her team or half the FBI.

There are so many variables that it's impossible for me to even begin to imagine things like odds or stats. All I know for sure is that the majority of the world knows nothing about what's really going on. If they did . . .

That's where my focus should be. Trying to convince people that there's an actual threat here. That there are aliens who will think nothing of destroying our planet if it means getting what they want—whatever that is. Who might even be gearing up for a full-scale invasion or something. I need to find more proof of what's happening. I need to turn They Walk Among Us into a movement. Maybe even an *army*.

And it all goes back to Sarah again. Not just because I promised—and *want*—to protect her, but because we need her to get to the other Garde. She's our connection. But I still have no idea how to find her. I need to step my search for her up to the next level. I think about posting a message to her on TWAU but realize that the dumbest thing I could do is get her face or name out there where some assclown might see her and try to tell me where she is, only to alert other authorities. I should discuss options with GUARD. Maybe he can pull some hacker moves and break into her email account or something. Maybe he can even track her face using security cameras.

We have to find her. Not for her sake or mine, but for the world's. So we can create a united front with the Loric.

And it would be great to have someone helping me out. In person. Someone I knew and trusted and cared for. Someone to keep me from being lost and alone in all this.

At a little drugstore just across the Alabama border, I stop to buy butterfly bandages. I try to remember a time when I didn't have problems like taking care of gunshot wounds or running from government agencies. It wasn't that long ago. Just a few months. A weird thing happens as I think about Friday nights under stadium lights and hanging out with my buddies after games. Usually when I do this, I wish I could go back and enjoy not knowing what's going on in the world. But now I'm glad I have a much bigger purpose. I can do great things.

Not that I wasn't great before. I'm just in a position now where I can do some truly capital-*A* Awesome shit.

The address GUARD gave me takes me through Huntsville, which looks like a pretty good-sized town, and then out into nothingness and a series of back roads and dirt trails that lead me closer and closer to the edge of a national park. I start to worry that the GPS has completely failed at its job of getting me to the base until a structure finally comes into view. It's almost completely hidden by hills and trees, set back from a dirt path. The GPS tells me that I've arrived at my destination just as I stop in front of a giant wrought-iron gate topped with the words "Yellowhammer Ranch."

It doesn't look like anyone's been here in a long time.

There's no lock on the gate, which is good for me right now but also means that the place probably has shit security. As I drive over a cattle guard and onto the property, my stomach starts to clench up a little bit. This whole thing feels really weird—as if I'm trespassing on someone else's property.

The house is one story and looks like a big log cabin. *Great. I'm attending Fugitive Camp.*

I stay alert. I'm not going to do what I did at the warehouse and just barge in—though, at this point, the FBI or Mogs would have to go pretty far out of their way in order to track me to this remote location. I knock on the front door since I have no idea if I'm actually in the right place or not. When no one answers, I circle the house just to make sure there's not some rancher out herding sheep or whatever it is people do in places like this. But there's only overgrown fields marked off by barbed-wire fences and a barn out back that's missing almost all of one side and is obviously empty. A big patch of grass in front of it has been flattened and burned in places, like something really big was sitting on top of it that was only recently moved. I shrug and look around, guessing that there was a tractor or something there that got hauled off.

Back on the front porch, I try the doorknob. The house is unlocked.

"Hello?" I call, but there's no sound or movement, so I head in and find a light switch. The place looks like I'd expect a country home to look. There's a lot of oversized furniture, mostly made out of wood. A cow skull hangs over the fireplace. A leather couch sits in front of a projector-style big-screen TV that's probably as old as I am and I'm guessing weighs a ton. I open up the refrigerator in the kitchen out of curiosity and see that it's stocked with essentials: milk, water, and even a few steaks. The pantry's got a bunch of food in it too. Everything looks fresh.

Thanks, GUARD, for making sure I don't starve.

I check out a few of the bedrooms, but there's nothing really interesting until I stop in front of a quilt hanging at the end of a hallway near the back of the house. There's a note on it that says *"Look behind me."*

Huh?

I pull back the quilt and find a solid sheet of metal that's got a little rectangle of reddish-colored glass on the right side where a doorknob or handle might normally be. It looks just like the little fingerprint scanner on my netbook.

"No way," I murmur as I raise my thumb to the little port.

There's a beeping noise, and the glass lights up green. The door starts clicking loudly, and I take a few steps back, concerned about what I'm going to find on the other side.

After a few seconds, the thick metal door swings open a bit, and I push it in farther as I enter the room. I immediately see about a dozen computer monitors covering one of the walls. Each of them is streaming footage from the areas in and around the house. There must be cameras located all over the grounds.

So much for laughing at the lack of security.

There's a sleek-looking computer set up at a desk opposite the other monitors. A couple of burner phones sit beside it. I turn one on and find that GUARD's number is already programmed into it, then pocket the burner.

"What the hell is . . . ," I say as I take everything in. But then I turn around and never finish the question.

The wall behind me is lined with shelves. There are several handguns, rifles, and knives sitting on them, along with a few things that I assume are weapons but don't immediately recognize. In the center is a folder with something written on it in black marker. I pick it up.

I hope you're ready for war.
-G

CHAPTER
NINE

I SETTLE IN.

Well, as much as I can in a house where I feel completely out of place.

I clean up the gash on my arm using a first aid kit I find in one of the bathrooms. The butterfly bandages don't seem like they're doing a great job of keeping the wound closed, so I try to figure out another way of dealing with it. After spending, like, an hour looking up advice on the internet, I dig through a bunch of drawers in the house until I find a tube of superglue, and then put a layer of the stuff over the graze. It feels weird as hell, but it's the best I can do. As badass as I've been recently, I don't think I have it in me to do my own stitches. Needles were never my thing.

Then, I get straight to work.

Whatever personal business GUARD was dealing with must be taken care of, because he's almost always online now. I get Purdy's computer hooked up to the big desktop in the back room, and GUARD uses his hacking skills to try to salvage any files that might be hidden on the hard drive, like the MogPro files that disappeared when the thing first shut down. He uploads basically everything from my computers to some secure cloud server. We start to build up evidence of what's going on behind the scenes. We read files about the specifications of Mog weaponry that have obviously been written for *human* users—proof we need to show the Mogs and FBI are working together. I take some screen grabs and upload them to TWAU under the title "Uncovered: FBI Training Manual for Mog Weapons." There's also a ton of transcripts that could take months to sort through, many of which have speakers who are noted using initials only.

The scariest thing I find repeated references to are upcoming "peace talks" with leaders from around the world. Could the Mogs be preparing to expose themselves and give Earth an ultimatum? Or have they already gotten to enough world leaders that they're relying on the humans to do that for them?

While GUARD focuses on recovering files from the hard drive, I go over Purdy's old emails, update the blog and try to keep up with the insane amount of emails I'm getting on my JOLLYROGER182 account ever since the Chicago story went viral. Most people who write me are assholes who just want to make fun of us and ask if we know where Bigfoot is hiding, but every now and then I get something that's worth following up on. A tattooed gang settling in the Everglades, weird-looking animals spotted flying overhead in Illinois—those sorts of things. I try to get as much info as I can from the sources, then scour local news stories, call police stations anonymously or anything else I can think of to back up any of the claims.

Our most promising lead is this dude named Grahish Sharma over in India. I get a dozen emails from different sources all talking about this commander or priest from some religious group that has something to do with one of the Garde. I'm not *exactly* sure they're legit, because a lot of the emails have contradictory information, which I'm guessing may have something to do with translation issues. All the messages have one thing in common, though: they all say Sharma shot down a Mog spacecraft and captured the pale-faced bastards inside alive.

When I bring this to GUARD's attention, he gets really excited about the idea of seeing one of the Mog ships up close—not to mention the fact that we could get footage of real-life Mogs. I respond to every email that mentions the Sharma guy, hoping that someone will be able to put me in contact with him.

Our most important break is when GUARD manages

to track down a recent photo of Secretary of Defense Bud Sanderson, the old, fat, bald guy who was getting Mog injections and plastic surgery done. Sure enough, the guy who looked more like a zombie than a human a few years ago suddenly has a full head of silver hair, smooth skin and a giant, shit-eating grin. If it wasn't for his eyes and the way his nose crooks to the side, I wouldn't believe it could possibly be the same dude.

I write a short exposé and post it to the blog. Once again, I feel like I'm actually doing something to help the fight. I just wish we could get more definite proof, something to show the world that the Mogs are real. That we're in danger.

That's why we need Sharma. Or Sarah.

I work through the night. Reading, speculating and taking notes. By the time the sun comes up, I need to get out of the back room and get some fresh air in order to stay focused. So I grab one of the handguns with a silencer on it and head outside. I set up empty aluminum cans in the old barn and start knocking them down one by one. I'm not a bad shot—would probably be better if I wasn't so jittery from caffeine.

The only drawback is that shooting the gun makes the wound on my arm hurt. How ironic. I just hope the superglue helps it heal like it's supposed to.

Shooting makes me think of my dad and the rest of my family. I wonder what they're doing. If they're still worried. I don't open their emails because I know I'll want to respond, and the last thing I want to do is put them in danger, or put *myself* in danger by saying something I shouldn't. But it's hard not to have them on my mind when I practice with the weapons. Dad taught me gun safety and used to take me hunting every year. He's the reason I know how to shoot at all. I hope that these aren't skills I'm going to have to put to use anytime soon, but if I do, in a weird way I think my dad would be proud of me, if he could see the big picture.

It hasn't been all that long since I left Paradise in the middle of the night, but it feels like an eternity. That freaks me out a little bit. I mean, I'm hidden away out in the middle of nowhere trying to track down an alien hunter in India instead of sitting at Nana's kitchen table eating bacon while going over scholarship offers or something. College seems almost laughable given what's going on. The future in general is too much to think about, too far away and unknowable.

We might not even be able to save the future, or the world. GUARD and I are stuck going through data that's weeks old. What if things have gotten so bad that we can't stop the Mogs?

I try to center myself. In Paradise, after everything went down at the school, I had Sarah to talk to, to keep me sane. And so after my shooting break, I go back inside and email her for the millionth time, knowing by now not to expect an answer.

> Sarah—
> I don't know why I keep sending these emails. Part of me hopes that you're reading them, using them to help the Loric, and can't reply for your own safety. Another part of me worries that you aren't even out there, that you're gone. I refuse to believe that but . . .
> I need to hear from you.

I start to write about Walker, but think better of it. Even if she was a Mog henchwoman in Paradise, she let me go in Dulce. She's working against them now. And if somehow the Mogs are intercepting my emails to Sarah, I don't want to blow Walker's cover if the aliens haven't completely labeled her a traitor. So instead, I'm kind of vague about my whole trip out into the desert.

> I thought I had a lead on you in New Mexico. All I found there was a deserted military base. It looked like a major battle went down. Way bigger and nastier than what happened in Paradise. I hope you guys got out safe.
> I hope like hell I'm not the only one left to fight these assholes. That would suck.
> A friend of mine set up a safe house for me. Way off the

grid. A place where we can work on exposing those pale freaks to the world. If you can get in touch, I'll find a way to send you the coordinates. We're on to something big. Something international. I don't even know what to do with it.

If you're reading these, if you're still in contact with John, now would be a really good time to show up. I need your help.

—Mark

I'm surprised my heart doesn't explode when my email dings later that day and I see that she's finally replied. Nothing long—just a note saying she's sorry she hasn't contacted me and that she's with John, and where the hell am I, anyway?

I type faster than I ever have in my life. I'm about to send her an email detailing exactly how she can get to me . . .

And then I stop.

I think again about how careful I've been not to give away too much about where I've been or what I've been up to since I left Paradise in the middle of the night. GUARD's got my IP address completely blocked, but that doesn't matter if I'm giving my location away in an email. My JOLLYROGER182 address at They Walk Among Us is on a secure server that GUARD himself designed, but my personal one is just a free email service. So is Sarah's. The Mogs or FBI could be tapping them. The same thing goes for the phone: if she hasn't been careful with burners, telling her where I am might be the same as calling up the FBI or the Mogs and giving them my address.

There's another possibility too. One I don't even want to consider. What if it's not even Sarah at all?

Think, Mark. Don't get lured into a trap again.

I email her back.

I'm okay. I was just about to make a pizza. What do you want on your half?

—Mark

The question is the first way I can think of to figure out if I'm talking to the real Sarah Hart. When we were dating, we had a standard order at the pizza place back in Paradise's downtown square. Every Saturday night we'd slide into a booth together and order the same thing.

I wait, staring at my in-box, hardly breathing as I will a new message to show up on the screen. Finally, it does.

Mark,

Things have been crazy here, but it sounds like it hasn't been easy for you either.

Veg for me, please. Don't let any of your gross all-meat

side cross the line. WHERE ARE YOU?
Sarah

It's her. That's our order. One medium half veggie, half meat. Soda for me, diet soda for her.

But I can't let my excitement about any of this cause me to make some kind of idiotic move that gives away my location. I take a deep breath, try to focus, and then pull up a map of Huntsville, the closest big city. I find a Waffle House on what looks like a busy intersection based on the size of the streets and email the address to Sarah.

Can we meet here? I'll have to make sure you don't have a tail or anything. I'm kind of wanted by a bunch of different bad guys. Come every day at 2 p.m. I'll be watching. When I'm sure everything's okay, I'll take you back to my base.

Ten minutes pass. I wonder if she's thinking about whether or not she wants to come. Or if she's arguing with John about what to do.

Whatever it is, she finally responds.

I'll be there. I'll head that way tonight.

I laugh, grinning to myself in the back room of the cabin out in the middle of nowhere.

Sarah's still alive and fighting. She's *okay*.

And she's coming to Alabama.

I know I told her she'd have to come to the Waffle House a few times before I took her back to home base, but as soon as I see her getting out of the taxi the next day, I know that's not going to happen. It takes everything I have not to burst out of my truck—which I've parked in a grocery store parking lot across the street—and cross six lanes of traffic to get to her. Instead, I try to play it cool, because I know I can't jump into this. We need to play everything as safe as possible.

But I can't just watch her leave the restaurant when she's done eating. I won't let her slip away again.

So I wait ten minutes and then call the diner. I describe Sarah to the woman who answers and manage to sweet-talk her into handing the phone over.

"Hello?" Sarah's voice comes out of the receiver, and it's glorious.

"Hey," I say.

"Mark, where are you?"

"What's the nickname those asswipes in Helena gave you?" I ask. I have to be sure.

"Huh?"

"I think they were from your bio class."

"Oh," she says. "Sarah Bleeding Hart?"

I grin.

"There's a parking garage two blocks north of here. I'll be on the second floor. Look for a blue truck."

"Can't you just . . ." But she must know how important it is to stay underground. To be incognito. If she's been with John since she left Dulce, she has to have caught on by now. "Okay. I'll see you soon."

I hang up and jet over to the parking garage—the one I scoped out after Sarah finally emailed me back. There I wait, texting GUARD to let him know she's shown up.

The waiting is terrible. I've been trying to rescue, find or even just be in contact with Sarah for weeks— ever since she disappeared—but the minutes it takes for her to walk from the Waffle House to the parking garage feel like years. With every second that ticks by, I can't help but imagine some terrible scenario that keeps her from getting to me, or some way that I've screwed up and doomed us both.

Finally, I see her wandering up the ramp and onto the second floor of the garage. I flash my lights, and she hurries towards me.

And then I'm out of the truck and running. It's like my body is operating outside of my brain's control. Everything in my head is saying *Get in the truck. Get both of you to safety. Keep your heads down and don't even talk until you're back at the base.* But my legs are moving, pumping on their own accord and bringing me sailing towards Sarah.

We practically collide in the middle of the parking garage, wrapping our arms around each other.

Finally. I'm not alone in this anymore. It's not just me and GUARD's messages.

"Mark," she says into my shoulder.

The way she squeezes me makes my arm hurt like hell, but I ignore it. I feel like some huge weight has been lifted off me.

"Jesus, Mark," she says again, her arms still around me. "What have you been doing?"

"You'd think I was joking if I told you," I say, squeezing the back of her neck.

"Try me."

"I don't even know where to begin."

She pulls away and takes a good look at me. I can see concern cross her face as she stares into my eyes.

"Don't take this the wrong way," she says. "But have you been sleeping at all? It looks like—"

But she stops and gasps. My fists automatically clench as I look around.

"What?" I ask. Shit. I knew I should have just got us in the truck and then out of here. "What is it?"

"*Mark,*" she says, pointing at my left arm. There's

blood dripping out from under my T-shirt sleeve. "Are you okay?"

I push the cotton of my T-shirt down onto the wound, hoping that stops the bleeding until we get back to home base.

"Would you believe me if I said I was shot while escaping from a bunch of crooked FBI agents?" I ask.

She nods, her eyes wide.

"I've been shot at a lot lately," she says quietly. "A few days ago I was stabbed by a Mog."

And then we just stare at each other. This is the moment when, months or even a few weeks ago, I'd probably have tried to kiss her. Or at least wished that was what I was doing. I'd have ignored the fact that I promised John Smith I'd keep her safe—ignored the fact that he existed at all. But in the parking garage, I look at her and she looks at me, and there's some kind of joint understanding. The dynamic has changed between us. *We've* changed. I can't be some hotshot football star trying to win back his ex when the fate of the world could rest on us. And she . . . there's some-thing different about her. Something fierce. She looks more like a soldier than the girl who used to wander around campus snapping pictures of flowers.

"I'm so glad you're here," I say. "And that you're okay. I'm fine. I'll patch up back at base."

"That wound is supergross, Mark," she says, her nose wrinkling a little. "You should probably see a doctor. . . ."

Her voice trails off. She knows that's not really an option.

"I should have brought a healing stone or something with me." She's eyeing my arm, shaking her head. I stare back at her, not knowing what she's talking about.

"We have a lot to catch up on," I say. I put out my arm, ushering her towards my truck.

"Let's start with why you're in *Alabama*," she says.

"Um, that's kind of a long story." I open the passenger's-side door for her. She's halfway inside before she stops and turns to me.

"Wait, when did you get this truck?"

I start to answer, but a huge bird lands on the hood of the truck with a loud thump. I jump, instinctively raising a fist.

"Jesus, what the hell?" I ask.

"Oh," Sarah says, smiling. "Do you remember Bernie Kosar?"

CHAPTER
TEN

SARAH FILLS ME IN ON WHERE SHE'S BEEN
since she was taken from Paradise. She glosses over
being imprisoned in Dulce. It kills me to think that
they might have tortured her or something, but I don't
push the issue, because how do you casually ask, "So
what terrible things happened to you when the FBI
threw you in a secret dungeon?" She goes into more
detail about everything after that, though, and walks
me through the escape from New Mexico, their time
at the John Hancock Center in Chicago—which I was
totally right about being a Mog attack—and then their
temporary hideout in Maryland, where she finally got
the emails I'd been sending her. She tells me about
a team of Garde sent down to Florida, and my head
buzzes as I think of all the weird messages that had
been sent to me about gangs in the Everglades and kids
with telekinetic powers.

One of the Garde died down there, and when she left John and the others, none of them even knew which one it was.

Shit is getting very real on Earth.

The more we talk, the more the puzzle pieces start to fit together. A bigger story forms. Notes and small leads start to connect, and I suddenly have information about people and places that I was just kind of guessing at before. I learn names like Setrákus Ra and Adam, and that there's a giant Mog base somewhere up in West Virginia, and that the Mogs have been doing all sorts of experiments with some of the dead Garde and alien animals—not that *this* is really any surprise, considering the crazy-ass stuff they've been doing to Bud Sanderson.

I type notes on one of the computers in the hidden room as fast as I can, trying to keep up with her as she talks.

"This stuff is incredible," I say. "I never could have uncovered all this on my own."

"What's your plan, Mark?" She stares at the security monitors on the wall. Sarah's still trying to wrap her head around the fact that I'm hiding out in some kind of spy base. Over her shoulder, I see BK travel across the monitors—a pet from another planet helping to make sure our perimeter is secure.

I pause. I've been going full throttle, alone, trying

to absorb everything. I haven't really had to put into words what my mission or whatever is.

"We tell the world what's really happening," I say, choosing my words carefully. "We wake them up and get them on our side."

Sarah smiles at me strangely, as if she wasn't expecting something like that to come out of my mouth.

"Next time I talk to John, I'll see what kind of evidence he can send our way."

As we work, I tell her about breaking into Sam's house and finding all the old newsletters, stealing Purdy's computer and my road trip across the country—first looking for her and then following GUARD's orders to Alabama. She listens carefully as I talk, her face twisting and lighting up as she calls me "lucky" and "stupid" and even "heroic."

Mark James, hero. That has a nice ring to it.

I'm pretty sure I blush when she says it, because afterwards she laughs and rolls her eyes. But it feels good. Especially since this is the first time I've really sat and thought about all the different things I've had to do in the last few weeks. I've been so focused on the stuff I've failed at—like getting caught in the FBI trap and not being able to contact Sharma or find Sarah—that I'd kind of forgotten that I've totally been living in, like, a James Bond movie lately. With aliens. And *I'm* 007.

John sends us crappy cell phone pics of a bunch of documents he recovered from some FBI agents—including my old friend Agent Walker, who has apparently switched sides completely and is helping out the Loric. At least for now. I'm happy she let me go, but I can't imagine that I'd trust Walker or her agents with my life or anything. I hope John and the others know what they're doing. I *can* say that this stuff combined with some of the other files we've salvaged from Purdy's computer make for some pretty epic breaking news. I'm talking stuff like photos of Mogs shaking hands with politicians and lists of who within the government is playing ball with the shark-faced mofos. I practically piss my pants with excitement when Sarah forwards them to me—before I send them along to GUARD for a second look. A story like this could be big, so we should probably make sure that we don't completely screw it up when we post it.

We print out everything and tape it to the walls of the back room, trying to piece together the larger story. This stuff is bigger than all of us. It's the truth, and the world needs to be able to see it.

I start working on articles: posts that incorporate all the new info that's suddenly been dumped at my feet.

"This shit is going to go *viral*," I tell Sarah.

"It's definitely going to piss off the Mogs," she says hesitantly. "You're sure they can't track us here?"

"Definitely. GUARD's got this place locked down."

"He'd better," she says.

It sounds like she might have some doubts about this. She's not exactly on Team GUARD and asks a lot of questions—about where all the stuff in the safe house came from, how he got a truck to me, *anything* about his actual personal life—that I can't answer because *I have no idea who he is.* I tell her that she should just trust him and be done with it, but that's not exactly her style—especially with all she's been through. I don't really blame her. I'm not even really sure why I trust in him so much. Maybe it's because, after Sarah disappeared, he was the one constant I had.

After Sarah's read over the articles, I upload them, and our hit counter on They Walk Among Us skyrockets. My post detailing MogPro—which, it turns out, stands for "Mogadorian Progress"—attracts a lot of attention thanks to the intel John gets out of Walker. Some commentators start guessing that the whole blog is viral marketing for some new sci-fi movie. Other anonymous users send death threats. Views and comments come in from all over the world—so many that I give Sarah the log-in to my JOLLYROGER182 account so we can split the work of sorting through them.

We make a good team. Things are looking up.

Until the next day, at least. I wake up from a power nap around dusk feeling a little off. Just weak, and a little sick to my stomach. I'm sweating a lot too, which I brush off as the fact that we're in the South and it's humid as balls. When I get up and start moving, I realize that my left arm is all stiff and sore. And so while I wait for coffee to brew in the kitchen, I pull up my T-shirt sleeve and take a good look at the place where the bullet grazed me.

It's not pretty.

The wound is swollen and a dark, sort of terrifying red color. It's kind of hot to the touch too. In short, it looks mad at me for not taking better care of it.

Sarah walks into the kitchen while I'm looking at my arm.

"Holy crap, Mark."

"It's not that bad," I suggest.

"No." She shakes her head. "That looks terrible."

"I'll just pour some more rubbing alcohol on it and pick up some superglue and . . ." I have to stop because she looks like she's going to simultaneously puke and smack me.

"It's infected. We have to do something about it or it'll get even worse."

"We've got a lot of work to do." I start for the back room.

"You could lose your *whole arm*, Mark," she says, standing in front of me so I can't pass. She puts her hand on my forehead. "Jesus, you've got a fever. You could get *sepsis*. We'll just . . . We have to do something. At least let's get some antibacterial stuff."

I relent. We could use some more groceries, anyway.

I grab my keys. Sarah clears her throat, holding out one palm.

"I'm driving," she says.

"Uh, no way," I say. Suddenly I'm feeling very overprotective of my shiny new truck, and the Sarah I know—or knew in Paradise at least—didn't have the best history with oversized vehicles.

"Mark."

"Sarah," I say. We lock eyes for a few seconds. "I'm okay to drive. I promise. Trust me."

She doesn't respond immediately but finally sighs.

"Okay," she says. "Okay."

Huntsville is the big city closest to us, but there are a bunch of little towns between there and the ranch. I try to go to a different one every time I pick up supplies, so this time I drive Sarah towards a place called Moulton, which is tiny but has a Walgreens and a grocery store at least. BK rides in the back, and I roll one of the windows down so he can stick his head out. The sun starts to set in the west. As we drive, we make supply lists out loud.

"Maybe we could get BK to sneak into the pharmacy section and steal you some penicillin," Sarah suggests. "Though, I'm not sure he can read."

"I'm pretty sure I'm allergic to penicillin," I say.

"You don't know?"

I shrug. "I'm, like, 90 percent positive."

She shakes her head.

"What?" I ask. "I've been going to the same doctor since I was a baby. He always just prescribed me medicine, and I took it."

"Give me a list of UN ambassadors," she says.

I don't know where she's going with this, but I start to rattle off the people I've been looking into based on the files we've uncovered. She stops me after a dozen.

"You can name all those people," she says, "but you don't know if you're allergic to penicillin. If it could *kill* you? If I didn't know any better, I'd say you'd been replaced with a Mog clone since we were in Paradise."

She's right. I start to laugh a little at just how absurd this is. How absurd all this is. Then she does too. It's like I haven't laughed in a really long time and now have to get it all out of my system while I can. I go into a *fit* of laughter. And it feels wonderful.

So wonderful that I end up running a stop sign.

I know this because suddenly there are flashing lights and a motorcycle cop behind me, pulling me off onto a side street in Moulton.

"Oh shit," I say. "Oh shit, oh shit, oh shit."

You're so fucking stupid, Mark.

"What do we do?" Sarah asks. She's sitting up

straight, her left hand white knuckled as she grips the console between us. "Please tell me your GUARD friend gave you a legit fake ID."

"No." I shake my head. It's not like I can give the officer my real license—I'm guessing everything with my name on it has been flagged by the FBI. "Let me think."

I never had to worry about traffic tickets in Paradise—perk of being the sheriff's son. I even talked my way out of a ticket for underage drinking once because this guy Todd, a former Paradise High football player, was the officer who caught me and my buddies with a case of beer out in a cornfield. But now my life is going to be monumentally screwed up because of a single stupid stop sign.

The officer dismounts from his bike. I pull my sleeve as far down over the wound on my arm as I can and then tighten my grip around the steering wheel.

"I might be able to lose him if I speed off while he's up here," I say.

"He's on a bike, Mark," Sarah says. "And you have no idea where you are, do you? He'd catch up to us."

She's right. Of course she is.

I glance into the truck's backseat. BK's tail is wagging, but his eyes are darting back and forth between me and Sarah as if he's asking what he should do.

"Worst comes to worst, can BK scare him off?"

Sarah just looks at me, shrugging. BK lets out a little

whine. I can't even tell if the damned dog can understand me.

And then the officer's tapping on the window.

"License and registration," he says as I roll it down.

"Uh, yeah . . . ," I start.

I launch into this whole story about how we're on vacation—hence the Louisiana plates—and we'd just run up to town to buy a few groceries, and, oops, we totally left our IDs and stuff down by the swimming hole at the ranch where we're staying.

I actually use the term "swimming hole."

The officer sighs and asks if the truck is mine. I say it is, and he tells me to stay put while he goes back to his bike. I use the time to take a few deep breaths and try not to completely lose my shit.

"This is okay," I murmur. "Maybe he'll just write me a ticket. I'll give him a fake name."

Sarah stares holes through me.

"What?" I ask. "Do you want me to make a break for it now?"

"Is this truck stolen?" She raises one eyebrow as she speaks.

"No, of course—" I stop talking because . . . it could be. I guess I really have no idea.

I look into the side mirrors nervously as the cop strolls back up to my side of the truck. He doesn't seem to be treating us like felons at least.

"All right," he says. "The vehicle's not listed as missing or anything. I don't see why I should ruin your vacation with a few tickets. I'm going to let you off with a warning, but I've reported it, so don't make it a habit of driving around without your license or you'll definitely get a citation next time." He grins. "Just make sure to watch for those stop signs, son."

I'm so relieved I could vomit.

He starts to walk away but turns back.

"Funny first name," he says. "I don't think I've ever heard it before."

"Huh?" I ask, confused.

"From your registration. Jolly. Jolly Roger." He thinks about this for a second and laughs a little. Meanwhile, my lungs fall into my guts.

"It's a family name," I mutter.

But all I can think about is how he just ran the plates to a truck that turns out to be registered to a guy named Jolly Roger. A truck purchased the morning after a shootout between JOLLYROGER182 and the FBI, in the same city. And how, at this moment, the Mogs are probably slobbering all over themselves to find out who this dickhead is who's unleashing all their secrets on the internet.

You're an idiot, Mark. How could you be so stupid as to use that name?

"You look like you're about to pass out," Sarah says. "Are you feeling okay?"

I swallow hard. Screw supplies. Screw my arm.

"I think we'd better go back to the ranch."

CHAPTER
ELEVEN

SARAH TRIES TO TELL ME THAT I'M FREAKING out about this too much, but I can tell she's worried too. She knows the lengths the Mogs will go to in order to get what they want—after all, she was their prisoner. As we drive, she goes into more detail about the rebel Mog John's recruited on to his team. Apparently, he's a hard-core computer wiz, and there are tons of evil ETs who've been trained on computers just like he has.

It doesn't bode well for us. I kind of wish I'd known this sooner. I have no way of knowing who'd win in a hacker battle between GUARD and a spaceship full of highly trained Mogs.

I have Sarah text GUARD, telling him what happened, more about Adam, and asking for his advice. She reads and responds for me as I drive us back towards the ranch.

GUARD: If the Mogs had no idea where you were, they'd never be able to track you down based on your IP address or any of your communications from the ranch.

GUARD: But if they know you're somewhere near a little town in Alabama, that could be trouble.

Me: SHIT. What should we do?

GUARD: That's your call. It should take them a while to pinpoint an area to search. Could take hours. Could take weeks. I don't know how skilled their hackers are.

GUARD: More than likely they'd just raze the whole area looking for you.

Me: All my notes and stuff are at the ranch. We need that info, but maybe it'd be better if we just abandoned the base? Can you get all my stuff off the computer?

A minute passes.

GUARD: No. It's either dead or turned off. I can track its location, but I can't get onto it remotely without juice.

Not charging my electronics is going to kill me.

Sarah looks at me.

"All the work we've been doing is on your computer, right?" she asks.

"Yeah, but—" I start.

"We can swing by and grab everything. Then, I don't

know, find one of those crappy motels you've gotten so good at scouting out."

"This is dangerous," I say.

She laughs a little.

"You don't have to tell me."

She texts GUARD back, telling him what we're doing.

GUARD: You're a true patriot for Earth. Keep me posted. Constant communication.

Night has completely fallen by the time we get back to the ranch. Everything looks just as we left it. Calm and boring.

"Bernie," Sarah says, letting the dog out of the backseat, "go take a look around, okay? But be careful."

I guess he understands her, because he darts off as we hurry inside. I head straight to the back room to pack up my notes and computers while Sarah grabs some of our clothes, food and other random stuff that might come in handy on the road. It's almost like we're getting ready to go on vacation instead of running away to hide from aliens and government henchmen.

I've just pulled my big messenger bag over my shoulder when all the lights go dark.

I hear glass breaking in the kitchen.

"Sarah!" I shout.

She yells back at me from the kitchen that she's fine. I trip over a chair trying to get to her—the windowless room is completely pitch-black now that the power's off. I curse as I hit the ground hard, my left arm throbbing. There's a sound like the air conditioner starting up and then suddenly the power's back on. I vaguely remember seeing a generator out at the back of the house—thanks again, GUARD. As I get to my feet, I kick the chair out of the way. Just as I'm about to leave the room, the security monitors boot up.

There are at least twenty Mogs closing in on the ranch house.

There's a split second when I freeze, can't even will my legs to move. And then adrenaline crashes over me and I react. I grab two guns off the weapons shelves and bolt to the kitchen, where Sarah's crouched over a few glasses she knocked to the ground when the lights went out.

"What was—" she starts.

"Mogs!" I whisper.

Before she can respond, an explosion blows the front door in.

Both of us duck behind the kitchen island. I'm about to tell Sarah to stay down when she grabs one of the handguns I brought from the back room and fires two shots through the kitchen window, nailing a Mog right in the forehead. It turns to ash and disappears.

Whoa.

"Did you bring ammo?" she asks as she fires through the front doorway while I cock the shotgun I grabbed.

Crap. Ammo.

"No," I admit.

"Can you use that?" She nods to my weapon.

"Yeah."

"Then cover me," she says.

As gunfire and Mog blasts tear up the living room and kitchen, I pop up from my cover and start pumping rounds through the doorway and windows, firing at every possible place the Mogs could be. I wonder how screwed we are—how many Mogs were just off camera on the monitors? Sarah makes for the back room, grabbing a big butcher's knife out of a block along the way and keeping it positioned at chest level, ready to strike.

I can't help but marvel at what a badass my ex-girlfriend has turned into.

She reappears with a grocery bag overflowing with ammo. We duck behind the kitchen island again to regroup and reload. I keep my shotgun pointed at the kitchen window.

"We could bunker down in the back," I say. "The door's thick."

"No way." She shakes her head. "We'd be trapped."

"Then we have to make it to the truck." I pat my pocket to make sure my keys are there. "If they haven't blown it up or something."

We nod to each other in agreement. The messed-up thing is that we've been in this sort of situation together before, back at Paradise High. Only back on campus, we had superpowered aliens on our side. Now it's just us against a bunch of Mogs.

But then, I tend to forget that I have friends who always seem to come through for me.

There's a giant roar outside, like a damned dragon has suddenly appeared out of the sky.

"Shit," I say, imagining some kind of huge Mog creature that's going to tear the roof off the house at any second. "We're dead."

"No," Sarah says as she reloads. Her face actually lights up. "We're saved."

Most of the Mog gunfire that had been focused on the house suddenly disappears. They're shooting at something else. The roar sounds again, but this time there's something almost familiar about it—something I recognize. It's not unlike a beagle's howl.

Bernie-fucking-Kosar is destroying the Mogs in the front yard.

I grin.

"Can BK hold the bastards off?" I ask.

"For a little while," Sarah says. "Probably."

"Now. Go. This is our chance."

We move in unison, running in a crouched position until we're taking cover on opposite sides of the front doorway. Peeking out, I can see a bunch of piles of ash around the lawn, as well as at least a dozen shark-faces attacking BK. I actually wasn't that far off when I thought there was a dragon in the yard. John Smith's dog is now a huge beast, all muscle and claws and snapping teeth. One of the Mogs blasts him in the leg with a cannon, and in response BK impales him with one of two horns that have grown out of his head.

"Holy hell," I mutter.

"Go!" Sarah shouts. "BK will catch up."

And so we run. Luckily, most of the Mogs are focused on BK, and the others we cross paths with are so distracted by the roaring of the beast and shouts of their fellow pale-faced douche bags that we catch them by surprise. A few shots and they're nothing but dust. We're in the truck quickly, and before any of them are the wiser, I've got the engine on and am gunning it down the little path that leads to the street.

A lone Mog stands between us and the open gate to Yellowhammer Ranch. He holds a blaster out in front of him.

"Get down," I shout to Sarah as he fires.

I swerve, losing control of the truck for a few seconds but missing the blasts from the Mog's weapon. I regain control just in time to ram into him. The alien rolls over the hood and roof, landing in the bed of my truck, where he tries to get up on his feet again. Sarah leans out the window and shoots him, and I swear to God we really are the heroes in an action movie.

"Bernie!" she shouts, her head still out the window.

In the rearview mirror, I can see Bernie's form start to change, and then suddenly he's soaring through the air as an oversized golden bird. He lets out a shrill call as his giant wings beat against the wind, propelling him forward. He lands in the back of the truck, returning to his familiar dog form just before he hits the bed. Half a second passes before his wet nose is against the back windshield. He barks and pants and looks like a worried, but totally normal, floppy-eared dog as we pass through the gate to Yellowhammer Ranch.

"Holy crap," Sarah says. She's breathing deeply. "Okay. We're okay. Whoa."

"We don't know that for sure." I hand my burner over to Sarah. "Text GUARD. Tell him we just escaped the Mogs."

It takes her a few seconds to get the text out because her hands are shaking a little. I keep my eyes scouring the road, the fields and the sky, terrified that more Mogs are going to show up at any moment.

"Okay, it's—" she starts, but she's cut off by the ringing phone.

GUARD is calling.

"Holy shit" is how I answer the phone.

"How far are you and Sarah from the house?" GUARD asks. His voice is the same slightly distorted, electronic-sounding one from the night when he warned me about the FBI trap.

I glance in the rearview mirror.

"I don't know. Maybe a mile? I can still see it in—"

I'm cut off by the sound of an explosion. I hit the brakes out of sheer confusion and instinct—and so I can whip my head around and see it for myself. The ranch, barn—the entire area surrounding our safe house—has gone up in a huge ball of fire. I have to shield my eyes.

"That should take care of any Mogs remaining on the property and thoroughly wipe our tracks," GUARD says.

Sarah turns to me, her mouth hanging open.

"GUARD, dude," I say. "Did you just blow up the safe house?" My voice starts to get louder. "Were we working on top of a *bomb* this whole damned time?"

"I can guarantee that the only way that bomb was going to go off was if I wanted it to, and that would only happen in an instance like this. You were both perfectly safe."

I don't know what to say. I just sit on the phone in silence, hardly breathing. Trying to wrap my head around this.

"Get the truck moving again," GUARD says. "The two of you are coming to my home base."

Suddenly, the GPS on my truck activates, plotting a course to some place outside of Atlanta.

"I'll see you in a few hours," GUARD says.

Then he hangs up.

CHAPTER
TWELVE

WE PASS A FEW OTHER HOUSES AS WE SPEED away from the ranch. They're secluded, just like Yellowhammer was, and separated by miles and miles of fields and land. All of them have little trails of smoke rising from their yards and roofs. Not completely destroyed like my base, but definitely messed up.

The Mogs must have narrowed our location down to one area and then systematically searched for us house by house. My brain shuts down as I start to wonder who lived in these homes. Who the Mogs slaughtered in their effort to find us.

It takes everything I have not to puke my guts out.

We ride in silence for a while, listening to BK's panting in the backseat. I think both of us are in shock. Finally, the quiet is broken when Sarah's phone rings. It's John.

"Before you say anything," she says when she

answers, "I just want you to know that I'm okay."

She talks to John on the phone, and I strain to try to hear what he's saying on his end. She tells him a little bit about what happened and where we're going. I'm glad she doesn't give him any specifics, because I don't know how new her burner is or how careful John and the others have been about using them.

Safe houses won't keep us alive, apparently. Paranoia might. Though I don't even know if I can call any of us paranoid, since our fears are totally justified.

"Tell John to kick some Mog ass," I say.

When she's off the phone I ask her how her alien boyfriend is.

"Fine," she says.

"Are you worried about him?"

"Every second."

We cross the state line into Georgia around dawn. Sarah yawns a lot but doesn't sleep. I offer her an energy drink from my stash in the backseat, but she turns her nose up at it. I down a can in one gulp.

Not long after that my fever comes back, and I start to feel a little woozy. My arm is so sore that I can hardly use it to drive, and Sarah makes me pull off the highway and into a drugstore parking lot. She goes in with some cash and comes out a few minutes later, demanding I move to the passenger seat. I down a few Tylenol at Sarah's insistence and despite the energy drink I've guzzled, I pass out.

I wake up to Sarah poking the side of my face. We're almost there. The landscape looks eerily similar to what it did at the ranch house. GUARD definitely has a knack for finding secluded hideouts. We come to a gate among a bunch of trees, and the GPS beeps that we've reached our destination. I can just make out a few structures through a dense thicket of incredibly green trees. Old signage says something about the place being a peach-and-pecan orchard.

That must be the place. GUARD's base.

"I can't believe I'm finally going to meet the man himself," I say as we start up an old trail that cuts through rows of thin, dead trees. I'm feeling groggy and drained, but knowing GUARD must be just a couple of yards away fills me with adrenaline.

"You sure this is where your friend is?" Sarah asks. I can hear the skepticism in her voice.

"He's the one who inputted it into the GPS," I say.

"It just seems so . . . ordinary."

I can see a few flashes of silver throughout the branches—cameras. Naturally. I point them out to Sarah and tell her that I'd thought the same thing about the ranch house before I went inside. I'm guessing cameras are up all over the place, just like in Alabama. Possibly even some remote-operated weapons too. I wouldn't put it past GUARD.

Eventually, the trees all give way to big, open lawns around a white farmhouse and a gigantic steel building behind it that looks like it used to be some kind of small mill or factory or something.

"He's here," I say, more to myself than to Sarah. He has to be here. Everything is going to work out. We're going to meet up with GUARD and figure out what we can do to bring down these Mogadorian bastards.

I jump out of the truck when we park in front of the house and am a little wobbly on my feet. My fever's getting worse. BK stares up at me with wet-looking eyes as if he's actually worried about me or something, but I man up and keep going. There's a note on the front door of the house that just says "Out Back," scrawled in messy handwriting. So we wander around the house to the big metal building. We walk through the front door and must trip some kind of invisible alarm, because suddenly the door locks behind us and there are four guns mounted on robotic arms trained on us.

"Shit!" I yell as I try to pull the door open.

"Mark," Sarah says quietly, but I can tell that she's freaking out.

I start to move forward but the guns stay on me, keeping their aim with every step I take. So instead, I take a few steps to the right and plant myself in front of Sarah. At our feet, BK starts to growl. The edges of his body begin to contort, as if he's just about to transform into a monster.

"I wouldn't go any farther than that if you don't want to end up full of holes," a muffled voice says.

There's a figure standing in front of us that's tall—taller than me—and wearing loose-fitting coveralls and a shiny, robotic-looking helmet. Something about it is familiar, but I don't know why. My head is fuzzy from the fever. A bunch of tools hang from a belt around the person's waist, but I'm more concerned about what's in their hands, which, based on what I can remember about the weapons in my dad's old office, is a semiautomatic combat shotgun.

Dozens of scenarios flash through my mind, none of which end well for us. My loudest thought screams that I've been duped again. That I've been a huge dumbass and somehow ended up communicating with another fake GUARD. Or maybe GUARD was never on our side to begin with. There's no mystery grenade to save me this time, though. With all the security stuff everywhere, I'm guessing even if we did make it outside, we'd still be goners.

Behind me, Sarah's breathing is heavy, and my entire body shudders with regret for bringing her into this.

I'm relieved when the figure lowers the shotgun, but that feeling is quickly replaced by confusion when the weird helmet comes off. The person in front of us is a black woman with strong, slightly masculine features. Her hair's shaved on the sides but fades into a short, flat Mohawk on the top of her head. A sheen of sweat shines on her face. She looks like a badass warrior, but she's also totally hot.

She stares at BK and mutters something in a language I've never heard. Her voice is commanding. Suddenly, BK heels.

So much for that line of defense.

"A Chimæra. Wonderful," she says. She turns her attention to me. "Mark James. You look even worse than the last time I saw you."

That's when I realize why the helmet looked familiar. I've seen this person before. In New Mexico.

She's the courier who delivered the first package to me.

"Wait . . . ," I say. "*You're* GUARD?"

She nods, raising one eyebrow as if she thinks I should have somehow figured this out already. As if I had any reason to guess that the person I'd been in contact with all this time wasn't a conspiracy-obsessed hacker shut-in but a woman who looks like she'd be equally comfortable on a magazine cover or a battlefield.

"You can call me Lexa. That was my name on Lorien."

Lorien?

My head pounds as my brain tries to make sense of the fact that GUARD is not only a chick, but an alien.

What the hell is going on?

"Mark," Sarah says, breathless. Her eyes are wide and staring at something farther back in the giant metal building, behind the woman.

And then I see what's got her attention.

"Welcome to the hangar," Lexa says. "It looks like we need to get you fixed up. I hope you're good with tools. I'm trying to get this thing to run off the primitive fuel systems available on this planet."

She turns away from us and walks towards the beat-up silver spaceship parked in the back of the hangar.

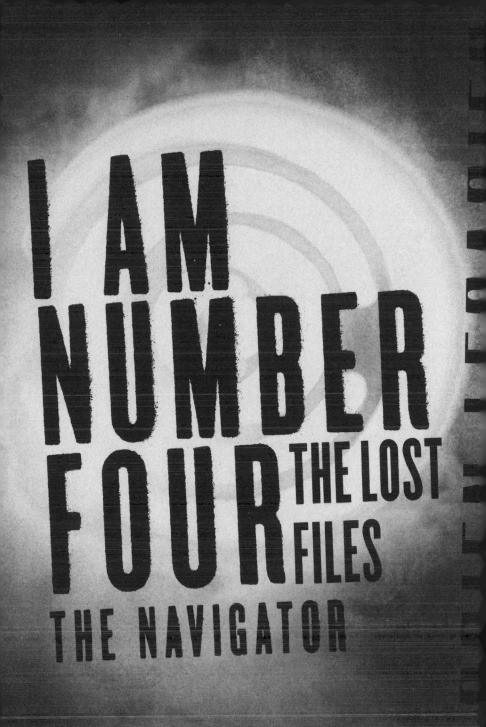

I AM NUMBER FOUR

THE LOST FILES

THE NAVIGATOR

CHAPTER
ONE

I'M WOKEN UP BY TWO POUNDING BANGS THAT reverberate through my basement apartment. There's shouting somewhere outside on the street. A single thought shoots through my brain: *They're here.*

My survival instincts take over. I jump out of bed and start shoving anything particularly damning out of sight, hiding data pads and electronic storage devices filled with stolen files in secret drawers and compartments I've built into my furniture. My heart pounds, but I move calmly, methodically, zoning in on my task. I've always worked best under pressure. It's a skill that comes in handy when you do what I do.

I'm leaning over my main computer when a few notes from a guitar or synthesizer filter in from outside, followed by the sound of a cheering crowd. It's only then that my brain starts to logically assess what's going on. I pause to take stock of the situation, my fingers hovering over a keyboard, ready to wipe a hard drive full of incriminating data logs. There hasn't been any more banging or knocking. There's no official from the Lorien Defense Council bursting through my door. Just some music and the sounds of people . . . laughing?

It's only then I remember it's the day of the Quarter-moon celebration.

The music riff stops. I pause and listen for a few seconds before closing my fingers into a fist and creeping over to one of the small windows located near the ceiling of my apartment. I step up on a chair and peel back a blackout curtain just a hair so I can peer outside. Across the street, Eilon Park is packed with people, its location on the outskirts of the city making it the perfect place for those living in more rural areas to congregate in celebration. A kaleidoscope of lights blinks over the dancing crowds, painting them in neon colors. Somewhere a stage must be set up. There are two more powerful bangs that once again rattle my apartment—a bass drum, I realize this time—before a band breaks into some synth-heavy song to the obvious delight of everyone in the park.

Part of me feels stupid for being scared by a drum, but mostly I'm angry. Not because my sleep was cut short—it's dark out, which means it was time for me to wake up, anyway—but because this sort of government-sanctioned celebration is just one of the many ways that the Elders keep the Loric masses placated. They put on all-night parties and erect flashy monuments and light displays they call Heralds, and we are supposed to thank them—to recognize these events as signs that all is well on Lorien. All is *perfect*.

But it's not.

My feet step back onto the cold stone floor. My heart is still pumping in my chest, and I try to slow it down by breathing deeply and stretching my limbs. The tips of my fingers drag across the ceiling as I stretch. On the streets of Capital City—on the rare occasions that I'm out in public during the day—I tower over most of the population, especially other women. Despite my height I rarely feel claustrophobic in my apartment, which is just one big room. If I ever did feel cramped, I could just clean up a bit, since most surfaces are piled high with books and electronics in various states of repair or modification.

I slip on black pants and a T-shirt before returning to my main computer. My adrenaline is still pumping. Best to put this energy to use.

"Talk to me," I say, logging in to my terminal. "What have you got for Lexa today?"

I open up a few of the data-collecting programs I've designed and find a treasure trove of intercepted messages, alerts and intel. The most useful type of currency: information.

A few weeks ago the Grid, which controls and monitors basically all communications and municipal functions in Capital City, had started to malfunction in various locations throughout my neighborhood. Usually the Grid is impossible to hack—even for someone as skilled as I am—but when my own scanners had alerted me to the issue, I saw an opportunity. A chance for me to gather confidential communications—to show the people of Lorien that there are pockets of corruption in our government and secrets that the Elders and high-ranking officials keep from us. I was able to get to one of the Grid workstations before the Munis lackeys got around to fixing it. I did their job for them—adding a bit of my own hardware to the system. Since then, the "impenetrable" Grid has been mine for the perusing.

And I've been stockpiling all kinds of data.

This is supposed to be one big, happy utopia. At least that's what the Elders—and therefore everyone who buys in to them being all-powerful and all-knowing—want us to think. In order for Lorien to be "perfect," all of us have to abide by certain rules. We fall into categories, which make us easier to classify and control. Garde and Cêpan. If you have Legacies, you're a soldier. If you don't, you're a Mentor or Munis or bureaucrat. You're told to follow certain tracks, and if you don't—if something happens that sends your life careening off your destined path—or if you question the system too vocally, then the rest of the Loric don't know what to do with you. If you aren't working in an expected role, you are flawed. You are different, which isn't a good thing. You might as well be actively working *against* the rest of the planet.

Granted, that's exactly what I'm doing. Not for the sake of anarchy but for freedom. What most people don't know—or choose not to believe—is that there are some of us who don't agree with the way things are run. We've realized that, while this may look like a model society, the cost is our free will.

Some of us have lost too much to Lorien. *I've* lost too much. And I want to see it changed. We need reform. We need *revolution*.

The sounds from the celebration across the street are so loud that my apartment has become an echo chamber of cheers and electronic music. I try to focus as I sort through the various communiqués my programs have intercepted throughout the day. Mostly they're harmless—orders for Munis workers, notes from schools about absent students, traffic statistics. What I'm interested in are the encrypted files. Those are the ones that get personal. You can tell a lot about people based on the words they don't want you to read. I've come across a lot of interesting tidbits—cheating spouses, conned business partners, less-than-scrupulous teachers at the Lorien Defense Academy. There are many people who would pay me well for the information. Or to keep it from going public. I know because, in desperate times, information has kept me fed and paid my rent. What I'm really looking for now, though, is something that will expose corruption in the Lorien Defense Council or the Elders—something that will force the people of Lorien to take a hard look at the way our government is run.

I know it has to be there. I just haven't found anything heinous enough yet. But I will. I have to have faith in that. It's the goal that keeps me going, that gets me out of bed. Besides, I'm not just doing this for myself. I'm also doing it in his memory.

I'm doing this for my brother.

My apartment shakes. A little stream of dust filters down from the ceiling. There are some heavy fireworks being shot off elsewhere in the city.

They're really going all-out with the celebrations this year.

An alert pops up that my decryption software is having trouble decoding a message that's just been intercepted from a communications channel I didn't know existed. I'm surprised my monitoring programs even picked it up. Either I'm getting much better at keeping tabs on Capital City or the higher-ups are getting really sloppy.

Whatever the case, an encrypted message broadcast

on a hidden channel like this is bound to contain something important.

I run a secondary decryption program, and an unin-
telligible mess of symbols and letters slowly begins to
form words. While it runs, I try to figure out who sent
the message and to whom. The former is a bust, leading me back to a computer terminal and address I don't
recognize, though I log it so I can track it down later. I
have better luck with the receivers. It appears to have
been transmitted to only nine ID bands—all belonging
to people whose names I don't know. Not a problem. I
run a cross-check against the LDC's database of every
registered citizen—a database that could really use
better firewalls—and sure enough, the names have one
big thing in common: they're all Mentor Cêpans.

Curious. Why would nine Mentor Cêpans be
contacted via an encrypted message during the Quartermoon celebration, a night when most people like to
pretend they don't have a care in the world? I wonder
if it's a matter concerning them, or their Garde—what
unnecessary risks they're asking those gifted with Legacies to take now.

I switch back to the decryption program. It's still
working, but I can pick out a few words. "Airstrip."
"Garde." "Loridas."

My entire body freezes.

Loridas.

This has something to do with the Elders. I've been trying to track down more information about their current locations ever since I intercepted a Grid message a few days ago mentioning they were all off-world. Why? What are they up to?

I grin as I lean back, putting my hands behind my head and rubbing them over my buzz cut. Regardless of the message's content, something like this—something straight from the Elders—will definitely be valuable. People get obsessed over the details of the Elders' lives. I could have just intercepted Pittacus Lore's grocery list, and I bet I could sell it for enough credits to pay my rent for a month.

There's a sound from across the room. My modified identity band—which looks more like a silver cuff now that I've integrated a communications system into it—vibrates on the table. Zophie's name flashes on the surface. I don't answer but slip the cuff onto my wrist, wondering why she's contacting me. Possibly for another museum gig, I suppose. Zophie's from what others would call "a good family," which really just means that they're wealthy and spend a lot of that money at charity galas and stuff like that. We were at the Lorien Defense Academy at the same time, friendly but not exactly friends. She was always with a pack of other students, but I preferred solitude, even then, back before everything changed and I went off the Grid. Later—years after the incident—we met again at a Kabarak in the Outer Territories, where I was reconfiguring a computer network. By that point she was heading the Department of Otherworld Studies at the Loric Museum of Exploration. She's the one who brought me back to Capital City to work on a restoration project at the museum, refurbishing the onboard systems of an old fossil-fuel spacecraft. It was good money—enough to upgrade most of my computer equipment, which inevitably led to where I am now. But we haven't spoken at all since my last day at the museum, and that was a few years ago.

Maybe it was a mistake. Maybe she just had too many ampules and wanted to wish everyone in her contacts a Happy Quartermoon.

The sounds of the crowds crescendo across the street. I continue trying to ignore them as I crack open a can of liquid stimulants and take a seat in front of the computer again. More of the message has been decoded, but it still doesn't make a lot of sense. Something about a prophecy coming true and the end of Lorien and . . .

"Evacuation?" I mumble to myself.

My ID band buzzes. It's Zophie again. I sigh and am about to answer when I realize that the music from the celebration has stopped. The crowds are still noisy, but their shouts are morphing. They're no longer sounds of jubilation or celebration but of fear and alarm.

What the hell is going on out there?

I rush over to the window and pull back the curtain. I can just see a bit of the sky.

It's red.

There's a surge in the panicked screams from the park, but since the small window is at ground level, the people sprinting past on the sidewalk mostly block my line of sight. My apartment shakes again, more violently this time. I see the light a few seconds before I realize what it is. Fire. Fire coming towards me in a huge wave, engulfing everyone in its path: men, women, children. I manage to take a few steps away from the window before the glass breaks and half the ceiling falls down around me.

CHAPTER TWO

I COME TO, CHOKING ON SMOKE AND DUST. MY ears ring. I can hear the sound of people yelling, but their voices are far away and fuzzy. At first I can't even tell where I am—it seems like a small, unlit room thick with haze—until I recognize the arm of a sofa that's in flames a few feet away from me. I'm still in my apartment. Only, the ceiling has mostly caved in and there are smoldering planks of wood where my computer equipment used to be, and I'm half buried in debris. My first instinct is to try to collect some of my personal belongings, but I can't stop coughing and my head is pounding, and I know that what I need to do is get up, out into some fresh air. It's too dangerous to stay here. And so I use the flaming couch as a point of reference and start towards the place where my window should be. I climb on all fours up a pile of rubble until I'm finally breathing in cleaner air and collapse on the lawn. My lungs are on fire. My dark skin is covered in ash and dust.

It's only then that I realize most of my building has been blown away, the apartments above mine completely obliterated. Razed, along with the rest of the structures on my block. I'm probably only alive at all because I was in a basement. Still coughing, I roll onto my stomach and look towards the park where the crowds had gathered for the celebration.

Only, there isn't really a park anymore. The trees are gone. Small fires dot the charred grass, smoke spiraling up towards a crimson sky. There are scores of blackened clumps throughout the park too. I tell myself they're tree stumps or the remains of the stage I never saw—anything to keep my mind away from the idea that these mounds were recently dancing around with their hands stretched up to the sky while drums and synthesizers blared.

My stomach lurches. My mind races, trying to make sense of the world I've climbed up into, which seems so different from the one I was just living in. What's happened? What caused this? I wonder if there's been some kind of gross miscalculation of celebratory pyrotechnics. Or if a Garde's new power has overwhelmed him, turning an unsuspecting kid into an untamable inferno and wiping out an entire block.

The streets fill with people, all shouting, adding

to my confusion. They're singed and bloodied. Some huddle over unmoving bodies on the ground. Others stumble unevenly before collapsing.

I realize that my identity band is vibrating—for all I know it's been going off constantly since I woke up. It's Zophie again. Not knowing what else to do, I accept her call.

"Lexa!" Her voice pours out of a hidden speaker on the side of the cuff. "Hello? Are you there?"

"Zophie," I murmur. My ears are ringing.

"You're okay! I thought you . . . Everything is so messed up."

"What's going on?" I ask, getting to my feet. It's the first of a million questions that are threatening to pour out through my lips. "My neighborhood . . . Eilon Park. Something's happened here."

"No. It's everywhere. We're being attacked. And not just the city. The planet. They're hitting us hard, Lexa. Their targets are strategic. . . . I think Lorien is falling. Everything we'd been warned about—it's all coming true."

The prophecy. My mind races back to the message I was decoding before everything turned to fire and ash. For generations, the Elders have been warning us that one day Lorien would face destruction and death. Some kind of global calamity. It's the entire reasoning behind our society's setup—with our super-powered children trained to be soldiers against some unknown enemy. I'd always thought it was a scare tactic. But as I stumble forward, stepping past the remains of a man dressed in the colorful robes of the Quartermoon celebration, I realize I might have been wrong.

"Lexa," Zophie continues before I can ask anything else. "You have to come to the museum. Right now. It's the only way you'll be safe. I need you. I have a plan."

"What?" I ask. My brain isn't functioning on all cylinders. I'm not sure if it's shock, or the cave-in, or both. "What are you talking about?"

"Just meet me there. I'm on my way now. As fast as you can, Lex. Run. Don't let anything stop you."

There's some kind of interference on her end of the line, and then the connection drops out. I look down at my cuff, thinking about who I should contact if the world really is going to shit. Who I should check in on. That's when I realize I have no one else to call. For the past few years I've been alone, refusing to get too close to anybody. Secluding myself. Making sure I had no strings, no one tying me down.

No one to worry or care about.

I look to the sky. The smoke from my neighborhood has created a layer of smog far above me, all but obstructing the Quartermoon and whatever else is out there causing this.

Who is attacking Lorien? Why? How could—

Beside me, the scarce remains of my building collapse farther, filling my basement apartment with fire and debris. I stumble away, coughing through the miasma of dust and ash that's kicked up.

This stirs something in me. A switch is flipped, and before I know it I'm running. On instinct. It's not until I'm at a full sprint that I realize my body is following Zophie's orders and that I'm headed towards the museum. My home is destroyed. My planet, flawed as it may be, is under attack. I don't know what else I'm supposed to do. I just have to focus and keep moving, heading towards the next goal.

The chaos is everywhere, widespread. Most people I pass are preoccupied with their own survival or with trying to find or help out their loved ones. They yell, asking no one in particular what is happening. I hear a short screech somewhere to my right—blocks away? Closer?—followed by an explosion and a rumbling beneath my feet that almost knocks me to the ground. Capital City is still under attack. And even after everything we did to prepare, we weren't ready. We were caught off guard.

The museum. It's not that far away now. Ten blocks or so. I just have to keep my legs moving and concentrate on the sound of my feet hitting the ground and . . .

Out of the smoke in front of me charge half a dozen figures unlike anything I've ever seen. They're pale, dressed in black and carrying blasters and swords that seem to glow with a light of their own. Dark circles ring their black eyes. Their gaping mouths are full of sharp, jagged teeth. The one in the front is huge, taller than me and three times as wide. He has a long black ponytail, but the sides of his head are shaved. Tattoos wind around his skull.

These monsters are definitely not Loric.

I stop too fast, and in doing so trip over a smoking tree branch, hitting the pavement hard. I'm trying to catch the breath that's been knocked out of me when one of the men—no, *creatures*—raises a blaster and fires at a woman crying over a lifeless body on the other side of the street. She falls forward.

My heart goes into overdrive as I fight the urge to vomit.

I stifle a cry and half-crawl to a nearby bush to try and get out of sight. The creatures continue forward. I look around to find something to protect myself with, but there's nothing. I'm alone—I don't even have a utility knife or anything with me, just the clothes on my back. I've always imagined there was no situation I couldn't handle by myself; I'm going to be proven wrong about this by being murdered on the streets of Capital City.

I clench my fists. I won't go down without a fight, at least.

Suddenly a blinding light flashes through the square. I squint and reel back. The burst appears to completely disorient the creatures in black, who take the brunt of its force. And then the strange men are flying through the air, battering against each other and slamming repeatedly into the ground.

Telekinesis. That means Garde are here somewhere.

The one who appears to be the leader is thrown far—well out of my range of sight. Another one of the sword-carrying bastards is impaled on a broken Grid pole. He roars, and then his body starts to disintegrate, turning to dust. A girl who looks far too young to be facing such creatures darts past the pile of ash, one hand in front of her as she uses her powers to crush another of the attackers. Her metallic red pants reflect the flames of a nearby club called the Pit, which smolders, threatening to live up to its name. Two other Garde flank her, their arms outstretched as the bodies of their enemies crash against each other, eventually turning to dust as well.

"This way," the girl yells to them, flipping back her unnaturally white hair. "I see survivors in the distance."

She points forward, and there's another flash of light. Then they're gone. Whoever those Garde were, I think they may have just saved my life.

CHAPTER
THREE

THE LORIC MUSEUM OF EXPLORATION IS A WHITE-brick building that looks mostly untouched. Whoever is attacking us must not think of it as being a worthy target. As I race up the stone steps, I wonder what I'm going to do if Zophie isn't here. What if she ran into some of those monsters and didn't make it past them?

Thinking about Zophie lying crumpled on the street makes me cringe in a way I wouldn't have expected. We're not close, but she was kind to me at a time when I had all but sworn off everyone in Capital City, and for that I guess I have some sentimental attachment to her. I grimace, steeling myself. This is no time to be getting caught up in emotions. I need to stay strong and focused.

One of the tall glass doors to the museum opens when I approach, and it's only when I'm inside and Zophie is closing it behind me that I realize it's because she was there, waiting for me.

I breathe a sigh of relief.

"Lexa," she says, stepping forward. She looks like she's about to hug me, but I hold out a hand instead. She pauses and then takes it, wrapping her fingers around it. Her curly red hair is pulled back into a tight bun, one strand falling haphazardly over her face.

"What the hell is happening?" I ask.

"Invasion," she says. "On a global scale."

"Who? I saw some . . ." I struggle to find the right word. "*Monsters*. They murdered a woman, but the Garde showed up and took them out."

Zophie nods, her eyes looking distant. "Those Garde were lucky, then. I saw some fighting on my way here too. But there were so many of the invaders. Armies of them, with beasts and weapons like I've never seen. The Garde were trying to defend some children and . . ."

She doesn't finish.

"Why are we here?" I ask. "Is there a bunker? Some kind of shelter we can hide in?"

"Bunker?" Zophie asks, her eyebrows forming a line of confusion across her forehead. "There is no bunker. There's only the ship. You're flying us out of here."

My mouth hangs open as I try to wrap my head around this.

"What?" I ask.

The idea is unfathomable to me. The ship Zophie's talking about is the one she'd hired me to work on, refurbishing the vessel to the state it would have been in when it was in use generations ago. But it was never actually meant to be flown. It runs on *fossil* fuel, something our society hasn't used in ages.

"Impossible," I say.

"Not impossible." She shakes her head. "It's our only way of getting out of here. The Elders . . . they don't expect the Loric to survive this. And even if we do, you saw those invaders, Lexa. Do you want to be under their rule?"

"Where do you expect us to go?"

"Earth," she says. "It's the closest inhabitable planet."

I know about this planet. When I was at the academy, I was on a team that specialized in modifying and upgrading technologies for Earth, a place we had been helping to advance and evolve for centuries. They had us to thank for several of "their" breakthroughs over the centuries. I can't believe Zophie is telling me that this planet that is so far behind ours in every conceivable way is our only hope for survival.

"There's no way," I say. "What would we even use for fuel?"

"You remember Raylan, the man who commissioned the ship restoration?" Zophie steps towards the glass doors, looking out warily. "Well, in order to receive his funding, the museum had to follow his very specific instructions. Part of that meant storing a tankard of synthetic fossil fuels in the display room. We all thought he was crazy. I mean, for the longest time he was living as a hermit in that huge compound. But maybe he was thinking farther ahead than any of us could. I've heard that he's a descendant of one of the Elders. Who knows—maybe he *knew* this was going to happen."

Zophie starts to wring her hands. I try to process everything that's happening.

"But there's a catch," she says, turning back to me. "Per Raylan's instructions, the fuel pump can only be accessed through a pass code—one only he knows. He contacted me right before communications went out asking me to oversee preparations. He was having trouble getting in contact with his pilot at the LDC. I told him I knew someone who could fly the rocket, but I wanted a place on the ship. He agreed. He's on his way now. Once he gets here we can fuel up and go."

I stare back at her, still not believing anything I'm hearing.

"Please," she says. "I can't fly this thing. You're the only one I trust to get us out of here alive. You *know* this ship. Even if you hadn't been on the refurbishing team—I know you used to program flight sims back at the academy. Those included older models like this, right?"

"That was years ago," I say. "I'm not a pilot. Call your brother."

Her brother, Janus, is a hot-shot pilot for the Lorien Defense Council. She shakes her head.

"I *did*. He's been called out on a mis—"

"Then call the LDC or the LDA. Call . . ." I struggle to come up with another viable option.

"There's no one else," she says. Her voice is firm but her hands are trembling. "I talked to my brother." She swallows hard. "He said these attacks were strategic. They've taken out our weapons, our ships—anything that's left is being used to fight. They've hit us hard. The ports, the academy . . . This is likely the only fly-able passenger ship left in Capital City. If we don't leave . . ."

She trails off, but I get the point. It's easy to see our situation. She doesn't believe this world is going to survive. Lorien, perfect Lorien, with its green forests and red-peaked mountains and Elders who always know what's best for us—this false utopia is going to burn.

"Besides, I've seen you fly before."

I wince.

"That was different," I say. "An accident. Besides, the only reason I got off the ground was because I was in a ship where almost every function was automated. Not like this ancient piece of crap you're suggesting we use."

"Lex . . ."

I stare into her big, pleading green eyes for what feels like a long time, but I say nothing. My mind is too overrun with the images of what I saw between my apartment and the museum. Everything Lorien has already lost. Everything *I've* lost. My home. My work. My brother. And now I stand in front of the only person I might consider a friend, and she's asking me to leave our world behind. Lorien, which I've been fighting to change.

But it is changed now. It can never be the same. And I realize that if I do go with her, all I'd be leaving behind is a planet. Not a home or family. My options are to try to escape or die fighting for a place that I had already grown to hate.

"There's more to it," Zophie says softly. "There are others going. There's another ship that's leaving. It may have *already* left. We have to join it. Janus is piloting it."

The doors burst open before I can respond. A small, floating trolley piled high with boxes and bags sails in. A dozen or so Chimærae follow behind it, and finally, a man. He's tall, with dark, curly hair and thick eyebrows. His pale-blue shirt is ringed with sweat.

"Crayton!" Zophie exclaims, rushing to close the doors behind him. "Where are Raylan and Erina. Are they . . . ?"

"They're staying," Crayton says. "They're Garde. They're going to fight."

Zophie's mouth hangs open for a few moments. Then she just nods.

"Who's this?" the man asks, staring at me.

"Our pilot," Zophie says, looking at me in a way that makes it obvious that she wants me to keep my mouth shut and just go along with her. "Lexa, this is Crayton. He's a caretaker at Raylan's estate. You may remember seeing him making deliveries to the museum when you were here. He's been our go-between with Raylan for years."

"What is all this?" I ask.

"Supplies," he says, waving to the boxes. "Food. Weapons. Water. Medicine. Even some bags of jewelry and valuables to barter with. Raylan had it all loaded up and ready to go at a moment's notice. I think he'd been anticipating something like this."

"I meant the Chimærae."

"They're coming with us." His voice gets quiet. "There were more of them when we left the estate. They fought bravely to make sure we got here."

I'm about to protest the idea of taking an animal horde on board the already-small ship—not to mention the fact that I don't even know if I can fly it—when Zophie steps forward.

"We need a pass code to access the fuel," she says. "Did he give it to you?"

"Yes." Crayton nods. "It's her name."

My head buzzes with confusion. Crayton shifts his weight, turning slightly, and that's when I realize that he's not just carrying a backpack. There's something moving inside the bag strapped to him, stretching beneath the dusty layer of fabric covering his pack and starting to fuss, as if just waking up.

A baby.

I must look surprised, because Crayton nods his head back over his shoulder.

"Her name is Ella. That's the pass code. I watched Raylan change it on his data pad right before I left. Something simple so I'd remember it."

Zophie pulls back the cloth covering the baby. She's tiny, pink and wrinkled. I haven't had much experience with babies, but she looks too small. Like a doll.

"She's so tiny," Zophie whispers, almost cooing.

"Everything happened very fast," Crayton says. "Erina wasn't feeling well, and then suddenly she was in labor. No time to trek into the city. But everything was fine. Erina and Raylan looked so happy. Then the sky turned red and everything went wrong. They entrusted her to me. I don't think . . . I don't think they believe this is something they will survive. I have to make sure she's safe. It's *bad* out there, Zophie. If they don't make it . . . their sacrifice can't have been in vain."

There's an explosion outside—close. Too close. Dust and debris fall from the ceiling around us.

"We have to move," Crayton says.

"This way." Zophie pulls on his sleeve. "Hurry!"

CHAPTER
FOUR

WE THROW ON ILL-FITTING SPACE SUITS PULLED
out of an exploration exhibit, slipping them on over our
own clothes. They're supposed to help with the changing pressures as we exit the atmosphere, but I'm more
concerned that the refurbished ship holds together
through liftoff at all. Besides, if we get to a point where
a space suit is the only thing keeping us alive, we're
probably dead already.

The ship is housed inside a cavernous domed
exhibit, alone in the center of the stone floor. Zophie
and I enter the room first, followed by the herd of
Chimærae and finally Crayton, who drags Raylan's
supplies on the floating lift. All three of us start shouting orders at the same time, trying to figure out what to
do. Caught up in the madness and fear of what's happening, I slip into a hyperproductive stupor, opening
the ship's main loading hatch and grabbing the first

of many boxes. Interactive panels line the walls of the room detailing the primitive nature of old vessels like ours. How inefficient and poisonous fossil fuel was before we switched to synthetics and then eventually the power crystals we use now. Zophie taps on one of the displays a few times, and it slides away, revealing a fuel pump. She plugs it into the ship and then joins Crayton and me as we load supplies as fast as we can.

"Can't these damned Chimærae help at all?" I ask.

"Feel free to ask them," Crayton says. "Not that they'll understand you. Besides, they're scared."

"*I'm* scared," Zophie says, her breath heaving as she somehow manages to lift a box that must weigh as much as she does up to me inside the ship. "I've never wished I had telekinesis more than I do right now."

When the supplies are taken care of, the Chimærae flood in, shrinking into smaller animals. They flank the sides of the cargo hold as I rush down the narrow hallway that leads to the cockpit, past the small private rooms, galley and common area. In the pilot's seat, I pause for a few moments as I try to recall the countless hours I'd spent inside this ship, helping to repair its systems—but I've crammed a lot of information into my brain since then. I think back to all the old guides and books I'd read and simulations I'd programmed; my fingers start pressing buttons and flipping switches. By some miracle I manage to get the ship powered on.

"We're ready," Zophie says as she appears beside me, taking a seat in the copilot's chair and buckling herself in. Crayton drops into a seat behind her, the swaddling backpack spun around so that the baby is in front of him.

"Everybody hold on." I press a few more buttons.

The loading door closes, and the ship tilts up, pushing us back in our seats. From the cockpit, we stare at the roof of the domed room, which is only a foot away from the nose of the ship.

"I'm guessing this thing's not retractable," I say.

Zophie shakes her head. She reaches out a hand and grasps my upper arm. A bead of sweat runs from my forehead down the side of my nose, stinging my eye.

"I guess we're about to find out how good a job we did of refurbishing this thing."

Zophie squeezes my arm. "Let's do this."

I flip a switch, and it feels like I've just detonated a bomb. Fire fills the room. The craft shakes so hard that I'm sure it's going to fall apart, ending our journey before it ever begins. But it doesn't, miraculously. Instead, we punch through the ceiling. The thick glass of the dome shatters, exploding out into the red night sky, glittering as it catches the light from the flames around us.

We're up in the air.

The cockpit offers a sweeping view of Capital City, and even though I'm focused on the control panels and onboard monitors, I can see how widespread the damage to Lorien is. Fire and smoke fill the horizon. On our right, a beam of purple light shoots down from the sky beyond the outskirts of the city. I don't know if it's a Herald or something far more ominous. From the air, many parts of the city are unrecognizable, smoldering scars where vibrant neighborhoods once stood. There's something strange about the skyline too, but I don't figure out what it is until I realize that we should be flying past the Spires of Elkin. But they're gone. The structures that held a third of our city's people have been obliterated.

I go numb. I can't look at it anymore. My focus shifts solely to the instruments in front of me.

"It's gone," Zophie whispers. "Our planet. Our home."

Our trajectory has more of an arc to it than it should, and I pull on the flight yoke, desperately trying to keep the ship's nose up. The sky is too dark, full of smoke from our burning city. But the ship presses on, and we punch through the haze. It's only then that we can see the enemy warships. Jagged and gray. Countless in number. Firing on our planet. Smaller ships shuttle down to the surface. In the middle is a pearly sphere, floating like a dim moon that the other vehicles orbit.

"How can this be happening?" Crayton asks.

We shoot past the fleet; by some luck our course sent

us through a hole in their formation. And then we're jetting into the blackness of space. Despite the ship's primitive nature, I have to admit it's *fast*. At least on takeoff.

And just like that—in the course of a few minutes— we've made it. We've left Lorien behind.

I tap on the radar screens, trying to make sure no one's following us, but I don't see anything. Once I figure out how to set the artificial gravity and autopilot, I finally allow myself to breathe. Clayton bounces the baby in his arms and whispers shaky reassurances to her, but his eyes are wide and watery.

"By the Elders . . . ," Zophie mutters. She leans forward in her seat, staring out into space. "Where's the other ship? Can you find it?"

It takes a little while to navigate the controls, but eventually I figure out how to expand the radar's search.

"I'm getting a Loric signature from a ship that appears to have stopped some distance from the planet," I say. "But it's a weak signal. We're so far away from it already."

"Turn back." She starts to nod. "Head towards it. We'll travel to Earth together."

After swiping through a few galaxy maps, I find Earth. Various figures start to populate the cockpit screens.

"I don't think we can." I stare at the instrument panels in front of me, doing calculations in my head. "It's too far away from us right now, and we barely have enough fuel to get to Earth as it is. We're going to have to rely on momentum more than I would want to already. Unless you know of a fueling station somewhere between here and there. Besides, we were lucky to escape unharmed. Turning back around and getting close to those enemy ships again could be suicide."

"Then contact the other ship," Zophie says, an edge to her voice. "They'll be operating on an emergency channel. Or maybe the official Council channel. I'm not—"

"We can't," I say.

"What are you talking about?"

"Those alien ships might intercept the transmission," Crayton says. "What if they use it to follow us?"

"We're in a giant white rocket that just shot into the sky," Zophie shouts. "We didn't exactly make a subtle exit."

"We *can't*," I say louder. The baby in Crayton's arms wakes up. "We can't contact them because this ship was refurbished to be an exact replica of the older models, meaning its communications systems were never upgraded. Their ship runs on a completely different comm system."

Zophie starts to say something but instead lets out a whimper. The baby begins to shriek. Crayton looks back and forth between us, confused.

"So what does that mean?" he asks.

I turn to one of the port windows. In the distance, Lorien burns. Our world is weeping fire and smoke and death, and for a moment memories flash through my head. Happier times long since passed—chasing my brother through lush green fields, laughing over home-cooked meals, the faces of people I haven't thought of in years. It's so overwhelming that I have to swallow down the urge to cry, or be sick, or scream.

In all my years of hating Lorien and the way it was run, I never expected to see it like this. I wanted to change the planet, not watch it be destroyed.

"It means we're alone," I say.

Crayton stares at the floor.

"We left them," he says quietly. "We left everyone to die."

He starts to mutter names and then apologies. Tears stream down his cheeks. Zophie isn't crying, though. Her eyes look out into space, searching for something but finding only stars and planets and other celestial bodies light-years away, and a cold, black expanse of emptiness.

I tap on the instruments again, confirming our course—breathing out a sigh of relief to find that the navigational system I helped to reinstall is actually working.

But that's the last of the good news.

"You've got to be kidding me," I mutter.

"What is it?" Zophie asks.

"We made a fast start, but it cost us a lot of fuel."

"Right . . . ," Zophie says, bracing for bad news.

"Which means it's going to be a long flight," I say.

"How long?" Crayton asks.

I turn back to the control panel, staring at the number on the screen in front of me.

"About one and a half years," I say.

CHAPTER
FIVE

CRAYTON FINDS SOME PILLOWS AND PUTS ELLA down for a nap in a pulled-out drawer in one of the private rooms. Afterwards, we sit on benches in the little common area beside the galley and go over the events of the last hour so many times that they begin to feel unreal, like an old myth told to scare children into doing their chores. I have to keep reminding myself that every word spoken is true. I think we're all in shock.

I know I am.

"All those ships," Crayton says. "Those bastards."

"Who were they," I ask. "*What* were they? When they were wounded, they just disintegrated."

Zophie narrows her eyes, staring at the ground. I recognize this look from the days at the museum when she would work out complicated problems in her head or try to figure out how we were going to get vintage wiring and fixtures for the refurbishment. Back when the rocket was just a project I was working on for some money and not the only thing keeping me alive.

"What is it?" I ask.

"Well . . ." Her nose crinkles a little. "There were always rumors at the museum of an old conflict between us and another planet. Tales archivists and historians told when too many ampules had been passed around at parties. There was no hard evidence to substantiate these stories, but there *were* hints that there was some truth in the claims—telling gaps in our historical record and allusions to terrible casualties and vicious otherworldly beings found in diaries and letters. We couldn't help but speculate."

"You're talking about the Mogadorians," Crayton says.

She seems a little surprised that he knows the word. It means nothing to me—and yet I feel as though I've heard it or seen it before. In encrypted messages I didn't think were important, or whispered in the halls of the LDA when I was there so long ago.

"Raylan talked about them often," Crayton says. "He had all these theories about secret wars just like you described. He was sure that his father had been not only a key figure in the conflict between us and the Mogadorians, but an Elder, and that there was some sort of conspiracy that led to the number of Elders being reduced to nine." Crayton shakes his head. "Raylan's claims changed all the time, but he was obsessed with trying to prove them. I always thought he was a little crazy, but . . . *this* is crazy."

Zophie keeps nodding.

"There were . . . *whispers* that Raylan's father had been a traitor to the Loric," she says. "Again, there's no hard evidence there even *was* a 'secret war,' but Raylan had probably heard these rumors at some point or another. I think it's one of the reasons he was so keen on donating money to the museum and getting this ship rebuilt. He wanted to show that his family was doing something positive for the people of Lorien."

"That's all well and good," I say. "But what else do we know about these . . . Mogadorians?"

Zophie lays it out for us—everything she's heard during her time at the museum. According to rumors and legends, generations ago the Loric reached out to the planet Mogadore, trying to form diplomatic bonds with the planet. But their civilizations were barbaric and not ready for contact with more advanced beings. Something happened there—the details vague and sometimes contradictory, depending on who was telling the story—but from what Zophie could gather, many Loric lost their lives during the expedition, and subsequently all contact with the planet and its people was forbidden.

We try to digest this. Eventually we sit in silence,

none of us knowing what to say. None of us sure how to react to the fact that our planet might be completely obliterated by these monsters.

My thoughts race as I try to make sense of all this, piecing together a bigger picture of what happened. I think back to the message I'd intercepted earlier. About the airstrip. The prophecy.

"The evacuation," I say. "Do you know who is on the other ship?"

"Janus wasn't supposed to say anything," Zophie says. "It was highly confidential. He was breaking his highest oaths by telling me."

"I understand," I say. "But it's not like the information is going to go past this rocket."

Her shoulders sag. She relents.

"I don't know much. Something about nine chosen Garde. The Elders assembled them. Or Loridas alone, I'm not sure. They—along with their Cêpans—are the ones in the other ship. They're the last hope."

"For what?" Crayton asks.

"For the survival of our people." Zophie smiles a sad little smile. "Well, other than us, I guess. I don't know why they were chosen, but that's what Janus said. They're going to be . . . *blessed* with something. Maybe they already have been. Some charm to protect them. It sounds crazy, I know. Why would the Elders try to save a handful of us while the rest of the planet is sacrificed?"

I clench my jaw. Of course this is how they faced the planet's destruction. By using us. By treating us as pawns as they always have.

"That can't be right," Crayton says.

"It is," I say. "Right before the first wave of attacks, I intercepted a message sent out to nine Mentor Cêpans telling them something about meeting at an airstrip—that the prophecy was coming true. The Elders abandoned the rest of us."

"That's insane," Crayton says. "What are these nine supposed to do on Earth? Everything I know about that planet sounds like it's far inferior to Lorien."

"It could be worse," Zophie says. "We could be headed to Mogadore."

Crayton opens his mouth to say something else, but the baby starts to cry again. He excuses himself and heads down the hall to tend to her.

"I guess we have to get used to that sound," Zophie says. She stands. "I'm going to start taking stock of our supplies. We'll need to ration. And I need to do something with my hands right now. Anything."

A question has been circulating through my mind.

"Why did you ask me to come with you?" I'm still trying to fit everything together. "Surely there was someone else. Someone in the department who's studied this damned relic. Why me?"

"You got us up here, didn't you?"

"It's going to be a long flight if we're keeping secrets the whole time, Zophie."

"Because I knew you wouldn't want to stay and fight," she says finally. "There was no time to argue with anyone about what our duty was. I don't know exactly what you've been doing for the last few years, but I knew, even when you were working at the museum, how unhappy you were with Lorien and its leaders. Not that I blame you after what's happened."

I stare up at her, not saying anything for a little while. I don't know how I'm supposed to feel about any of this.

"And you?" I ask. "Why didn't you stay and fight?"

She turns away from me, staring out one of the portholes.

"My parents died last year. Janus is the only family I have. I thought we'd be able to talk to the other ship. I thought . . ." She wipes a tear from one of her eyes. "I was stupid. Everything happened so fast. As soon as I disconnected from Raylan, I called Janus and told him to meet me at the museum, but he was already being taken to the airstrip. He told me to find shelter. He was going to Earth. I didn't understand. That's when he told me about Loridas and the Garde. And then everything was on fire, and I couldn't reach him. I didn't even know where his ship was. At first I thought he was breaking all his sworn oaths as a member of the LDC by telling me this classified intel, but now I realize he only told me because he assumed I wouldn't survive. He was saying good-bye."

"Why didn't he bring you with him?" I ask.

Zophie shakes her head. "Loridas was there. The LDC was involved. You know how strict they would be about who could be on that ship. Besides, if they made allowances for one person, they'd have to start letting everyone on."

"Heaven forbid they protect their people," I mutter.

"I had to come," she says. "I had to go. I had to follow Janus."

"And you needed a pilot who was a shitty citizen and wouldn't have anything to leave behind."

"He's my family, Lex," she says, not looking at me. "He's all I have. You of all people know how important that makes him to me."

And with one sentence the already-tiny common room seems to shrink around me as I think of my own brother. My chest buzzes and my throat tightens—after all these years, he can still take me by surprise, causing my heart to clench and dragging me down into a deep, palpable hurt.

Zophie smiles weakly. Unconvincingly.

"Earth is ten times bigger than Lorien, Lex. And it's so different. How am I supposed to find him there?"

I stare at the metal floor of the ship, trying to think of something to say. Some kind of reassurance.

"You don't give up faith," I say. "Even when common sense tells you that you should."

She must know I don't believe this, but she does me the favor of not pointing that out.

CHAPTER
SIX

I EXPLORE EVERY INCH OF THE SHIP, REMIND-
ing myself of its layout. It doesn't take long, since the
rocket is basically just one long hallway. There are four
small personal rooms. The Chimærae stay at the back
of the ship, nesting around the boxes and supplies we
brought on board. We're lucky in that, as part of the
refurbishment and exhibition, the closets are stocked
with clothes, and the galley has some useful tools and
appliances. For the next year and a half, we'll be living
in a model home, surviving off of Raylan's supplies.

I find an old data pad in the cockpit outlining the
functions and capabilities of the ship and show it to
Zophie and Crayton. I tell them it's my duty as their
pilot to know this ship as well as possible and excuse
myself for a few hours, choosing one of the tiny private quarters to call my own. It's cramped and sparsely
furnished with a dresser, a chair and a bed that is six

inches too short for me. I toss the data pad onto the bed without turning it on and sit in the chair, staring out the dense glass of the porthole window. And I think of him. It's not what I want to do, but it's impossible not to, being out here, flying through space.

Zane. My younger brother.

There was a time when Zane was a constant, sunny figure in my life. He was a Garde who was going to make my grandfather the proudest Loric on the planet. At least that's what he always said. I remember one morning when he was eight or nine, sitting around the breakfast table. He suddenly stopped eating, put down his fork and turned to our grandfather.

"Papa," he said, his voice as serious as I'd ever heard it. "When I grow up, I'm going to be an Elder. And if there are already nine Elders, they'll look at me and make me the tenth. I'm going to make our family proud."

I'd stifled a laugh, but my grandfather just nodded and smiled.

"I believe you, Z," he said. "But if you're going to do that, you'll need to start by eating the rest of your breakfast."

When I think back on my life, the shining bright spot is when the two of us were both at the Lorien Defense Academy. He was just a kid—thirteen years old—but I was already in my second year as a technology specialist for the LDA. Much younger than my classmates. I'd had a knack for electronics that sent me rising through the ranks, allowing me to work on projects other people my age wouldn't have dreamed of being a part of. Stuff like programming simulations and satellite navigations. I even helped tweak a few of our Loric technologies to be taken to Earth. I thought I'd found my calling. I had no desire to be a Mentor Cêpan. Aside from Zane, I'd never felt the urge to train or supervise a kid with Legacies. But numbers and computer programs made sense to me. I felt at home there, at the LDA, working more hours a day than was probably healthy.

I saw Zane often. Mostly during meals or when he'd show up in the tech labs wanting to brag about how well he'd done in training. He'd study in the corner while I worked. Sometimes I'd have to wake him up and drag him back to his room when he'd fallen asleep over a book. We seemed like the perfect siblings. Both excelling. Both with promising futures ahead of us.

Zane was partnered with a Cêpan named Dalus, whose qualifications I had questioned from the very beginning. He was too new, too green to be training someone like Zane, who was headstrong and eager to show what he was made of. I didn't think Dalus could handle him. The man was meek, with a quiet voice you had to lean in to hear. I'd spent enough time chasing Zane around our grandfather's house to know that he needed an authoritarian figure keeping him on track.

I even complained to the higher-ups at the academy. All they said was that the bond between Garde and Cêpan had already been established and that it would be damaging to both of them if they were separated. So were the ways of Lorien. The LDA spoke on behalf of the Elders, and whatever the Elders said went. There was no room for complaint. And so I tried to accept that the system knew what was best for Zane. That as his older sister, I was maybe overreacting. Being too overprotective. Caring too much.

After Zane developed the Legacy of flight during his second year at the academy, I hardly ever saw him with his feet on the ground. Several of the Garde could fly, but Zane flew with such grace and speed. It was as if he was teleporting, darting from one end of the campus to the other in the blink of an eye.

He was living up to the promises he'd made our family. He was becoming something undeniably special.

Dalus saw promise in him too. Not just as a pupil, but as something he could exploit. If Zane ended up being the fastest flier on the entire planet, there was a certain level of respect that would be given to his Cêpan, whether Dalus deserved it or not. People would look at Dalus and say, "Ah, look at how well he trained this magnificent Garde." And there were other perks as well. Even in my station in the engineering branch, I'd heard stories of older, wealthy members of the LDC betting on Garde races and other trials. If he played his cards right, Dalus could make a hefty profit off of my brother. So he pushed Zane to the brink, always insisting that he could fly faster, farther, for longer periods of time.

And then it happened.

I'd been at one of the council's airstrips working on improving navigational systems in the newest ship models when I found out. An LDC higher-up I'd never met before was the one who told me. I remember seeing his tan robes as he stepped out of his transport and knowing something bad had happened. That he was there to see me.

"It was an accident," he said. "Zane was performing long-distance training. He was flying at incredible speeds—far faster than should have been allowed. There was a Kabarak supply ship coming into the city. We don't think Zane saw it until it was too late."

At first I didn't understand, until the man started telling me something about how Zane's training band— the one that tracked his speed and location—went dead, and that *something* had to have brought down that ship. They were still trying to excavate the site where it crashed, but they wanted me to know as soon as possible. They wanted to tell me that my brother was dead.

"Again," the man said. "We're sorry for your loss. It was a terrible accident."

The minutes that followed were a blur. I just kept thinking that there had been some kind of mistake. Zane wasn't gone—he'd just ditched his training band and was hiding in the clouds somewhere. It was a joke. My beautiful, smart, talented, loving baby brother was still floating up there in the sky somewhere.

Zophie had been at the airstrip—she'd been there for some other LDA matter—and tried to calm me down, but I don't remember what she said. I couldn't hear anything but my own thoughts, shouting at me over and over again.

You just have to find him.

I wanted to run and scream and fight and cry. What I ended up doing was climbing into the cockpit of a ship I had no permission being in and taking off. It was the first time I'd flown alone, but the system was advanced and did most of the work for me. I knew how to take off and engage the autopilot because I'd helped design updates for the navigation system. And before I knew it I was soaring through the air, looking for Zane. I had no idea where he'd been training, but it didn't matter. I just couldn't live with myself if I didn't try to find him.

Eventually, exhausted, I landed somewhere out in the country. LDA officials tracked the stolen ship and brought me back to campus. By that time, they'd finally located Zane's training band at the crash site. And his remains. I wanted to see Dalus—to tear into him—but they wouldn't let me near him. Eventually he was shipped off to a remote Kabarak—no one would tell me where. He must have gone completely off the Grid; I never found him.

I tried to stick it out at the academy, but it just seemed so pointless now. People kept using that word—"accident"—as if it was supposed to make things better. Then, for the first time, I started thinking about how truly messed up Lorien was. How tenuous our freedoms were and how our leaders were never held accountable for anything, not really. What if Zane hadn't been forced to go to the LDA? To be trained to fight and protect. What if he'd just been allowed to be a normal kid? What if he'd had any choice of his own in the matter? Or if the LDA had listened to me when I'd told them Dalus wasn't a good match for him?

"Accident." That word hit me like a sucker punch every time it was spoken. Because what happened to my brother wasn't an accident. There were people to blame. Dalus being the most obvious. But the LDA, as well. And I couldn't forget the Elders, who had ruled that our society's most gifted children must be trained as soldiers based on a prophecy that I didn't even believe was true. Not then.

And me too. I was to blame for buying into all this—into the idea that the LDA and LDC would keep Zane safe. That they had our individual interests in mind instead of their own.

I couldn't handle hearing the word "accident" anymore. I left the academy. I never returned.

In my tiny little room on the ship, I can't get Zane out of my head. It's been five years since he flew too fast through the sky, and even though I know he's gone, there's still a part of me that expects him to randomly show up and reenter my life.

Losing Zane left a hole in me. It's for this reason above all others that I tried to stay free of too many responsibilities these past few years. People included. I couldn't get close to anyone—couldn't even say goodbye to our grandfather. I refused to be hurt again like I was by Zane's death. If that meant I'd be alone for the rest of my life, so be it.

Only now do I realize that some of my assumptions about Lorien and the way it was run were wrong. The prophecy was real. We needed soldiers—some of the Garde even saved my life. But at what cost? Lorien is most likely gone. Burned away. And if Zophie's intel is right, the Elders only saved eighteen citizens. Nineteen if you count Janus.

Why them? What makes them so special?

What makes them more worthy of saving than me? Or Zophie and Crayton and Ella?

Or Zane?

CHAPTER SEVEN

THE WEEKS WEAR ON.

The Chimærae adapt faster than we do. I suppose that's the story of their lives, though, changing to fit the present situation. They are mostly small, furry animals now. Rodents hibernating in storage bins. They seem to know that there's not enough food on board for both us and them to survive and so they sleep away the days. Crayton spends too much time watching over them, stroking their backs when Ella is napping. Every few days he wakes them up one by one and goads them into drinking a bit of protein-based slurry pressed out of a little gold pouch. I hope that we make it to Earth before I have to know what the gray globs that fall out of that package taste like.

At first, we talk a lot about Lorien, positing theories and asking the same unanswerable questions we'd had when we could still see the planet's scorched surface through the portholes. We spend hours trying to come up with answers we can't confirm. Everything is hypothesis, conjecture. We don't even know the status of the planet itself. It doesn't take long for us to realize that we're having the same conversation over and over again, and without any of us having to say it, we make a conscious effort to keep our focus on the future. The time for answers will come when we're on Earth, when we can track down Janus and the evacuated Garde and Cêpans. They'd be taking a different course than us, given their ship's capabilities. They'll be on Earth months before we are.

Zophie won't entertain the idea that anything will happen to Janus's ship on its journey or that the Mogadorians tracked or intercepted it. Crayton seems just as determined to believe that the others will be on Earth too. I think he feels unprepared to raise Ella, which is something I can't blame him for. If she ends up a Garde like her parents, she'll need a Mentor Cêpan to train her, and there are likely only nine of those left in the universe.

I try to remain optimistic that the other ship successfully escaped the Mogs and will make it to Earth unharmed. There are so many questions I have that only the chosen survivors can answer. Maybe Loridas himself is with them, and I can pin him down and ask him why. Why after all our training we weren't ready.

Why the Mogs came for us.

Why so many had to be sacrificed.

Finding the others once we're on Earth, though . . . that's going to be the real challenge. Zophie had enough foresight to bring a data pad from the museum with her, and so over the course of our months in space she gives us a crash course on Earth, trying to acclimate us so that when we get there we don't stand out too much. The planet hasn't made contact with any extraterrestrial life—at least not that they know of—and Zophie is unsure of how they might react to the discovery that they're not alone in the universe. Perhaps with hostility. But blending in ends up sounding much more difficult than I had expected it would be. On Lorien, the customs and cultures didn't really change much whether you were in the middle of Capital City or shoveling Chimæra dung at a Kabarak. But Earth appears to be nothing like that. It's so much bigger and split up into different sections that are all so different from one another. There's no ruling body directing all the planet's people, or "humans," as Zophie calls them. That sort of diversity sounds great in theory—it sounds like the kind of world I always imagined Lorien might turn into if we just opened our eyes—but as someone from another planet, it makes trying to get a grip on humans pretty damned difficult. Fortunately, we have a lot of free time, so learning about Earth is at least a distraction from the monotony of our journey.

Not to mention the anxiety of watching our food stores slowly dwindle. By Zophie's calculations we should make it to Earth just fine, but we all start eating smaller and smaller amounts of food as the months progress. We survive on dried Karo fruit and protein chews.

Zophie insists we try to have a rudimentary knowledge of several languages before we land—enough to ask simple questions and sound like tourists or travelers from other Earth realms instead of three people who can't speak a single Earth dialect. Again, I'm astounded by how different the people who all inhabit the same planet could be. How strange that these billions of people can't even all communicate with each other. We start with a language called French, as its vowels are most like our native Loric tongue, then switch to others I've never heard of: Spanish, then English and then Mandarin. Crayton and Zophie excel at the languages, and before long they are laughing at jokes in one known as German while I'm still stumbling over "*Ich heiße* Lexa." This is probably because I spend most of my free time writing down everything I remember from my days working on Earth's communications systems instead of studying new languages. I am more at home with the vocabulary of electronics—ones and zeros and carefully formatted lines of code. Based on my time at the LDA, I assume Earth has reached a point in its technological evolution that means it's interconnected by machines and relying on them in the same way we were on Lorien. The internet was one of the many gifts that the Loric brought to humans over the centuries. Not that they know it or that any of the other treasures we bestowed on them actually came from us. Or even that some of their brightest minds were not of their planet at all but Loric. I used to wonder why we'd spent any resources helping a planet so far away when there was nothing in it for us. Not even recognition of our contributions. But now I'm beginning to wonder how long the Elders knew about the Mogadorians. How much of the "secret war" was real.

Had they been preparing for a Loric migration to this new world this whole time?

Six months into the trek, I find Crayton hyperventilating, sitting on the ground beside the makeshift crib we've put together for Ella—an oversize plastic bin fastened to a side table and filled with blankets. Crayton's face is white, and his forehead is shiny with sweat.

"What's wrong?" I ask, taking a few quick strides to the baby's side. But she's fine, sleeping without a care in the universe.

"What am I supposed to do with her?" he asks. "I watch over animals. That's it. I just make sure they have food and water and aren't sick. I don't know how to raise a child."

I stare down at him. I'm not sure if he really wants an answer or if he's just talking to himself. He continues.

"Even after all our studies, I feel like I hardly know anything about Earth. How am I supposed to make sure she's okay? What *language* am I even supposed to speak to her in? Loric? And what if she asks about her parents? What am I supposed to tell her?"

I glance towards the cockpit, where Zophie's lost among the stars, staring at everything and nothing at once. I guess this is something I'll have to handle on my own.

"You'll tell her whatever you want," I say.

"That's a great bedtime story," he scoffs. "That her mom and dad are most likely dead and that they sent me with her on a ship with a bunch of animals to make sure she was safe. How do you explain that to a little girl?"

I don't know what to tell him. What I'd tell Ella. What would I tell Zane? My first instinct is the truth, without question. But what if the truth is terrifying? How do you find the middle ground? What if the truth puts her in danger?

"Maybe you don't explain it," I suggest. "Maybe you tell her something that will help to keep her alive and safe. Even if that means lying to her. You'll have to ask yourself if her knowing the truth is more important than her being able to fall asleep without the fear of everyone she knows being destroyed in a hail of fire in the middle of the night."

Crayton looks up at me. His eyes are bloodshot.

"I'm not going to lie to her," he says.

Ella starts to wake up, stretching and cooing. Crayton is on his feet in an instant, bent over her. I shake my head.

"When the time comes," I say, "you'll do what you have to in order to protect her."

I leave him with the baby and retreat to my room.

CHAPTER EIGHT

BY THE TIME WE HAVE A VISUAL ON EARTH, Ella has a full head of auburn hair. The rest of us are looking unkempt.

Crayton sports a bushy dark beard that hangs almost to the middle of his chest. There's a puff of black hair an inch thick on my own head. Zophie keeps her long, red locks tied back with a piece of cloth.

Actually seeing our destination is reassuring, as we're starting to run out of supplies. Without ever talking about it, we've all been doubling down on rationing, and the result is three gaunt Loric with dark circles under their eyes. Ella is the outlier. She's practically chubby, which leads me to believe that Crayton has been giving her some of his own food. Not that I mind. The girl can stand now, and will run a little if we're not careful—the ship wasn't really made with children in mind and is full of sharp corners. She can even say a few words. Maybe more than a few. It's hard to keep track of whether she's making gibberish noises or trying to form words in one of the languages we practice.

She definitely knows our names at least, even if she does struggle with some of the consonants. We have become "Ex," "Zoey" and "Ray-un" to her, the last of which is the strangest to hear coming out of her mouth since it could just as easily be her trying to pronounce her father's name. But there's no denying that it's Crayton she's calling for when she wakes; her eyes light up whenever she sees him.

And for his part, the way he looks at her has begun to change. No longer is it only with worry, like she's a fragile bubble he has been tasked with protecting. That's still there, but under a thick layer of affection.

When I call everyone to the cockpit to see Earth, even though it's only a blue pinhead in the distance, Crayton brings Ella with him.

"You see that?" he asks her, pointing into space. "That's our new home. That's where you're going to grow up."

She just coos and pulls on his beard with chubby little fists.

It's a few more days before Earth looms large ahead of us and we can discuss where and how we're going to land. We don't exactly have the luxury of time or travel, as we're coasting on the fumes of synthetic fossil fuels by this time. Based on our angle of approach and the rotation of the planet, we have a very narrow window of where, geographically, we might land. We're so low on power reserves that we'll be relying on the force of Earth's gravitational pull to bring us down to the ground as it is.

Zophie pores over scans from Earth's surface, seated in the copilot's chair. Finally, she points to a spot on the digital map she's pulled up on one of the cockpit monitors.

"There," she says. "It's a desert."

"So, lots of sand?" I ask. It takes a few seconds for me to understand what this means since deserts weren't exactly abundant on Lorien.

"Right. And more importantly, it's largely uninhabited, so we won't have to explain where we came from to a bunch of bystanders. We'd be able to set the ship down and journey a day or so to a major metropolitan area—a city called Cairo."

I bring up the coordinates on a navigational panel.

"It looks like that's doable," I say. "Tell Crayton he needs to strap down with Ella. When we enter Earth's atmosphere, things will start to get bumpy."

The three of us remain quiet as we start our final approach to the planet. Even Ella is silent, as if she realizes that this is important. I keep my eyes locked on the instrument panels, monitoring the increasing heat outside as we shoot through the atmospheric bubble.

"This isn't so bad," Crayton finally whispers. "At least there's not a fleet of ships hovering around—"

The ship begins to shake violently, shutting him up.

"Is everything—," Zophie starts.

"We're fine." I keep my eyes moving back and forth between the instruments and the quickly approaching surface of the planet in front of us. The ship continues to jostle back and forth, as if it's trying to tear itself apart in the sky. But it holds together as we sail head-first towards a golden expanse of land.

A readout from one of the monitors beeps. It's time to deploy our reentry measures: a dozen outboard thrusters that will rapidly slow our descent until we're hovering above the sand.

"Hold on!" I shout, and flip the switch.

Only, nothing happens.

I hit the switch again. And then again. Still, there's no response.

"Shit!" I mutter. My heart and brain begin to race. "Shit, shit, shit."

"What is it?" Crayton asks.

"The reentry thrusters aren't working."

We're traveling too fast. We have practically no fuel. There's no way we can eject ourselves at this velocity. Alarms and warnings start to go off around the cockpit. I tap on the controls until I'm given a readout that helps explain what's going on—we never properly rebuilt the thrusters during the restoration. I've got two front thrusters I can engage, but it's a one-time deal, and they'll only change the direction of our much-too-rapid descent slightly.

We're going to crash.

Somewhere behind me the Chimærae shriek and Ella cries as the cockpit instruments make terrible whining noises that seem to say "It's too late; you're dead."

I try to remain calm, going over options in my head. There's nothing we can do—not even a reentry parachute we can deploy.

And then, suddenly, an image comes to me. Zane. His favorite way to scare me after he developed flight was to race towards the ground until I was screaming for him to slow down, to stop, always sure he was going to end up crashing into the lawn or street. He'd wait until the last conceivable second and then finally pull up, shooting past me horizontally. A tornado in the form of a little boy.

"Everybody get ready," I say. "I'm going to try something."

I hear them shout things at me, but I don't listen. I have to be completely focused. We're getting closer and closer to Earth, but I wait. I have only one chance at this. *We* have only one chance.

The sand is almost upon us now. Zophie screams.

Crayton wraps his arms around Ella.

I punch the front thrusters.

We straighten out for a split second, until we're parallel to the earth. That's when I blow the last of our fuel in one hard boost straight ahead. It works—by some miracle, we don't crash. Not exactly. The surface of the desert is a blur as we skim across it. We start spinning. I'm sure that at any moment the ship is going to break in half and send us spilling out, our bodies breaking against the sand. But it stays together long enough to smash into a giant dune. Sand covers us, blacking out the cockpit but for the still-beeping emergency lights.

Everything is calm except for the howling of the animals. And the child, Ella, cries.

I'm almost afraid to look away from the controls or let go of the flight yoke. And then I hear Zophie gasping for air and Crayton talking to Ella, and I know that they're alive. I look at them. They glisten with sweat and their eyes are wide, but they're okay.

I hadn't even realized I'd been holding my breath, but I exhale finally, peeling my shaky hands off of the controls.

"You did it," Zophie says.

And I can't help but laugh a hysterical, confused laugh as I try to gulp for air.

CHAPTER NINE

GETTING OUT OF THE SHIP PROVES TO BE A challenge.

The only way we're able to escape is thanks to Raylan's weapons cache—one of the few boxes we haven't touched in the year and a half of our journey. My landing might have kept us from crumpling against the earth, but it also deeply embedded us in a sand dune. The loading door is blocked, and without any fuel to punch the thrusters or engine, it's impossible for us to dig ourselves out of the sand. After a little bit of brainstorming, I find an old incendiary grenade in one of the boxes from Lorien and blow a hole in the side of the cargo bay while we huddle in Crayton's living quarters along with the Chimærae.

On one hand, it's perfect that we've crash-landed in the middle of nowhere, with no humans to catch sight of us. On the other, seeing nothing but sand and dunes surrounding us isn't the most welcoming sight imaginable.

"How's the radar on Earth?" I ask as I jump down into the hot sand, wearing the T-shirt and black pants I had on the night everything changed on Lorien. They're a little baggier on me now, but I hardly notice. It is so good to be breathing air that hasn't been recycled and to feel sunlight beating down on my skin. I don't mind the heat. I *welcome* it, just as I welcome the solid, stable ground under my feet.

"Their systems aren't exactly unsophisticated," Zophie says, climbing out through the smoking hole. "It's possible someone caught our entry. We're in northern Africa. Egypt. We're close enough to their capital that they may have had eyes in the sky."

"Can someone take her?" Crayton asks, and then he hands Ella down to Zophie.

Soon the three of us stand at the top of the dune our ship has crashed into. The sand stretches out for what seems like an eternity.

"Which way do we go?" Crayton asks. He's now got Ella strapped to his chest, holding his hand over her head to shield it from the sun.

"I'm not sure." Zophie bites her lip. "I was charting us visually from space once we were close enough."

"Isn't there something on the ship that can point us towards civilization?"

"None of our tech is made to work with the satellites here," I say. "I might be able to reconfigure something, but I have no idea how long it would take."

"If the humans tracked our entry they might be coming this way." Zophie raises her hand to her eyes, squinting.

"Then we should move," I say. "Try to find a populated area and blend in."

There's some kind of commotion below us, and I realize that the Chimærae have all flown out and are now stretching their bodies, morphing between shapes and wrestling with one another in the sand. They seem as happy as we are to be outside again. A few of them take avian forms and soar up in the air.

"I've never seen them so riled up," Crayton murmurs.

"They should get it out of their systems here," I say, "while we're out of sight."

I can't help but wonder: What are we going to do with all these beasts now that we're on Earth?

One of them—a giant blue bird—flies higher than the others, golden eyes shining like a beacon in the sky. It lets out a shrill call and then swoops down, looping around us in two tight circles. It flies so close to me that I can feel its wake in the air on my face. Then the animal is in the sky again, beating its wings against the wind but looking back at us.

"Did I go completely insane in space or is that Chimæra beckoning for us to follow it?" Zophie asks.

"Possibly both," I say.

"Her name is Olivia," Crayton says. "She's always been one of the brightest among them." He turns to us. "I think we should follow her."

Zophie and I exchange glances. She shrugs. "That direction looks as good as the others."

Before we leave, I take a closer look at our ship. Or what's left of it. Even without the gaping hole we've blown out of the back hull, the main propulsion units look like they were fried in our reentry. Without the necessary parts and materials, there's no way the vessel is ever moving again.

"I think this ship's seen its last flight," I say, suddenly feeling very much stuck on this new planet.

"So do we just leave it, or what?" Crayton asks.

Zophie suggests we blow it up if we don't want the humans to find it and suddenly come face-to-face with the realization that they're not the only intelligent life in the universe. I can't tell if she's joking or not, but either way I argue that it's a bad idea—I'm not exactly thrilled by the thought of destroying what might be one of the few remaining Loric computer systems in the universe. Besides, the ship is almost completely embedded in a sand dune anyway, obscured. After a few days, it will likely disappear beneath the sand completely. So we gather the few supplies we still have and distribute them among bags for equal carrying weight. There's little food and only a handful of weapons—knives, concussion grenades and a few blasters. Raylan didn't skimp on other resources, though. We split up the jewelry—rings, bangles, necklaces—and precious stones.

We walk. It is perhaps the first time that the enormity of our situation has dawned on me. We are now refugees. Four beings without a planet. We are a species on the brink of extinction. Trusting the guidance of an animal because we have no better plan or option. Even though Earth has been our intended destination for months, being on its sandy ground feels surreal. It feels so foreign.

It's been so monotonous on the ship that I've let old fires grow cold, but now that we're on Earth, I remember all the hatred I had for the way Lorien was run. And for how it fell. I silently curse the names of each and every Elder. It's something I've done countless times, usually thinking of Zane. Or for the Loric who died in the Mog attack—even those who were a part of the system, whether they realized it or not. At this moment, though, with the child crying and our feet sinking into the sand, I curse the Elders for me and Zophie and Crayton and Ella. For everything they might have kept from us. For getting us into this situation.

For thinking that we weren't worth saving.

We follow Olivia. The rest of the Chimærae trail behind us. Eventually, when our pace slows, a few of them transform into four-legged beasts and carry us and our supplies. We march on until they too begin to grow weary. And then we camp.

Night falls. Zophie guesses that it must not be summer or winter, otherwise the temperatures in this climate would be extreme. It's chilly, but we make do. One of the Chimærae morphs into a large animal with long, soft fur, and after a little hesitation I give in to leaning on it. I fall asleep quickly, my mind drifting to other times. Zane and I playing games at our grandfather's home. Our mutual excitement on his first morning at the academy. Perfect afternoons on Lorien.

It's the middle of the next day before we spot structures in the distance. Tall, sand-colored triangles jutting out over the horizon. When Zophie sees them, she cries out, running forward a few steps.

"The Great Pyramids," she says. "They're ancient constructions—one of the first projects the Loric spearheaded here on Earth ages ago when we were still trying to assess the capabilities of the life-forms here. This is it. The Chimærae led us in the right direction."

And so we soldier on with renewed vigor.

A few hours later, we begin to pass small buildings

and finally hit roads. The Chimærae shrink down to smaller sizes. Some scurry through the gutters as lizards. Others perch on rooftops above us as birds. I swear I see a small rodent crawl into one of Crayton's pockets.

We stand out, with our bags and sallow expressions. A few men congregated in front of what looks like a small market ask us questions in a language I don't recognize. But Zophie does. It must be one of the ones she studied on her own. She converses with them for a few minutes, finally laughing a little.

"What is it?" Crayton asks in Loric.

I shoot him a look. "That's not our language anymore," I say in French.

Zophie smirks. "They say we look as if we just walked across the desert. They say that would be a long journey indeed."

"Ask them where we can find a place to stay."

She goes back to talking. The words come rapidly, and it sounds as if things are getting heated.

"We're in Giza," she says. "I told them we need to find a place to sleep, but they're trying to sell us a tour of some local landmarks. They think we're visiting from another place on Earth."

I take a few steps forward, scowling. I have several inches on these men, and when my boots plant in front of them, I can feel their apprehension. I reach into my pocket and remove a small, glittering ring from Raylan's stash, holding it out to them in my palm.

"Tell them it's theirs if they can get us to comfortable beds," I say.

Zophie speaks. The men grin.

CHAPTER
TEN

WE BARTER. WE SHOWER. WE SLEEP FOR WHAT
seems like a very long time.

We try to adapt.

We check into three rooms at what I understand
to be a nice temporary dwelling called a hotel using
names Zophie assigns us. We split the Chimærae
among us, letting them sleep at our feet in the oversize
beds. We try to cobble together some kind of semblance
of normalcy. After being stuck in a metal tube for a year
and a half, the ability to wander around a city for an
hour—just moving my legs and feeling the wind on my
face—seems like a blessing.

I sell much of Raylan's stuff to pawnshops around
town once I discover what a pawnshop is. A few of the
nicer things I take to places that specialize in jewels.
The shop owners there look at me suspiciously when I
say they were heirlooms passed down from my family

in what I'm sure is butchered English. They buy things from me anyway, and we amass a stockpile of the currency used in Giza—though, to be honest, the wads of paper and coins are fairly meaningless to me without context of what it costs to survive on this planet. But Zophie's the one in charge of the finances, and she says we have plenty of money to live on for now.

The city itself seems safe enough, but I take to carrying one of Raylan's blasters in my pocket whenever I leave the hotel. I've learned too well how everything can change in an instant. Also, Earth doesn't have the most reassuring history when it comes to violence and war.

I take a portion of the money to buy a laptop, which on this planet is considered state of the art but to me is an archaic machine that I imagine my grandfather might have used. Still, primitive as it is, some of its hardware is based on Loric systems I know well. I disassemble the computer that must weigh more than Ella and reassemble it, incorporating components from the two data pads we had on the ship. The result is a decent upgrade.

The communications systems on this planet are just as rudimentary as the computing gear, but they'll suffice. I get to work harvesting data, scouring the internet for any information on the other ship, anything that might be related to the Loric at all. But this planet is so large, with so many places to hide, in so many different languages. Progress is slow. I feel at home, at least, back in the world of ones and zeros and code.

But the days wear on Zophie. Each hour that goes by without an idea of where her brother might be puts another crack in her shell. It's unsettling to see. In the ship, we were frustrated because we were trapped, unable to do anything. But now on Earth, where we can actually do something, our inability to find any leads weighs heavy on her. It doesn't help that—although she is the specialist in otherworldly cultures and affairs—I am the one who is plugged in. The one she has to rely on. She might be able to type something into a search engine, but I can really navigate the internet on this planet. I know its back doors and recognize the things that are hidden in plain sight. She feels helpless. With each day, the bags under her eyes grow larger.

It's a few weeks into our indefinite residency at the hotel that I finally find a solid lead to Janus and the others. I run across a forum of people posting "evidence" of close encounters with alien species. Most of the photos are grainy and blurry, and I can see the wires hanging from a few of the flying saucers users are trying to pass off as legitimate extraterrestrial spacecrafts—what a strange thing it must be to live on a planet without any knowledge of what cultures and species exist in the universe. But I find a picture from a few weeks ago that's got an unmistakable silhouette in it. A Loric ship.

Spotted in the United States.

Zophie and Crayton are out buying grocery supplies. Ella sleeps behind me in a crib rolled in from Crayton's room. I'm alone and can focus on the task ahead of me. My fingers fly across the keyboard.

Through a little digging, I track the IP address of the user who posted the photo. This points me to a small county in the northern part of a state called New York. A population map tells me the place is secluded, sparsely inhabited—the perfect place to hide a ship. I continue investigating, trying to find more information on the user who uploaded the picture. He hasn't responded to any of the comments on his post—most of which are banal or useless. In fact, his online presence on the forums seems to completely disappear a few days after the picture goes up, which is strange, since I can tell he's normally a heavily active user. When I email him through the address connected to his username, I get an automated response saying the message was "undeliverable."

I pick out clues about the man's identity based on the large amount of personal data he leaves behind in his comments on the forums and track his username across several other websites. It doesn't take long before I discover his true identity: Eric Bird. After a little research,

I dig up property records in the New York area with his name on them.

And a home address.

It's not much, but it's something to go off of.

There's a phone number attached to the address, but when I call it, I get a busy signal. I keep trying, every ten minutes, for the next hour. Eventually, Zophie and Crayton come back. When I tell them what I've learned, Zophie drops her groceries and rushes over to me. She's hugging me before I can even get out of my chair.

"I knew you'd do it," she whispers. "Oh, thank you, thank you."

I can't help but smile. Zophie has needed news so desperately. It feels good to be able to deliver it to her.

"We'd need certification of some type to go to another country, right?" Crayton asks. "Identification?"

"Passports," I say. "We need passports. I can handle that."

"How?"

"Earth isn't so different from Lorien. There are people willing to do anything for the right price. I've been investigating a portion of the internet most humans probably don't even realize exists. It's mostly used by criminals on this planet. I've found people nearby in Cairo who will help us."

"We have to go," Zophie says. "We have to find Janus and the others."

"We don't know that they're still in the United States," Crayton says, his voice full of skepticism. "Besides, I don't feel comfortable trusting Ella's life to the hands of . . . what, some counterfeiters? *Criminals* on a planet we barely know?"

"It's the best lead we have." Zophie slams her palm down on the desk, her voice getting louder. Crayton stares at her for a few seconds before turning to me.

"When was this picture taken?"

I hesitate, glancing at Zophie. "A few weeks ago."

"They could be anywhere by now," Crayton says. "Look, I don't want to seem like I'm not excited about this, because I am. I'm just trying to be practical."

"Janus is smart enough to know that zipping around in a ship on a foreign planet is a bad idea," Zophie says. "This picture is probably from their landing. Janus said they had a contact here, someone Pittacus set up for them. They'll want to be incognito, just like we're trying to be. To blend in. I think the best lead we're going to get on them is this photo. And the longer we wait to follow up on it, the colder their trail will get."

Crayton looks to me, his eyebrows raised, waiting for me to respond. I bite the insides of my cheeks, staring at the lush green landscape in the background of the photo.

"Let's take a day to think this over," I say, even though I know what the decision will be. Of course we will track this down. Zophie wants to find her brother.

And I want answers.

There's only one problem.

"It's going to be incredibly expensive to get fake travel documents," I say. Even though I'm not really familiar with the cost of things on this planet, I know that the price of arranging for fake passports is going to take a serious chunk out of what we've accumulated. "We have a couple of options. I can look into this planet's banking systems and arrange for some funds to be siphoned into an account for us from other businesses and corporations. I've been so focused on finding leads that I haven't looked into this, though. I don't know how long it would take."

"What's the other option?" Zophie asks.

I walk over to the hotel dresser and pull out a small box. I toss it to Zophie, who opens it and finds a gold ring with a chunk of glowing Loralite in the center. One of the more ostentatious pieces from Raylan's collection.

"There was a jeweler who said he'd pay me good money for any more items that had this 'strange stone' in them. Emir, I think his name was. I can probably make enough to pay for most of the documents that way. Maybe as soon as tomorrow."

Zophie grins.

CHAPTER ELEVEN

ONE OF THE PIECES I SOLD TO EMIR THE JEWELER—
a silver necklace with a small Loralite pendant—is on
display in his front window. Crayton stops to look at
it before we go inside. Ella reaches a chubby fist out
towards the glass.

"I probably should have saved some of these for her,"
he says quietly, brushing Ella's hair out of her eyes. "I
think they were her grandmother's."

"She'll be served better by safety and answers than
by baubles," I say.

He frowns a little. He's seemed a little uneasy—
unsure—since I broke the news of the photograph last
night. Zophie has had the opposite reaction, of course.
While Crayton and I are out selling the belongings of
a man who is almost certainly dead, she's packing our
things up at the hotel.

"Come on," I say, holding the shop door open for him.

We've come early, and Emir is the only person in the store, standing behind a counter in the back. He freezes when he sees me, obviously recognizing me as the woman who brought him the necklace with a stone he'd never seen before in it. His expression isn't as excited as I'd hoped it would be, and I worry that maybe we won't be getting as much for Raylan's ring as I thought we would.

"You're here," he says as I cross the shop.

"You did say you'd be interested in any other . . . *special* pieces I had," I say. I take off my backpack and start to dig out the ring.

Crayton pauses at one of the many tall jewelry cases that dot the store to point out some glittering trinket to Ella, who giggles at the sight of all the shiny objects.

Emir's eyes go wide when he sees the child. He starts to say a few different things but stammers, never quite getting a full word out. Something about seeing Ella seems to have deeply unnerved him.

"Is everything all right?" I ask, narrowing my eyes.

Emir shakes his head. I slide my hand into my coat pocket, curling my fingers around the hilt of my blaster.

He takes a few seconds to compose himself as he

stares at a photo taped to the side of his computer. It's of him and a young girl who looks to be a little older than Ella. His daughter, I assume. A bead of sweat drips from his temple, which he ignores. It's only then that I notice the bruises—peeking out from his hairline and the collar of his shirt.

Everything suddenly seems very wrong.

"Oh, yes, the piece in the window," he says as if I'd asked about it. He springs back to life, smiling for the first time since I walked in but in a forced, anxious way. "You're right. The necklace *is* beautiful. But I'm afraid it's not for sale. We've had very particular interest in that piece. Buyers who are *very* interested in where it came from. I'm afraid I can't let you try it on."

We stare at each other. His eyes flit to his right, nervously looking at something across the store. I follow his line of sight to find a camera mounted on the wall.

It becomes all too obvious that we shouldn't be in here. Someone's been asking questions about the Loric jewelry—someone who has obviously scared him. Someone is watching us, and I don't want to find out who. At least, not like this. Not unprepared and with the child here.

"A pity," I say, keeping one hand on my weapon as I turn away from Emir. "Good day."

I grab Crayton's arm with my free hand and pull him towards the door. He starts to protest, but I shoot him a look that causes him to go quiet. He follows, clutching Ella to his chest.

We're almost to the entrance when a big, white van pulls up onto the sidewalk in front of the shop. Figures spill out of the back. I recognize them, even if they're in dark, human clothes instead of the body armor they wore on Lorien.

Mogadorians.

"Run!" I shout. Crayton and I both turn—there has to be a back way out of the shop.

Emir is saying something about how sorry he is— that he'd already described me to "the monsters" and that he didn't know there'd be a baby. He's stopped midsentence by a bolt of energy that drops him to the ground behind the main counter.

"Going somewhere, Loric scum?" a huge Mog standing in front of the back door asks. He's bald, but his head is completely covered in tattoos similar to the ones I saw on an invader the night Lorien burned.

There's a blaster in the bastard's hands.

I fire at him through my coat pocket but miss. At the same time, the windows behind us break as the Mogs from outside pour in.

We jump behind a jewelry case. Glass falls down over us as the top display is shattered in a barrage of blaster fire. Crayton huddles over Ella, protecting her and shouting desperate prayers to her in Loric. I peek around the corner. There are six Mogs advancing towards us and one—the big guy with the tattoos—blocking our exit through the back.

It's not exactly the best odds.

I fire over the counter. The snarling bastards duck out of the way and behind cases. We have to do something—we're outnumbered, all our exits are blocked and the only thing we have to protect ourselves with is a single blaster that I barely know how to use.

Actually, that's not exactly true. We have something else.

I dig into my bag and pull out one of the small grenades Raylan included in his supplies. It's a short cylinder covered in markings that identify it as a concussion and electromagnetic short-range hybrid bomb—in other words, not exactly a precise weapon but one that should be enough to knock down most of our assailants. I've never actually used one before, so I can't be sure. Crayton looks back and forth between me and the grenade.

"You can't be thinking—," he starts, but another barrage from the Mogs causes chunks of our shoddy cover to shatter around us. I return fire, noting where our enemies are. The big guy has moved and is closing in on us fast.

We don't have time to plan or argue. I see only one way of us—of Ella—getting out of here.

"It's our only chance," I say. "Make for the back exit after it goes off. I'll hold off any survivors."

"What about you?" he asks.

"I'll meet you back at the hotel."

Before he can protest, I click the top of the grenade and toss it over the jewelry case. There are a few beeps as I dive to the ground, pulling Crayton and Ella down with me. And then a wave of force explodes from the center of the room, flattening us. Jewelry, glass and pieces of displays crash into the walls. The lights go out. The Mogs grunt, and I can't help but grin when I see one of them slam into the cinder-block wall of the shop and disintegrate.

Not all of them are dead, though. A few have been blown outside and are already picking themselves back up when I check. The big guy from the back of the store is laid out on the ground, seemingly unconscious.

"Go!" I shout, pushing Crayton.

He hesitates for only a moment before running towards the back door, Ella in his arms. I try to fire at the Mogs outside, but my blaster has powered down due to the EMP. *Shit.*

Fortunately, the Mog weapons don't seem to be working either.

Crayton's almost to the back door when I see the big Mog move. Something shiny flies through the air and catches Crayton's calf. Crayton falls onto his side, Ella still in his arms, a big sliver of glass sticking out of his leg. The monster crosses the room in just a few strides as Crayton struggles to get up. Ella starts to babble. Crayton looks back at me and then to the big Mog, now just steps away from him. I can see some kind of calculations being worked out behind his eyes. He knows there's no way he's going to outrun the big guy. Not now.

He winces as he shouts to me.

"Catch her! Don't let them take her."

Ella's body flies through the air. She doesn't cry. In fact, I think I actually hear her giggle. I catch her with one arm, pulling her in to me, trying to protect her. When I look up again, the big Mog is holding Crayton up off the ground, a sinewy hand around his neck. The monster's black eyes are furious as he snarls. The creature pulls a small dagger from his belt and rears back, ready to plunge it into Crayton's chest.

"No!" I shout. But it's too late.

There's a bang, and the Mog stops. His arm falls to the floor. Another shot sounds, and the Mog begins to disintegrate. Crayton falls to the ground, gasping.

It's only then that I realize Emir is standing again, blood pouring out of a wound on his shoulder as he reloads what I think the people of Earth call a shotgun.

"Get that child out of here," he says to me.

The two remaining Mogs look so stunned that their leader has fallen that Emir has just enough time to fire off a few shots and take them by surprise. They turn to ash as Crayton picks himself up off the ground and hobbles over to me. Emir babbles in a language I don't understand, shaking his head. His eyes dart back and forth between the piles of ash, trying to comprehend what's happened.

There are sirens coming from somewhere down the road, and we can't be here when they arrive. I grab Crayton, and we sprint out to the van that brought the Mogs, our enemies, to us. We climb inside. The engine seems to be running, so I pull on various levers and push buttons until the vehicle is moving. The controls aren't so different from a tractor I'd driven once or twice out on the Kabarak. Crayton and I barely speak to one another as we try to come down from the shock of what's happened. Cars honk as I pass them, sometimes screeching to a stop—I'm probably breaking dozens of traffic laws. But I keep going. Eventually we park the vehicle far, far away from our hotel. From a small market, I buy some water, alcohol and gauze that Crayton uses to clean up the wound on his calf in a side alley. When he's finished, we climb into a taxi to return to Zophie.

It's only then, as we shoot through Giza, that Ella starts to cry, and Crayton turns to me, his face contorted with desperation.

"We're not safe on this planet" is all he says.

CHAPTER TWELVE

THE BLOOD DRAINS FROM ZOPHIE'S FACE WHEN we tell her what happened, and she starts to shake. We decide to leave. Immediately. None of us feels safe in Giza anymore. Fortunately, Zophie's already packed most of our things in anticipation of our trip to the United States. The Chimærae shrink, and we take them and our bags down to the lobby. Then we're in a taxi to Cairo, which is a city that doesn't feel far enough away, even though it's large and full of millions of people and is the kind of place where it should be easy to disappear. But without passports, we can't leave the country yet, so our options are limited. Besides, this is where our documents—our tickets out of here—will be made.

The Mogs are on Earth. They're seeking out the Loric here—they must be, if the Loralite necklace is the reason they found us at the jewelry store.

Why? What do they want? They already took our

planet from us. What more could we possibly have to give?

In Cairo, we check into another hotel. It's similar to the one in Giza, but it feels different. *Everything* feels different. The illusion of safety this world offered us has been destroyed. No one says it, but I know what we're all thinking: What if the Mogs have gotten to Janus and the others already? And if not, are they aware that they're being hunted?

While Zophie and Crayton unpack in their rooms, I refocus my efforts to try to find hints of the Garde and Cêpans online, anything that could be connected to them. We must find them now not just to reunite Janus and Zophie and get answers, but also to warn them.

Later that night I go to the restaurant on the first floor of the hotel to grab dinner and let my eyes take a break. I find Crayton at the bar, huddled over a glass of brown liquid.

"Do you mind?" I ask, motioning to the seat beside him. He shakes his head.

"Ella?" I ask. It's unlike him to leave her alone.

"Zophie has her right now," he says. "She wanted to feed her dinner for once, and I couldn't say no to an evening that didn't end with me smelling like mashed peas."

I nod and order some food to take back to my room. We sit in silence until finally I speak again.

"How's your leg?"

He shrugs.

"I'll live. I don't think I'll be running much for the next few weeks, but it's the least of my worries right now."

I nod. We sit in silence again.

"Tomorrow morning we need to have photos taken," I say. "For the passports. All of us—even Ella."

He shakes his head, not in disagreement but in despair.

"You still aren't sure we should be going after this photo lead, are you?" I ask.

"I think it sounds dangerous." He stares down at the bar for a few seconds. "I know it's what we always intended, but now that we're on Ear . . ." He grimaces, and lowers his voice. "Now that we're here, the idea of traveling all around the world looking for Janus and the others seems crazy. Especially because we know the Mogs are here. And *looking* for us. Or the Loric in general. By chasing after the Garde, we run the risk of chasing after the Mogs too."

"You're worried about Ella," I say.

"Obviously." He gives me a weak smile. "I've been thinking a lot about what you said to me on the ship. About how I'd do anything and tell her anything to keep her safe. I don't think I realized what you meant until we got here, where everything is new. I just want to make sure I'm making the right decisions. How do I know? How do normal parents know?"

I think of Zane. Even though I wasn't his parent, I was so overprotective of him. And look where that led.

"I guess you just have to figure it out as you go."

He nods, motioning for the bartender to pour him another drink.

"Be careful," I say. "I don't think the drinks here are the same as the ampules back home."

Crayton laughs a little at this, but then his face goes serious. He reaches into his pocket and then slides a key to me.

"What's this?" I ask.

"To my room." He holds up his glass, shaking it back and forth before downing the rest of its contents. "Just in case I'm sleeping so deeply in the morning that I'm not up and ready to be photographed. One of you might have to drag me out of bed."

My food arrives, and I tell Crayton good night. He leans over and hugs me unexpectedly. I stand there, one hand pinned to my side and the other holding a Styrofoam container. I wonder if he's had too many drinks, or if this is just affection brought out by the fact that we came so close to being captured or killed by the Mogs earlier.

"I'll keep her safe," he says quietly. "Everything's going to be okay."

CHAPTER
THIRTEEN

WHEN WE WAKE UP, CRAYTON AND ELLA ARE gone. There's a letter on his bed, written on the hotel's stationery.

Zophie and Lexa,

I'm not great at good-byes, but we have to go. The focus of my life now is to ensure Ella's safety, and I know I can't do that if I'm traveling the world in search of Janus and the others. It's too dangerous. Soon, Ella will be able to speak well, and before I know it, I'll have to explain everything to her. I don't know how I'll even begin to try to describe what our homeland was like, but I know it will be easier to do if we are nestled somewhere safe, somewhere hidden. Maybe I'll be more open to finding the rest of the Garde later, but for now, I cannot go to the

United States with you. I know you have to make
this journey, just as I have to protect Ella.

I'm taking Olivia with us—Ella seems to like
having her around, and I can use a spare set of
eyes and claws. I'm leaving you the rest of the
Chimærae. It pains me to do so, but I cannot travel
with a menagerie. They are kind, gentle beasts,
and they'll protect you until their last breath.

The Mogs are on Earth looking for us. Chances
are they're following the same leads you are.
There are so few of us left. Please, please be
careful.

And please understand.

- Crayton

Zophie's eyebrows draw together in confusion as she reads the letter over and over again, but I can only think of my conversation with Crayton the night before. How he gave me his key. He knew then that he was leaving, and he didn't say a word to me about it. Only hugged me. If I had been thinking more clearly, maybe I would have realized what was going on. Instead, I left him in the bar and returned to my room so I could get my eyes back onto my computer screen.

I take the letter from Zophie, find a pack of hotel matches on the desk and then set Crayton's good-bye on fire.

"What are you doing?" Zophie asks.

"We leave no trail behind," I say, walking to the bathroom and tossing the burning note into the toilet.

"How could he . . . ?" She keeps shaking her head.

"He's doing what he thinks is best for her," I say, all too aware of how my previous conversations with Crayton about Ella's future may have inspired him to run. "He's her guardian. It's his decision."

"Maybe he didn't leave that long ago." Zophie starts for the door. "Maybe we can still catch him."

"Even if we did catch him," I say, "what then? We drag him to the other side of this planet against his will?"

She stops and stares at me for a little while, her face falling.

Finally, she whispers: "That bastard left us."

"Yes," I say. "But we're not alone."

We move on. Zophie buys us plane tickets. Two passports are much cheaper than four. I have them made for us by men who also try to sell me guns, which I decline only because I've read enough about airport customs to know I'll have a difficult time getting them on a plane. Instead, I pack up the weapons from Raylan's supplies and leave them with the concierge at the front desk of the hotel, along with several large currency notes. When we are more settled in the United States, I'll phone him and have the Loric weapons shipped to us.

I scour our rooms, making sure we leave nothing behind. And then we say good-bye to Egypt, our first Earth home.

Getting the Chimærae across an ocean is a complicated task, but we manage to figure out ways. They shrink down to tiny lizards and insects, and hide in our pockets and luggage. It's a little awkward but necessary, and as soon as we're locked inside the primitive airplane, I'm much more concerned with not falling out of the sky than with the Chimærae in my coat.

The counterfeit passports get us into the new country. We change over our money and rent a big SUV using the fake driver's license that my passport people created for me as well. We pile in, the Chimærae filling the backseats, and then we're off.

It takes me a little while to get used to the handling of the SUV and traffic customs in the United States. Drivers in yellow taxis scream at me as I wander in and out of lanes or go far too fast or slow for their liking. But I get the hang of it. Zophie sits in the passenger seat giving me directions from a big map of New York State she has spread out on the dash.

We reach the village of Newton Falls in an area known as the Adirondacks shortly after noon. This is the place where I've tracked the forum post to. Tall green trees line streets that occasionally narrow to small wooden bridges crossing thin bodies of running water. Yesterday we were surrounded by desert. The change of scenery might seem drastic if it wasn't for the fact that not long ago we were on a ship, and before that another planet.

I suggest we find a hotel to stow our things and let the Chimærae out, but Zophie won't have it.

"We're here," she says. "We should find out what the man knows immediately."

And so we track down the cabin located at the edge of the little town where Eric Bird is supposed to live. There's a truck in the driveway. We park behind it.

I knock three times before someone finally opens the door, and even then it's only cracked. I can barely make out the shape of a man's face through the darkness of the entryway.

"Hi," I say in my improving English. "I'm looking for—"

"Go away." The man's voice is rough and cracked. He tries to close the door, but I put my boot in the way.

"I just have a few questions. Mr. Bird?"

"I have nothing to say."

The man pushes harder on the door, all but crushing my foot. I'm about to shout and possibly ram the door in when Zophie steps forward.

"Please," she says, her eyes wide and dewy. "It's

about my brother. He's missing. You're our only lead."

Her voice bleeds with desperation. Eric takes some of his weight off my foot. He lets the door open just enough for the chain lock to catch.

"I don't know anything," he says, a little calmer but no less resolutely.

"You posted a photo of a spaceship," I say. "We're looking for it."

Eric crams his head into the space between the door and the doorframe. I can finally see part of his face now. Dark circles sit underneath his bloodshot eyes. He's got a scraggly red beard and hair that shoots out in every direction, like it hasn't been washed or combed in days. His skin is sallow.

"I already told him everything I know," he says. "I saw the ship. I snapped a picture. It looked like it was headed for the mountains, but I didn't follow it. What more do you want from me?"

"Who?" I ask.

"Huh?"

"You told *who* everything?" I lean forward a little bit, and he flinches.

"The man who came." Eric's lips quiver a little. "He was a giant. His eyes were so black. Like a demon's."

My fingers ball into fists at my sides.

"Did he have tattoos on his head?" I ask, thinking

about the other big Mogs I've seen.

Eric begins to nod, his whole body shaking now.

"How did you know?"

Zophie lets out a small cry beside me as my stomach twists and clenches.

CHAPTER FOURTEEN

THE MOGADORIANS ARE SEARCHING FOR JANUS too. How long have they been on Earth? These monsters that annihilated our planet are several steps ahead of us—is it possible they've already tracked down not only Janus, but the Garde and Cêpans too? And if so, why? To what end?

More questions we can't answer. More knowledge we don't have.

Zophie is broken. I can tell by the dullness in her eyes. All her hopes had been tied up in finding Janus easily after we came to this country, no matter how blindly optimistic that seemed. Now she looks as though she's a breath away from bursting into tears. At first I wonder if Crayton had the right idea—if we should be hiding instead of looking for the others. But I tell myself we've done the right thing. We have a better idea of what's happening on Earth now. We have to soldier on. We have to outsmart the Mogadorians and warn the others, keeping faith that they're still out there somewhere, free.

I do my best to keep us going. The day after we talk to Eric Bird, I find a cabin thirty miles away, in the mountains he said the ship was headed toward. We rent it and set up camp.

I buy more computing equipment and a cheap station wagon for us that I get secondhand from someone in a small town nearby who doesn't ask for identification or a signature, just hands over the keys. I have the weapons in Egypt shipped to a post office two towns over. The cabin is only a few rooms, already furnished with homemade wood furniture. I set up an office in a spare bedroom, and wire cameras and alarms all around the outside just in case anyone comes snooping around. The Chimærae split their time between keeping guard over the perimeter and nesting in a garage in the backyard. For a while, we wake up early every morning and take them into the mountains, searching for the ship. Zophie makes us stay out longer than we should, until night has fallen and she's so exhausted she can barely stand.

We have no luck. It starts to get cold. We go back to the world of internet searching that I'm familiar with but that Zophie is still learning. We endure.

After a month in the cabin, I find Zophie in the living

room, huddled over the small laptop I bought her. She spends most of her free time on it, clicking randomly through websites and news articles, trying to find anything that might be related to the Loric. I've warned her a million times about being careful, about not sharing any personal information with anyone or mentioning anything related to Lorien directly. She mostly sticks to news sites, so I don't worry much. Besides, I've blocked the computer's IP address and location.

"Lexa," she says when I come in. "I have a few articles that look promising. Maybe you can look into them? One is from this guy in Vermont who swears a young girl caused his car to levitate after he yelled at her to get off his lawn. Doesn't that sound like—"

"Is it from Occult News Daily?" I ask.

"Well, yeah, but that doesn't mean—"

"I checked that lead out last night. In the last year the same man has also reported that his town is infested with creatures that survive on the blood of virgins, that a restaurant was serving human meat and that a foreign government was preparing an ancient dragon for warfare. And that's not even the craziest stuff."

"Oh," Zophie says, dejected.

Her eyes go dewy, and I feel terrible. Hard truths always worked when I spoke with Crayton—they were the only kind of advice I felt qualified to give. But I don't know how to talk to Zophie now that she's become so fragile. I can empathize, but I don't know how to fix anything. To fix *her*. I knew her brother only by name and reputation. To me, he's the means to an end—a way to get answers to all my questions and figure out what all this was for. Sometimes I forget that to her, he's everything.

"Sorry," I say quietly. "I'll look again. Maybe I can get into the police reports from around the area. It's worth another go."

"No." She shakes her head. "Don't bother. The Mogadorians are tracking this sort of thing too, right? They've probably already tortured the man and gotten every ounce of information from him. Or a confession that he made the story up." She runs her fingers through her hair, pulling it back. "Where are you, Janus? Where are you?"

I stand there awkwardly, not knowing what to do or say. One of the Chimærae has taken the form of a cat and rubs against Zophie's leg, trying to comfort her. She looks up at me.

"Do you think . . . ," she begins. "Do you think the Mogs have him?"

"No," I say. "I'm sure they don't."

And she's desperate enough to believe me, even though she knows I have no evidence.

It pains me to see her like this—so lost and hopeless. If it wasn't for her, I would have died on Lorien. I would have been killed by the Mogadorians. So I owe her.

I have to find the others. No matter what the cost.

I leave Zophie in the living room and retreat to my office. I've been extremely careful when it comes to seeking out information on the internet. I haven't typed "Lorien" into a search engine for fear this might sound a Mog alarm somewhere—that despite my best efforts and all my digital cloaking they would use something like that to be able to find us. But we can't keep living like this, waiting for one of the Garde to screw up and get his or her face spread across news sites for using a Legacy in public.

We have nothing to go on. We're lost, and Zophie needs a reason to hope again. We both do.

So I take a more direct approach to our search.

In a particularly busy forum about alien encounters, I set up an account. My IP address is encrypted. My location signal is bounced across a dozen satellites. I should be untraceable. A ghost.

I bite my lip and stare at the screen, typing a few words. Finally, I hit Submit.

The post goes up, written in our native language:

Where are you?

It's a long shot, but if for some reason Janus or the other Loric or maybe even the contact Zophie said they were meeting on this planet sees this message, they'll recognize that there are more of us here. That they're not alone on this planet. That we're looking for them.

There's nothing to do now but wait. I open up my email and find a dozen news stories Zophie has forwarded me. I flit through them, seeing the obvious holes that she's overlooking, or refusing to acknowledge. Spaceship sightings that don't really match descriptions of any of Lorien's ships. The teenage boy who claims to have telekinetic powers but also has an online presence dating back several years, well before Lorien fell.

"Lex!" Zophie yells from the living room. "Check out what I just sent you! I think this could be it!"

I find another message from her in my in-box. Reports from two different media outlets in Montreal about a small gang of men with tattoos on their heads who were allegedly seen chasing a young boy into the woods on the outskirts of the city—though neither the men nor the boy were found.

Now that sounds much more promising. And potentially damning.

I'm about to tell Zophie that she may have just found our first real lead since Eric Bird when my computer beeps again. This time notifying me of a comment on my post in the forum.

The response is written in Loric.

Anonymous: I'm here.

CHAPTER FIFTEEN

MY FINGERS HOVER OVER THE KEYBOARD, UNSURE of how to proceed. I have to be careful—if the Mogs found Eric Bird, it's entirely possible they're watching this forum as well.

I try to be smart when I reply, still using our language:

Who are you?

While I wait for a response, I try to track the user's data, but it appears to be completely blocked. Or if it's not, it's encrypted and hidden well beyond my skills. I hope that means one of the Loric from Janus's ship happened to be a tech prodigy.

A response comes:

Anonymous: A friend.

Me: You're from Lorien?

Anonymous: Yes.

Me: Where?

Anonymous: The capital.

Me: When did you come to Earth?

Anonymous: You ask many questions.

Me: I have to be careful.

Anonymous: So do I.

My heart pumps in my chest, threatening to break out. I rack my brain, trying to come up with a way to prove this person is not a threat. The responses are coming quickly now, and I want to keep our interaction going.

I need to know—I *have* to know—if I'm talking to someone from the other ship.

I focus.

Me: I miss our home. I miss the red Spires of Elkin.

Anonymous: So do I.

The Spires of Elkin were green. Before the Mogs destroyed them.

My cheeks get hot as my pulse pounds. This is not one of the Cêpan or Garde—certainly not Janus. It's no one who has any real working knowledge of Loric culture.

But someone who knows our language.

I press on, clinging to remote possibilities that this person is a friend. Maybe this is a Loric ambassador, someone we'd planted on this planet long ago. I have to know more.

Me: I'm here on one of the Lore envoys. Are you?

Anonymous: Yes, a Lore envoy.

There's no such thing.

Me: Have you heard from our home lately? I haven't got a message in almost two years.

Anonymous: I have new orders, but I cannot share them here. Where are you?

This is a trap.

My mind goes back to the destruction of Eilon Park

when the fire rained down. I remember the woman who the Mogs murdered in front of me and all the terrible sights and sounds and smells from that night that I've been trying *not* to think about.

I tap out each word with quiet, seething rage:

Die, Mogadorian trash.

This time I don't get an immediate response. I just sit staring at the screen for what feels like a very long time, waiting for my breathing to settle down. I assume that our little exchange is over when a new message comes in.

Anonymous: Let's try this another way.

Before I can formulate a coherent question, a new private message from Anonymous pops up. There's a file attached—an MPEG movie.

My hands start shaking with uncertainty, but somehow I manage to calm them. I download the video to a secure folder—one that's cordoned off from the rest of my hard drive—and run every test I can imagine on it. But it seems clean. No viruses. No backdoor lines of code. A simple video.

I glance over my shoulder. Zophie is still in the living room. I think about calling her in, but being so unsure of what I'm about to see, I think better of it. Instead, I quietly close the door and sit back down, putting on my headphones.

Then I play the video.

The image that appears at first fills me with relief. I can't help it—seeing Janus after looking for him for so long immediately sparks joy in me. That fades almost instantly as I remember who sent the movie and realize how terrible he looks. There are bruises all around his green eyes. His red hair—the same shade as his sister's—is shaved off in places, seemingly at random. He's shirtless, gaunt, and tied down to a chair. There are blue bands around his arms and neck with cords leading out of them to something off camera.

I gape in horror, covering my mouth with one hand, trying not to cry out.

There's a gravelly voice from offscreen.

"Speak to your kind," it says in accented Loric.

Janus shudders. Then he starts talking.

"I . . . I'm sorry," he says. His voice is thin and shaking. "I tried to hide our ship. I was in the mountains for a while. I thought I'd been careful. . . ." He stares into the camera. Tears fill his eyes. "They destroyed our planet and when they found me . . . The things they've done to me . . . Forgive me, but I couldn't hold out. I told them everything. Everything I know about the Garde children. I'm so sorry. . . ." Suddenly there's a fierce look in his eyes. His nostrils flare as he turns to someone off camera and shouts. "By now they've scattered to every corner of this world. You'll never find them! And soon they'll wield the powers of our Elders and destroy every—"

Some kind of shock surges through him. After a while he stops screaming. Soon after, he stops breathing. The video ends.

I clench my fists. Before I know it I'm on my feet, my chair knocked over, and I'm storming through the office, throwing every framed photo and vase the landlord decorated my rented room with.

There's a knock at my door.

"Lexa?" Zophie asks.

I close the file. I want to delete it from my hard drive and my memory, but all I have time to do is pull up a Montreal news site Zophie sent me before she comes in.

"Is everything okay?" she asks.

"Yes," I lie. "I was just . . ."

But I don't have any words. I look at her. Everything she's done since the first missiles hit has been in order to reunite with her brother. But he's gone. The Mogs have killed him, as they killed our planet and our people. I look at Zophie, and I wonder how she will ever handle this news. I can never show her the video, I know that. But how do I even find the words to explain things to her? How do I deal with the fallout of the knowledge I can barely deal with myself?

Because Janus being captured means we have failed. I have failed. We couldn't save him, which means we might lose the other Garde as well. Just like Zane slipped away.

"What is it?" Zophie asks. "Lexa, you're scaring me a little."

There had been only a small window of hope after they'd told me about Zane—when I was flying through the sky of Lorien, looking for him, for evidence that the officials had made some kind of mistake. But then they'd found him in the wreckage. He was dead. I couldn't pretend he might come back. He was here one instant and then gone.

Zophie still has faith, though. And knowing that, I make a decision that I hope I can live with.

I let her continue to dream.

"Nothing," I say. "It's nothing. I was just feeling a little claustrophobic and helpless."

She smiles sadly, and it's like a dagger in my chest. I can't look at her.

"But I wanted to tell you that I think we should look into the Montreal case you sent me. It's only a few hours' drive from here. I may go up there tomorrow."

She seems excited by this—the first time I've seen her light up since we talked to Eric.

"The fresh air might do us some good," she says, and

I try not to cringe at the word "us" because I know I can't sit beside her in a car all day tomorrow knowing what I know.

"You look stressed," she continues. "I'll make us some tea."

She leaves. I realize my fists are still balled up, my fingers aching. I stretch them as I turn back to my computer, clicking once more on the forum.

There's another message from Anonymous. From a Mog.

> **Anonymous: He is not the only one we have.**
> **There are many more. Loric and Human.**
> **Comply with us, and you can save them. Turn**
> **yourself in, and they won't suffer the same fate**
> **as this one.**

I clench my teeth. The Mog could be lying. From the way Janus spoke, it sounded as though they hadn't captured any of the passengers from his ship.

Even if this bastard is telling the truth, there's no way the Mogadorians are ever releasing their captives. Not after what they did to Janus. Not after they slaughtered our people and razed our cities.

Every ounce of anger I ever had towards the Loric Elders or anything else from Lorien seems inconsequential compared to the rage brewing inside of me towards the Mogadorians now. And I finally realize that they are also to blame for Zane's death. The Elders made the Garde train as solders, yes. But only because they knew a threat was on the horizon. That the prophecy was true.

If it wasn't for the damned Mogs, we could have lived our lives in peace. There wouldn't have been cause for such severe training.

Zane might have lived to see his fourteenth birthday.

I tap out one more message before deleting my profile and post, my fingers hammers on the keyboard:

I will destroy you.

CHAPTER
SIXTEEN

I AVOID ZOPHIE FOR THE REST OF THE NIGHT, trying once again to find out where the video came from. But the Mogs' tracks have been covered too well. There's nothing for me to latch on to. I'm good, but our enemy is apparently better. And so I do the only thing I can do: I watch the video of Janus over and over again, frame by frame, trying to find any hint of where the Mogs were filming. But it's just some brick room. It could be anywhere.

I hardly sleep. When I do, it's restless. I rise with the sun and map out my route to Montreal.

I have to get out of this cabin. I need time to think about how I'm going to break this news to Zophie. How do you form the words that you know will destroy someone? I have no idea. What I do know is that I can't spend the day with her—can't spend any time with her—because knowing what I know and seeing the glimmer of hope still alive within her is torture. I think about sending her to Montreal instead of me, but this is a good, hard lead. There very well could be Mogs still running around, and while I'm no soldier, I'm probably more of a fighter than she is. I can't send her into harm's way.

So I decide to go alone.

I try to sneak out, already formulating an excuse to give her later—"I wanted to let you sleep and surprise you if there was any news!"—but she walks out of her bedroom just as I'm heading for the door.

"Lex, what are you . . . ," she starts. Her eyes are heavy with sleep.

"I just wanted to get an early start on the trip," I say.

"I thought we'd go together. If there's anything that could lead us to Janus or the other—"

"No." I cut her off a bit too harshly. She seems taken aback. I sigh and try to think of a valid excuse. "I mean . . . I just need to do this on my own. I'm so glad we're in this together, but . . . I'm much more used to being by myself. That's how I lived on Lorien. I just need a little space."

I'm painfully aware of what terrible reasoning this is, given that I've spent the better part of the last two years in a tiny ship with two other people and a baby. So I keep talking.

"It'll only be a few hours. I'll be back by dark,

unless I uncover something."

She's quiet for a few seconds.

"I'll make dinner then," she eventually says. She hands me one of the prepaid phones I've bought for us. "Call me as soon as you get there. And if you find anything. Just stay in touch, okay? I'll be here looking for more leads."

"Great," I say.

I start to leave, but she steps forward and hugs me.

"Thanks for checking this one out," she says quietly. "We're going to find him."

I hope she doesn't notice that I tense in her arms, or that I can't look her in the eyes when she lets me go.

"Be careful," she says.

"I'll see you in a bit," I call over my shoulder.

In the car, I toss a bag that contains my souped-up laptop and a few of Raylan's weapons onto the passenger seat. Zophie waves to me from the porch, and then I'm on the road.

The drive is scenic. Peaceful, even. The leaves are turning brilliant shades of orange and red. I would enjoy it if I could just get Janus and Zophie out of my mind. Every time I think of her waiting at home, still believing that her brother is out there, I feel sick to my stomach. I start to wonder if I've made a bad decision— that knowing that something terrible has happened to Janus is better than not knowing where he is or if he's even alive. Eventually she'll have to find out, or it might drive her mad.

When I get back, I'll tell her. Maybe not the exact truth, but I will tell her that Janus is gone. I just have to figure out how.

An hour or so after I cross the Canadian border, I pick up my phone to check in with Zophie, but it has no signal. It's only then that I realize the burner is only set to work off US cell towers. I glance at my map—I'm only half an hour from Montreal. I decide to soldier on.

At a gas station outside of the city, I buy a calling card and sidle up to a pay phone. I call the cabin's land-line, but in response I get a fast, repetitive beeping—the kind of noise I've only heard once before while chasing a potential lead on Janus, when I called a number that was disconnected. I try again and get the same sound.

When Zophie doesn't pick up the other burner, I start to panic. I try two more times but get no answer. I tell myself she's just gone to the store, or she's acci-dentally left the phone off the hook—any number of excuses that could result in her not answering.

I call my burner's number so I can check my voice mail remotely. There's one message. Of course it's from her, left an hour ago.

"Lexa!" she shouts. "Lexa, you have to come back now! As soon as you get this." She's so *excited.* "I stum-bled onto this Listserv of people calling themselves

'Greeters' who say they were recruited by an Elder. I posted on it anonymously, and someone's already contacted me. I know you said to be careful about this stuff, but I just couldn't wait. And besides, I made him prove he was one of us. He knows about Loridas and the Garde. He was on the other ship. He's one of the Cêpan."

My heart jumps into my throat.

"I asked the person what the pilot's name was. He said Janus. He knew all about my brother."

There's a pause in the message. I can hear Zophie sniffling, fighting back tears.

"Lexa," she says. "He says Janus is with them. My brother is on his way here. Everything's going to be okay."

My heart collapses, and before I realize it, I'm back in the car with my laptop open in front of me, connected to a satellite uplink. It's not too late. I can still contact her. If she's on her computer, I can send her a message. . . .

I pull up the live surveillance feed of the cabin on my laptop and choke. There are dozens of Mogs on our lawn. They wrestle with the Chimærae, who claw at the intruders. But the animals are being overpowered—there are hideous, gnashing beasts alongside the Mogadorians, and they tear into the Chimærae with terrifying ferocity. A few of our animals are already being bagged and loaded into a truck. Some fall and don't get back up.

And in the middle of it all is Zophie. I scream at her, dozens of things that she can't hear. I tell her to run. I tell her to fight. I apologize. She struggles valiantly alongside the Chimærae, tearing out of the grip of one Mogadorian, only to be grabbed by another. She has some kind of tool in her hand that she swings at him. A hammer or wrench—it's hard to tell. She must have been caught off guard, without a real weapon. I watch in horror as she finally escapes, running up the porch and towards the front door. Blasters fire, missing her, creating smoking holes in the wooden cabin wall.

She's intercepted by one of the Mog beasts the size of our station wagon—all horns and teeth, running at her on four legs. It catches her in its jaws, but she's not done fighting. She swings the tool in her hand down straight into the monster's eye. It howls in pain, dropping her, and I see that I completely underestimated her fighting abilities.

But it's not over.

The Mog beast lets out a roar and swings its head at Zophie. The creature's horned snout impales her. She stumbles towards the front door, a dark spot appearing and then growing on her stomach where the creature struck her. And then she falls. A few of the Chimærae surround her, turning into fanged monsters in order to protect her. But they can't help now.

Seconds pass. Her chest stops rising.

She joins her brother.

The Chimærae must know this, because they leave her side, trying to save themselves. It's no use, though. They're overpowered. Captured. The Mogs seem furious with their horned creature—the one that just murdered my friend—and begin to beat it. Flames start to lick the sides of the cabin, the multitude of blaster shots having caught something on fire.

Soon afterwards, the video feed cuts out.

I begin to shake. Slightly at first, and then violently. For the first time in as long as I can remember, tears start to stream down my face in hot, wet rivers. I can't stop them. My nose begins to run, and when I open my mouth to breathe, a sound comes out that isn't Loric—it's animal.

I start the car, ready to speed down the highway, to fly back to our cabin.

But it would be pointless. Zophie is gone. The Chimærae will be gone too by the time I get there. The cabin is burning and is probably still being watched by the Mogs.

I can't fight those Mogadorian bastards and win. Not hand-to-hand or face-to-face. Not that many of them.

The noise comes from my mouth again, raw and full of rage.

And then I'm driving, as fast as I can. Night falls and I continue, aimlessly, without any destination, until the car runs out of gas on the side of the road. Then I get out and run. No one is here to find me this time. No LDA squad tracking the ship I'd stolen and taking me back home. It's just me. I run until I'm so exhausted that I feel like I can't take another step.

And then I keep going.

CHAPTER
SEVENTEEN

TWO WEEKS AFTER THE MOGADORIANS KILLED Zophie, a seemingly unrelated story is published in someone's online journal. It's a short account of an incident at Philadelphia International Airport. A man refused to let a piece of carry-on luggage go through the airport scanner. He and his companion, a young boy, were scheduled to fly to Africa. There's a picture of the two of them, the man older and flustered, the boy four, maybe five years old and freckled. The man holds one side of a chest that's covered in Loric symbols. A member of airport security holds on to the other. I don't know who they are, but they are almost certainly one of the Garde and his Cêpan. I want to reach through the photo and shake the old man for being so foolish, but I unfortunately don't have that Legacy. I only hope he will learn. That he will do better.

I destroy every line of the journal's code and overload

the host site's servers for good measure. Then, over the course of lunch in a diner in South Carolina, I track down the writer and photographer's email address and send her a message containing a computer virus under the guise of it being a note from a fan of her journal. By the time I finish dessert, she's downloaded my worm, which rapidly eats up her hard drive. I pay my waitress and leave, continuing my aimless wandering.

Zane is dead. So is Zophie. And Janus.

I'm alone again, just as I was on Lorien.

Well, not technically, I suppose. Assuming the other Garde and Cêpan survived and that Ella and Crayton are still in hiding, there are twenty other Loric who I know of on Earth.

I consider flying back to Egypt, trying to track down Crayton and Ella. But they must be long gone by now. And even if I did find them, what if I unintentionally led the Mogs to them? What if somehow my presence ruined things?

I do better on my own, anyway. Sitting behind a computer screen. Gathering information. Piecing things together.

When I think of what happened to Zophie, I have to swallow down the urge to vomit. I blame myself. I should have been up-front with her about Janus as soon as I knew he was dead. I realize that now, but there's nothing I can do. She's gone.

My blood fills with rage and fire when I think of the Mogadorians. I'm still not sure why the Elders chose to send such a small number of our people to Earth, but I know that they must be important. Why else would the Mogs be here, going after them? Janus said they had scattered. I don't know if that was the truth or one final lie he was able to keep from his captors, but going their separate ways would make the most sense. The photo of the duo headed to Africa seems to corroborate his claim.

And so, what Zophie and I were trying to do—to find them all—was really dangerous for everyone. For the remaining Loric. I realize that now. It would be much better for them to stay hidden. At least until the Garde are strong enough to fight.

I can still help, though, and by doing so hurt the Mogs. From afar. Because the closer I get to people, the more they tend to get hurt. And I can't go through losing someone else. I just don't think I have it in me.

What I *can* do is work behind the scenes. I can be a phantom. Anonymous. The ghost in the machine. Just like I did with the blog—I can watch out for my people in the digital world. Cover up their tracks when I can. Help ensure that their mission, whatever it is, is completed. Find any information that might help them along the way. Train myself in this planet's technologies until I can control them fully.

I can try to help protect my people.

Maybe I'm not a ghost. Maybe I'm something else. Something more like a guardian.

I can gather resources for them should the day come when they are ready to rise against the Mogs. There are many powerful and dangerous weapons on Earth. And some not of this world too. There's still a Loric ship that can fly. Janus's ship. Maybe the Mogs have it. Maybe it's still hidden somewhere.

I wonder how hard it would be for me to find it.

CHAPTER ONE

ON LORIEN I LIVED IN MY GRANDFATHER'S house on the outskirts of the city, the dormitory of the defense academy, a basement apartment across from Eilon Park—even a Kabarak in the Outer Territories for a few years after my brother died, when I was happy to be lost and disconnected from Capital City and everything it stood for. None of those places exists now that the Mogadorians have destroyed my planet. Now I have only Earth, a world where I am not just a stranger, but one of the last of my people.

I've been on this planet almost two years, but I'm not sure it will ever feel like home. It almost did in a rented cabin in upstate New York for a brief period of time a few months ago. Thanks to the Mogs, that home no longer exists either.

It seems like all of my homes are eventually destroyed. Death tends to follow me wherever I go, taking those I care about most. And so I've made it a priority to stay alone, away from others.

That's how I end up buying a secluded piece of land I've never set foot on in Alabama.

It's dusk when I first see the property with my own eyes, parking in front of the huge wrought iron gate that opens up to a tree-lined drive. The name Yellowhammer Ranch is spelled out in rusty letters arching over the top. The gate looks imposing, but it's mostly ornamental. As a security measure, it's laughable. There's not even a lock on it. The fencing on either side is just as bad, consisting of a few strands of barbed wire: a barrier that will keep out nothing but stray animals. I wonder if the former owners actually felt safer because of these crude strings of metal. Possibly, I suppose. But then, they probably never imagined that their enemies would come from the sky instead of the winding dirt road that leads to the ranch.

I know better.

Still, the gate and fence aren't completely useless. They'll both come in handy when I install perimeter security cameras. Maybe a few remote-operated weapons too, just in case any Mogadorians manage to find me here.

With a little push, the wrought-iron gate moves, squeaking on old hinges. I get back inside my SUV and drive over the cattle guard. The actual house is located a short drive past the gate and is mostly obscured by rolling hills and trees. It's all thick beams of wood on the outside. I ignore the carport off to the side and drive onto the grass, straight up to the porch. The lawn is yellowed and rises just above the ankles of my black boots when I step into it. I circle the house once, taking in the area, keeping my eyes peeled for anything that seems out of the ordinary or that might pose especially glaring security problems. There's nothing around for as far as I can see in any direction other than more barbed wire and empty fields and an old barn out back. I'm alone here. No one to disturb my work. No attachments other than to my mission.

At least if this place goes up in flames too, no one will be hurt but me.

I step over a broken stair at the bottom of the front porch and walk to the wooden door, where there's a big envelope hung up by a thick strip of clear tape. I pull it down and slide out a small stack of paperwork that proves I'm now the owner of Yellowhammer. None of the documents actually has my name on it—I haven't given anyone my real name, Lexa, since I discovered that Mogadorians were on Earth hunting down the Loric. Not that it would mean anything to a Mog if he heard it, anyway—I'm not Pittacus or one of the other Elders. But I *am* careful. Yellowhammer Ranch is technically now owned by a shell corporation I set up, a subsidiary of another organization of my inventing, all of the paperwork looping together in a way that could never be traced back to me.

Lately I've started to collect identities. I've been dozens of people in the past weeks, sometimes in real life and sometimes in the virtual world. I was Julie when I bought the big black SUV in Pennsylvania. I borrowed a man named Phil's IP address when I attempted to hack into the CIA's intranet. I think it was Lindsey who purchased all the firearms in Kentucky and Patti who bought all the computer equipment in Tennessee. I take the names from waitresses, magazine covers and overheard conversations, changing aliases daily, sometimes hourly. Organizing information and data has always been a strong suit of mine, and I bounce between these identities without faltering, storing Julie and Lindsey and Patti away in the back of my head when I'm done with them in case I ever need to use them again.

The people I buy things from at pawnshops and computer stores never suspect I'm not who I say I am. Or if they do, they don't say anything. It's amazing how few questions get asked when you're willing to overpay in cash. And, thanks to the fairly primitive internet firewalls and security systems used by banks on this planet, money is easy to come by if you're someone who's good with ones and zeros and moving them around like I am. In the past few weeks I've skimmed minuscule amounts of currency from millions of bank accounts across the world. Money is one of the few things I have a lot of. Money and questions and anger.

I tip the envelope farther, and a set of keys falls into my open palm.

The ranch was trickier to come by. I knew I wanted somewhere far away from crowded areas, or even the nearest town if possible. Remote places like that were easy to locate, but it took me awhile before I found someone willing to part with their property in a hurry, and without ever even meeting me face-to-face. All I needed was to wire some money and forge a few signatures, and suddenly I owned a piece of this planet.

I take another look around the porch, and I can't help but think of how much Zophie would have liked this place. She spent many nights at the old cabin in New York out on the veranda with a cup of tea, staring at nothing in particular. Probably thinking of her brother, Janus. Back when there was still hope that he was alive.

A shallow ache rises in my chest. It's a feeling I'm familiar with, the hurt that comes when thoughts of Zophie or Janus or my brother, Zane, settle in my mind. No matter how hard I try to numb myself and keep memories of them buried, they always manage to find me again. I remind myself that it's not sadness I should be feeling, but anger. That, at least, I can use. It's what fueled me on Lorien when I wanted nothing more than to take down the Elders and uproot our society. Now, rage against the Mogadorians is what keeps me going half the time. A burning desire for vengeance in the name of everyone I've lost.

But to make the Mogs suffer, I have to get to work. And so I swallow hard, shake my head a few times and unlock the front door.

Inside, the house is dusty, all the furniture covered with white drop cloths. The skull of a big, horned animal hangs over the fireplace mantel. Why the people of Earth choose to decorate their dwellings with the corpses of animals, I have no idea. Killing for sport was an unthinkable crime on Lorien, but based on a few appalling stories I've overheard at hunting-supply stores in my travels here, I gather it's not exactly uncommon on Earth. I can only imagine what Crayton's reaction would be if he were with me, knowing his fondness for Chimærae. There's a pang in my chest as I wonder where he is now. Are he and Ella safe? How big has she grown in all this time since I last saw her?

Again I push these thoughts out of my head and keep going.

I pull one of the white cloths off a table and toss it over the skull, obscuring it. Then I explore the other rooms. The refrigerator in the kitchen has a huge freezer, meaning my grocery trips to the towns half an hour away can be infrequent. The hall closet can serve as my miniature armory, where I can stash a few of the weapons I've picked up lately. I leave the furniture in the spare bedrooms covered and scope out the office located at the end of the one hallway running through the house. This will be where I spend most of my time—the sanctuary in my new base of operations.

I start to unload my SUV.

Until recently I traveled light, mostly because Mogs had destroyed almost everything I had on this planet while I was out chasing a lead on the Garde. For a few weeks I traveled aimlessly, making my way across the United States, an outsider in a world not my own. I thought about searching for the rest of my people: the Garde and Cêpans from the other ship. According to Janus, they'd scattered. That's what he'd said shortly before the Mogadorians executed him on camera and sent me the video. The evidence I've discovered online seems to back this up. I've found hints of them here and there: pictures of an older man and young boy with a Loric chest trying to find passage to another continent, reports of tattooed men chasing a kid in Canada. I'm not sure why they've split up, but for the most part they're covering their tracks well, staying off the grid. I guess their Cêpans are competent, for the most part. Being impossible to find bodes well for their survival, but not for me finding them.

There's some bigger game at play here, but I can't

figure it out. Why are the Mogs after these kids? What's so special about them? Why spend resources trying to destroy the last of the Loric?

These are the questions I've been trying to answer, all while doing my best to help the Garde stay out of sight. If I see something on the internet that sounds like it could be related to them, I try to wipe it away or bury it in broken code. But staying on the move has made this difficult to do. That's why I'm here now, at Yellowhammer. It's a base of operations for a coming war. Because, if the Mogs are here on Earth, it's probably only a matter of time before they do to this planet what they did to my home.

Most of the boxes I have are full of computer equipment I've purchased on my trek across this country. Once everything is piled up in the back office, I begin to piece things together, breaking down machines and wiring them in more efficient ways, building a system that will incorporate the highly upgraded laptop I created in Egypt using Loric data pads. The custom laptop is fine, but the machine I'm building will allot me more processing power and storage space. The work is tedious, but I remain focused. Night falls and then the sun rises. I pause only a few times for water and to stretch my legs.

When my head starts to pound from concentrating for so long, I take a break and walk around outside, taking note of all the places where I can add some cameras and heighten security once the computer is up and running—something a little more substantial than barbed wire. This place will take a lot of work, but by the time I'm through it will be a fortress of knowledge and power. I plan to collect every scrap of information I can about the Mogs. Those bastards who destroyed my planet, who *murdered* my friend, will pay. I'll figure out what they're up to and help the other Loric bring them down. Somehow. Someway.

I pull open the half-rusted doors of the big barn out back. They squeal as if they haven't been moved in a long time. Light filters through a missing section of roof, illuminating a few bales of hay and a scattering of tools hanging on one wall. The place isn't much—in fact, it looks as though one good shove could send it clattering to the ground—but it'll do.

With any luck, soon I'll have a ship in here. The one that brought the chosen Garde and their Cêpans to this planet—maybe the last Loric ship in the universe for all I know.

Because whatever it is that the Garde are here to do, they'll need all the help they can get. They're being hunted. *We're* being hunted. And when they're masters of their Legacies and decide it's time to strike against the Mogadorians, they'll need the ship.

Hell, I'll fly them to the Mogs myself.

CHAPTER
TWO

ONCE MY DESKTOP SUPERCOMPUTER—OR AT LEAST what passes for one on this planet—is set up in the office, I get straight to work.

I start with the information I have from Zophie and Janus. It's not much, but that's what I'm here to fix.

Since tracking the Garde has proved to be nearly impossible, I take a different approach. A lifetime ago when we were still drifting through space in a refurbished ship, Zophie mentioned that Pittacus Lore had set up a contact for the chosen Garde here on Earth. If I can find that person, I may be able to get a better sense of what's going on. He or she might even know where Janus's ship is.

And there's always the possibility that maybe Pittacus survived the fall of Lorien. Who knows where the Elders were when our planet was destroyed? Maybe he's even here, on Earth. His contact might know.

So I focus my investigation on a simple question: How would Pittacus Lore go about recruiting a human to help the Loric?

I spend countless hours thinking about this, trying to get inside the head of an Elder. Would he have sought out a great thinker? Or a military leader? Or perhaps he would have chosen someone with extreme wealth who would have the resources to protect the last of our kind. These inquiries only lead to more questions, though: What Earth languages did Pittacus speak? How *many* contacts might he have had on this planet? In my time at the Lorien Defense Academy, I worked on improving technologies for Earth but never thought to ask how those technologies were given to the beings here. For the first time in my life, I regret not sticking it out at the LDA after my brother's death. If I had, maybe I'd have more information to work with now.

I barely sleep and rarely leave the back office. With blackout curtains on the windows, I hardly even notice whether it's light or dark outside. Eventually I realize I may be looking at this the wrong way. Maybe Pittacus didn't find a contact on Earth. Maybe someone on Earth found him.

This is something I can use, something narrower. I start looking into Earth initiatives to contact other planets. There are relatively few, and I'm struck, not for the first time, by how strange it must be to think your small world of dirt and grass and water might be unique in its ability to support life. Over the course of a few days I follow leads that go nowhere. I break into email accounts and track the browsing histories of a dozen astrophysicists, cosmologists, astronauts—even a few crackpot conspiracy theorists. I uncover nothing that even alludes to Lorien or Pittacus Lore.

Finally, I stumble across a promising candidate. I find information about a man named Malcolm Goode, who was outspoken in his belief of extraterrestrial beings—so much so that it apparently cost him his job at a place of education that sounds not unlike the LDA. More important, he published several articles detailing his attempts to broadcast messages to other planets.

His research and methods, while primitive, are sound.

Once I have a name and a little bit of history, it's not long before I find Malcolm Goode himself. He appears to be living in a small town in a state named Ohio. I do more digging and find a few email addresses linked to his name. From there it's hardly any work to hack into his accounts, where I sift through the everyday corre-spondences of what seems to be a very uneventful life.

Except for one email I discover that leads me to a private online forum. It has been inactive for years, and the correspondences all seem innocuous. Still, I dig around, until I find a deleted post still lurking in the lines of code that make up the message board:

Hello? Malcolm? Is anyone still on here? Has there been any more contact from the Pittacus? -Ethan

I consider trying to contact Malcolm online or over the phone, but I figure that if he *is* the person Pittacus talked to, he's probably been sworn to secrecy. I don't want to risk having him disappear on me, so instead I load some gear and weapons back into my SUV and drive from Alabama to Ohio for most of the next day. I hate leaving Yellowhammer unfortified, but tracking down this lead takes priority. Besides, I can't imagine I've done anything there to set off alarms for the Moga-dorians.

Not yet, at least.

Malcolm lives on the outskirts of a town called Para-dise. When I arrive, I park down the street and watch his house for a while, trying to get an idea of who this man is. Through my binoculars I see him pass by the windows, along with a woman and young boy, about six or seven years old, if I had to guess. His wife and son, I assume—I remember mention of them in some of his emails. I watch him water some flowers in the front yard, then wash and dry dishes in the kitchen.

His existence seems perfectly ordinary—so normal that I'm concerned I've got the wrong guy entirely.

When his wife leaves and the boy runs out into the backyard to play, I make my move. I pull in behind a truck in Malcolm's driveway and park. A few seconds later I'm standing on his porch, knocking on the door. I keep one of Raylan's blasters tucked into the pocket of my long, black coat. I've taken to carrying it with me wherever I go, just in case.

Malcolm Goode answers the door with a smile. His hair is a little unkempt, dark and wavy. His eyes are bright, brows raised in anticipation.

"Can I help you?" he asks, pushing thick glasses up his nose. He's on the scrawny side, and I'm much taller than he is. Good—if this goes badly and he ends up less than pleased that I showed up on his doorstep, I'll have that advantage on him.

I get straight to the point.

"I'm here about Pittacus Lore."

He pauses before responding.

"I think you have the wrong house."

"We both know that's not true," I say, but not in English. I use the language of Lorien. It feels so strange on my tongue at first—I haven't spoken the words of my people in months. Malcolm twitches as I speak. His eyes go wide for an instant, and then he blinks a lot, staring at me in a mixture of confusion and astonishment. This is exactly the type of reaction I'm looking for.

"What language is that?" Malcolm asks quietly, unconvincingly. "I've never heard it before."

I switch back to English.

"I know who you are, Malcolm Goode."

He starts to shut the door, but my foot is in the way before he can get it closed.

"Listen," I say firmly. "I have no intention of hurting you. I'm only looking for information."

"I don't know what you're talking about," he says, trying to kick my foot out of the way.

I put my hand on the door, flexing my fingers and pushing back a little. Malcolm must feel the resistance, because his nostrils flare.

"I just want answers," I say.

"I don't know anything." His voice is higher now, verging on panic. "If you don't leave now I'll call the police."

"And tell them what?" I ask. "That I came asking about a Loric Elder? You don't want something like that getting into the papers. It'd lead the Mogs right to you."

Malcolm's face goes white. He stops pushing so hard against the door.

"They're here," I continue. "The Mogadorians. He told you about them, right? Pittacus must have known what was going to happen to Lorien if he set up things with you in advance. The Mogs are on this planet.

They've come to Earth. I just want answers."

Malcolm looks up at me. He searches my face. I can see him doing calculations in his head, trying to figure out what to do next.

"How do I know you're not a—a Mogadorian?" he asks.

"Malcolm, if you'd ever seen one of those bastards, you'd realize that's the most insulting question I've ever been asked."

He nods a little. "From what I've heard . . . I can imagine."

"I know about the ones who came from Lorien. The nine Garde and their Mentors. I'm a friend. If I wasn't, I'd have shown up with an army."

After a few moments he takes the rest of his weight off the door, opening it just wide enough for me to pass through. While he pokes his head out the front doorway and looks around, I investigate the first few rooms in his house, taking in my surroundings, preparing for anything. Just because this man was chosen by one of the Loric Elders doesn't mean he's to be trusted. Not by me, at least—not when I barely have any faith in the Elders themselves. I keep one hand in my coat pocket, ready to draw my weapon at the first sign that Malcolm isn't going to cooperate.

But he does. He ushers me into his office. Dark wooden shelves line the walls. They're filled with books, files and papers all piled on top of each other haphazardly. The stacks spill out onto virtually every surface of the room, and for a moment I'm reminded of my small basement apartment on Lorien, packed with all sorts of computer equipment and various electronic projects.

Malcolm peeks through the window and looks into the backyard, where his son runs around with some big spaceship or airplane held over his head. When he seems satisfied that the boy is safe, he closes the blinds and turns to me.

"How did you—," he starts.

"An old message board," I say.

"But . . . we abandoned that well before the ship landed. And we only ever spoke in code. Anything conspicuous was deleted."

"Nothing is ever really deleted from the internet, Malcolm. One day your people will figure that out. If it's any consolation, it took me quite some time to find it."

He shakes his head. "But we were so careful. There were never any actual details mentioned. That was all reserved for face-to-face meetings."

"Someone didn't follow the rules," I say.

He considers this for a moment, and then his face twists into a scowl.

"I thought I'd gotten rid of . . ." He sighs. "Nothing is

ever really deleted." He purses his lips a little. "Ethan. I always figured he'd end up being trouble. That's why we cut him out before the ship ever landed."

"How did Pittacus recruit you?" I ask. "Through your messages sent into space?"

He looks at me quizzically before nodding.

"I've done my research on you," I explain. "Are you still in contact? Could you get a message out to him?"

Malcolm's eyebrows furrow together, and his gaze falls to the floor.

"I'm sorry," he says. "But Pittacus is dead."

These words land in my ears, but I feel them in my core, my stomach twisting so hard that I almost double over. This had always been a possible, if not likely, scenario. Still, hearing this for sure takes a little bit of air from my lungs. I always wanted the Elders out of power, but never dead. Not really. We are fewer and fewer.

"You're sure?" I ask.

"Quite positive," he says. He glances to the window overlooking the backyard and then back to me.

"What about a man named Loridas?" I ask.

"Another of the 'Elders,' yes? From what Pittacus told me . . . I think they're all gone as well."

I nod slowly.

"Was there anyone else on the ship other than the nine children and their guardians?"

PITTACUS LORE

"No. Well, there was a pilot too, but he took the ship to hide it. I'm not—"

"Janus," I say. "His name was Janus. He's dead too."

I turn away from him, taking a few steps toward a wall of bookshelves as I let all this information sink in.

"Who are you?" he asks. "You speak their language. Are you from Lorien as well?"

I'm about to answer when I see it—tucked under a few pages of loose paper on a bookshelf. A white tablet.

I recognize it; it's Loric. A tracking device used to keep tabs on ships, inventory and sometimes even people, depending on how it's programmed.

If it's here . . .

In a few quick strides I'm across the room and the tablet is in my hands, the papers on top of it tumbling to the floor.

"He gave you this?" I ask.

"Pittacus did, yes," Malcolm says. "Though I'm afraid he didn't give me any instructions other than to keep it safe. He was wounded and . . . do you know what it is?"

I pull my laptop out of my bag and find a connector cable from one of the old Loric data pads. It slides into a port at the bottom of the white tablet, connecting it to my computer. Within seconds I've got a map of Earth pulled up on the device.

275

"How did you . . ." He trails off.

"I'm good with computers," I murmur. "And I used these once or twice back on Lorien."

There are blue blips pulsing across the planet. Blue blips that represent people. Ten in all. Could this be the nine Garde plus one more? Maybe Ella? Given her parents' powers, I wouldn't be surprised if she developed gifts early on.

Or is there another that I'm not accounting for?

And there are two triangles too. One triangle is in Egypt—my crashed rocket. The second lies in the southwestern United States.

The other ship.

My pulse quickens until I can feel it throbbing at my temples.

"Do you know this area?" I ask.

Malcolm leans over my shoulder. "Let's see. That looks like it would be . . . Oh." He snorts a little. "Yes. I believe that's where the Dulce Base is supposed to be located. A secret government operation. Most people are more familiar with Area 51, but *this* is no tourist trap like Roswell."

"Dulce," I say to myself. That makes sense. If the American government stumbled across Janus's ship, they'd likely want to keep it hidden. At least that means it's not in Mog hands.

"What's in Dulce?" Malcolm asks.

"This is perfect," I say, ignoring him. "I'll get the ship back. With this tablet I could easily collect the Garde too."

"You can't," Malcolm says, shaking his head rapidly. "They have to stay separated."

"They won't stand a chance against the Mogs if they're found alone," I say.

Something flashes on Malcolm's face. He shakes his head a little.

"You don't know about the protection that's been placed on them, do you?" he asks.

I narrow my eyes. "I think we need to have a very long talk, Malcolm Goode."

CHAPTER
THREE

I KNEW THE ELDERS MUST HAVE BEEN UP TO something when they'd sent Garde to this planet. I'd even assumed that they'd in some way endanger the young Loric in the name of the greater good—the sort of thing I expected from Lorien's rulers. Never did I imagine that they would give these nine children the order in which they would die and call it "protection." In terms of survival, maybe it makes sense. But all I can do is think of the poor, unlucky kid who was picked to be Number One. What kind of burden is that to carry around with you?

These nine Garde—somehow they're to be the saviors of our people. That helps explain why the Mogadorians have come to Earth: if the escaped Garde will one day bring Lorien back to power, it's not a stretch to assume that they might do so by somehow toppling those who destroyed our planet to begin with. Of course the Mogs want to eradicate them.

It's obvious now why they separated. The reason they've scattered so far, these tiny blips on my screen located across this planet. I'd been wary of reuniting them, but now I see for certain that this would be dangerous for everyone. The Mogs could take them out in a single attack that way, destroying all the children at once. Better that they stay separate. At least for now. At least until they're older and stronger, with Legacies to fight with. I hope their Cêpans are skilled—that they've been given the strongest, most capable Mentors from our planet.

I have to let them be. As much as I hate to do it, I have to rely on the wisdom of the Elders and the capabilities of the Cêpans. Even seeking the Garde out individually would mean I was running the risk of leading the Mogs right to them, no matter how careful I was. That leaves me with one clear goal.

I'm going to Dulce to get that ship.

"I'm taking this with me," I say, staring down at the white tablet.

"What?" Malcolm asks. "No. Why? You can't."

"You don't have a choice," I say. The tablet is Loric. It belongs with me.

"Pittacus told me to protect it. He said it would prove to be useful."

"Exactly. I'm going to use it."

"No." Malcolm curls his fingers into fists and plants his feet in front of me. "It's my responsibility. I've put everything on the line to help your people. My life. My *family*. Pittacus told me to keep this tablet safe for the Garde, and that's what I'm going to do. One of the Cêpan—I believe his Loric name is Brandon—said he'd be back for it if there was trouble, or when his charge was at the age when he would start developing powers or whatever you know them as."

My hand moves towards my weapon. I don't want to threaten Malcolm with violence—he's right when he says he's sacrificed much to help my people, after all—but I'm not leaving this piece of technology in the hands of someone who doesn't even know how to use it properly.

There's a clattering from the hallway. I turn and see Malcolm's kid standing there. A plastic robot is on the floor in front of him. He's wearing a shirt with an image of Saturn on it, the sixth planet from this solar system's sun. I recognize its rings; I've seen them up close, on my journey to this world. The boy is pale and thin and has sandy-blond hair, and even though physically he looks nothing like Zane, there's something in his expression—full of wonder—that immediately makes me think of my brother. It hurts a place inside me I thought had finally begun to heal.

"Sam," Malcolm says, letting his posture slacken.

"Go outside, would you?"

Sam just stares up at me. Malcolm looks back and forth between us a few times before crossing the room and pushing Sam out of my sight.

I think about the fact that this family in a small town in Ohio has perhaps saved the last of my people. And about how I was considering taking out my blaster and forcing Malcolm to let me have the tablet. What would Zophie say? What would Zane say?

I'm not some Mogadorian thug. I'm not going to threaten this man and his son. That's not who I am.

Besides, if the Cêpans are counting on the white tablet being in Paradise, I can't very well take it back to Alabama.

"Your son can stay," I say, setting the tracking device down on Malcolm's desk and packing up my gear. "I should be on my way."

Malcolm looks confused but nods.

"Tell whoever comes for the tablet that the ship in Egypt is wrecked," I say, moving past Malcolm and his son towards the front door.

"Wait," he says. "Who are you? How did you get here? You haven't even told me your name. Where are you going?"

"New Mexico." I stop on the porch, turning to him. "Malcolm. Take my visit as a warning. I found you. It took me a while, but I did. And that means the Mog—"

I glance at Sam, hiding behind his father's legs. "That *others* might be able to as well. Others who aren't as friendly as I am."

Malcolm stares hard at me, nodding a little bit.

"Keep your family safe," I say, stepping down onto the Goodes' yard. "And the tablet too. At least *hide* the damned thing. The last thing we need is for that to fall into the enemy's hands."

Malcolm is still on the porch when I back out of his driveway. Sam lingers in the doorframe. As I start down the road, he waves to me.

The drive from Paradise to Dulce is a long one. Lush green fields eventually give way to flat plains that seem to stretch on past the horizon. I rest at a motel in Kansas for a few hours, hardly sleeping because, for the first time since I arrived on Earth, I know *exactly* where Janus's ship is. And because I'm worried about how I'm going to get to it. I run through what history I can find of this "secret base" online. Most of it seems to come from conspiracy theorists and quacks—though, considering that Malcolm was viewed as one of those by the rest of his profession, perhaps I shouldn't be so quick to pass judgment. It seems that most believe this base is some sort of research facility, which I hope means it won't be guarded too heavily. Maybe I'll even be able to tap into its communications once I'm close by

so I can get a feel for what the security is like inside—
something I dare not try to do on the motel's unsecure
network.

Perhaps. Maybe. The uncertainties are many, and I
have to remind myself that this is something I cannot
rush. I can't just cut through a fence or hop over a gate
and storm the base, rushing headfirst into this situation. Only a fool would be so brazen—or naive—to
do so.

I get a sense of the area where the base is supposed
to be via online maps and photographs, and then try to
sleep. The next morning I rise before the sun and drive
through the mountains of Colorado, which eventually
give way to the arid terrain of New Mexico.

Once I spot a chain-link fence topped in razor wire
and covered in signs warning against photography and
trespassing, I figure I'm in the right place. The base's
perimeter is barely visible from the trail-like road I'm
on. It's the middle of the afternoon, and I'm not exactly
inconspicuous driving around the desert area in my
big, black SUV, so I don't test my luck by getting any
closer to the fence. Instead, I head to the nearby town of
Dulce and pay for a week at a cheap motel. I stash most
of my things in a shoddy little room in case I manage to
get the ship and have to leave my car behind. I keep a
few weapons with me, then round up some additional
supplies from a sporting-goods store. Night-vision

goggles. Some wire cutters, just in case.

At night I return. I park a half mile from the fence and scope out the site with my new goggles. I don't notice any cameras or alarms. It's not until I get closer that I can finally see the tops of buildings and some of the grounds of the base. I stand a few feet from the fence and observe.

And I see things I can't even begin to comprehend.

The base is owned by United States government agencies—that's obvious from the information I found online and the signs dotting the fence line warning that I've approached a "military encampment." I can also see plenty of vehicles with government plates and markings. There are a handful of armed personnel around, wearing camouflage, pacing back and forth.

But that's not what causes my mouth to drop open and my hands to shake.

There's a ship sitting beside a tall watchtower. Not a Loric ship, but one I recognize all the same. Hundreds just like it swarmed the skies during the invasion of Lorien, raining fire and death down upon my planet, dropping off battalions of soldiers who slaughtered my people.

It's Mogadorian.

"Holy shit," I whisper. "What are the Mogs doing here?"

My mind reels with the implications. Either the

Mogs have taken over this base and are somehow forcing humans to work for them or . . .

I swallow down a mixture of anger and disbelief.

Or the Mogs and the American government are somehow working together.

This just got much more complicated.

I slowly lower the night-vision goggles, trying to make sense of what I'm seeing. It's only then that I hear the footsteps behind me.

CHAPTER
FOUR

"HANDS IN THE AIR!" A MAN SHOUTS. FLASH-
lights go on. I hear a few metallic clicks behind me.

One glance over my shoulder tells me these aren't
Mogs. Four men in brown law enforcement uniforms
form a half circle behind me, pinning me up against
the fence. Their guns are aimed at my back, but the
weapons shake a little. They seem almost scared.

I take a moment before moving, going over my options.
I've got a shotgun in the backseat and Raylan's blaster in
my coat pocket. I could try to make a run for it. . . .

But these are humans. They're probably just doing
their jobs. What are the chances I could make it out of
here without accidentally killing one of them?

Part of me says I shouldn't care—that me escaping
would be for the sake of the remaining Loric. But that
sounds an awful lot like something the Elders would
say. And I am *not* an Elder.

I'm reminded for the second time in the last twenty-four hours why I like to work behind the scenes.

"I said, hands in the air where I can see 'em!" the same voice shouts.

I turn slowly, raising my hands. The officers look startled at first, but I'm not sure what aspect of my appearance they're surprised by. Maybe the fact that I'm not a man. I've come to learn that just like on Lorien, the people of Earth aren't used to a woman being so tall. After the flash of surprise, though, there's a wave of relief that rushes over them. The one with the big hat on—the one who I assume is in charge—gets in close, putting his flashlight up to my face. He looks at my recently shaved head, then into my eyes for a few moments.

"What are you doing out here?" he asks.

"Sightseeing," I reply.

He lets out a grunt, but I can see his posture soften. The others lower their guns a little.

"This is government property," he says. "Trespassing isn't taken lightly."

"I'm on this side of the fence," I say.

He grins. "Which puts you under my jurisdiction. Now, I know just about everybody in Rio Arriba County, and I've definitely never seen you before, which means we need to get acquainted. Why don't you start by telling me why you're sneaking around in the dark with those hunting goggles?"

He motions to one of his men. The officer moves behind me and is patting me down before I can object. He pulls the blaster out of my coat pocket.

"What the . . . ," he whispers, wrapping his fingers around its hilt.

He's obviously never held a blaster before and doesn't realize what a sensitive trigger it has, because the weapon fires with an electronic sound and melts a hole in my front driver's-side tire. The SUV leans as the tire deflates.

"Dammit," I mutter.

Suddenly everyone's guns are on me again, and the man in the big hat's got my hands behind my back. I think about resisting, but there's no way I can outrun them now. One of the men starts asking me questions about some deputy I've never heard of, but the leader shuts him up.

"No one talks to her until we're back at the station. This is my interrogation."

"Do you want us to keep patrolling the perimeter?" one of the officers asks.

"Lights off." The man in the hat nods. "Stay quiet. I don't want anyone seeing you—on either side of the fence." He turns to me. "You have the right to remain silent. . . ."

My mind races as I try to remember everything I've learned in passing about the American justice system, any tidbit of knowledge that might be helpful.

"What crime am I being charged with?" I ask as he pushes me towards a car I can barely see in the darkness. "I haven't done anything wrong."

"Possession of an illegal firearm," the man says. "And suspected murder of a police officer."

I piece together what I can from the back of the squad car based on the conversation between the man in the hat—the county sheriff—and one of his deputies. Apparently two officers went investigating reports of bizarre lights near the base, which I gather isn't that strange a call for this area. But something went bad. Only one officer returned, his body shot full of cauterized holes from some sort of unidentified weapon. Before he slipped into a coma, he said something about men with tattoos on their heads and black eyes.

No wonder they reacted so strongly to the blaster firing.

Panic starts to settle in my chest once the shock of being arrested wears off. I have no identification. I'm not even human. And I'm handcuffed in the back of a locked-down police car with a thick layer of metal grating separating me from the front seat.

I have to escape this somehow.

As we shoot through Dulce, sirens blaring and lights flashing, I try to figure out where we are in relation to the motel where my computer and several extra weapons are stashed. The town is small, so it doesn't take me long to get my bearings—though that also means there aren't many places for me to hide if I do escape from police custody. Once I spot the motel's sign in the distance, I memorize the turns we make.

They take me to a small station in the center of town. I guess Dulce doesn't need much of a police presence. The deputy pulls me out of the backseat and escorts me through the front doors into a small lobby, where a woman with a headset sits behind a cluttered desk. The back wall is mostly frosted glass. The woman updates the men on their wounded officer's condition—which isn't looking good—and then I'm taken through a swinging door.

The rest of the station is mostly one big, open room lined with wooden desks. My eyes dart around. There's a weapons cabinet in the back corner of the room, but it's padlocked. The blinds are down on the windows, and I silently curse myself for not checking to see if there were bars on them when we were still outside.

"You want her in holding with Tony?" the deputy asks, motioning to the back of the station, where I can see a man sleeping inside a small cell. "He'll probably be passed out until morning."

"Just cuff her in a chair for now," the sheriff responds. "I want her processed by the book."

My left cuff is taken off and attached to the handle on the front of a short metal filing cabinet that has an empty coffeepot on top. The deputy points to a stool beside it, and I begrudgingly sit, pulling on the cuffs as I do, testing the weight of the cabinet. But it's solid. There's no way I'm dragging it out of here. I take in my surroundings. The deputy flips on the coffeemaker before walking over to one of the desks. He drops my confiscated blaster—now sealed in an evidence bag—on top of a stack of papers.

"By the book," he murmurs, taking a seat. "Sure thing."

The deputy types on the computer, the sheriff looking over his shoulder. From their conversation I understand that they're writing up some sort of report about my arrest. The desktop computers they've got here look ancient, and for a second I think about how easy it would be to hack into them and steal every bit of information I wanted. But that's the least of my concerns right now.

Eventually, the sheriff walks over.

"Name?" he asks.

I stare back at him. Neither of us blinks. I don't know how long this goes on—minutes? Finally he speaks again.

"Lady, I can do this all night, but eventually you'll probably get tired or hungry. Me? I'll just have the deputy bring me a cheeseburger. Now, you're not going anywhere anytime soon, so you might as well cooperate so we can make your stay more comfortable."

Our standoff continues. He pours himself a steaming cup of fresh coffee, never taking his eyes off me, even when he sips from it. The only thing that interrupts us is when the woman from the front desk comes through the swinging door.

"Um, Sheriff," she says, clearly concerned about something. "There are two men here who insist that—"

Before she can finish, the door swings open again and two men in black suits walk in. The first one's older, with thinning white hair and a wide nose. The second man has dark skin, like me, with a thin mustache running over his top lip.

"Special Agent Purdy with the Federal Bureau of Investigation," the first man says, holding up some identification I can't see. "I've got questions for your detainee."

"Now hold on just one goddamned minute," the sheriff says, starting toward the man. "How the hell did you even know we'd arrested someone?"

Purdy smiles. "We're always watching, Sheriff."

Of course they are—if the government is working with the Mogs out here, then they're likely monitoring all sorts of communications. I was probably scanned or filmed the entire time I was out by the fence, even if I didn't see any cameras.

So much for being careful. Again I remind myself

that I should be back at Yellowhammer, safely behind a computer screen.

The deputy and sheriff have a heated, quiet conversation at the front of the room. Purdy walks over to me. He pulls back his jacket and flashes a heavy-looking pistol at me before crossing his arms over his chest.

"Now, why don't you play ball and start by telling me your name?" he asks.

"Sir," the other man—special agent?—says.

Purdy turns and finds his partner holding up the bag with my blaster in it. He nods, and the man pockets it. Then Purdy lets out a whistle and turns his attention back to me. When he leans in close, I can smell stale coffee on his breath, and something else. Something rancid.

"Powerful little weapon you had on you," he says. "Where'd you get it?"

I don't say anything. He doesn't seem to mind.

"Thanks for picking her up, boys," Purdy says, motioning to the sheriff. "But I'm officially taking over this investigation." He smiles at me. "You and I are going to have a long conversation back at the base."

"What are you talking about?" the sheriff asks. "That woman's *our* suspect, and if you think—"

"You can argue with me all you want, but I believe this woman may have information about acts of terrorism planned against this country. And if you think that means the government is going to let her stay in the hands of this Podunk police force, you're delusional."

I can practically hear the glee dripping off Purdy's words as he pulls rank on the others. The sheriff sneers, but he doesn't say anything. Still, his hand is on his hip, close to his gun. The other agent puffs out his chests and walks over to the officers.

I silently panic. I can't go back to that base. Not as a prisoner. Not if the Mogs are involved there. They'll figure out I'm Loric somehow and use me, *destroy* me, like they did Janus.

I know too much. About Ella and Crayton. About the white tablet. They can't get into my head. And I don't know if I'm strong enough to withstand whatever torture it is they used to make Janus spill all his secrets.

I have to escape. I've tried not to hurt any of the people on this planet—they're just caught in the cross fire of all this. But I don't think Purdy counts. If he's working at the base, he's working with the Mogs. I don't mind hurting him; in fact, I think I'd take great pleasure in it.

He leans close again. "Hope you enjoy your last few minutes of fresh air. Because if you don't start cooperating, I'll see to it that you never set foot aboveground again."

I've got one chance.

"This is for Zophie," I mutter.

And then I attempt a desperate escape.

CHAPTER
FIVE

MY BOOT CONNECTS WITH PURDY'S STOMACH. AS he reels back, I slip off the chair, crouch as much as I can and then leap forward, pulling hard against the cuffs. The square drawer of the filing cabinet jerks out behind me. The cuff digs into my flesh as the drawer catches, but I continue in one fluid motion, pulling at the metal with both my hands. It's my greatest luck in life that the drawer is full of coffee supplies and not actual files; I'm able to pull it out. It swings over my head in a sprawling arc, threatening to tear my hand from my body.

There's a loud metallic bang as the edge of the drawer smashes against Purdy's face. Suddenly blood is everywhere.

"My nose!" Purdy gropes blindly at the desk behind him. "She broke my fucking nose!"

He half collapses into a rolling chair. The other agent

has my blaster, so I lunge for Purdy's gun and then slide over the tile flooring, the now-empty drawer trailing behind me. I fire a warning shot into the ceiling as I duck behind one of the desks. It's enough to make the sheriff and his deputy take cover.

Purdy pulls a walkie-talkie out of his jacket pocket and yells something into it. Suddenly there's a scream from the lobby, and I can see a couple of dark shapes on the other side of the frosted glass before they come bursting through the swinging door: two Mogadorians.

Shit.

I don't hesitate to fire a few shots over the desk at the Mogs, just enough to keep them at bay. The kick-back from the weapon is stronger than I expected, and I don't manage to actually hit any of my targets.

Blaster fire fills the air and shreds the monitors, papers and picture frames on the desk. I hear a yelp behind me—Tony, the guy in the holding cell, is on the floor, hands over his head.

"Tony!" I shout. He seems genuinely startled to hear his name, but he looks up and locks eyes with me. I point to my handcuffs. "The key?"

He shakes his head, lips quivering. I don't have time for this—I'm not going to get out of here dragging two feet of drawer behind me, and from what I can intuit, Tony's something of a regular in this station. If he doesn't help me out, my options are to lose my hand or try to shoot off the cuffs.

I fire two more shots over my shoulder and then turn back to Tony, pointing the gun at him.

"The key," I say firmly, directly.

His finger quivers as he points to the desk a few feet away from me.

"S-second drawer," he says.

There's a pause in the blaster fire. I peek around the desk corner to see that the sheriff and deputy have both gone white staring at the Mogs. In turn, the bloodthirsty bastards look back and forth between the lawmen and Purdy as if asking what they should be doing.

"Goddammit," Purdy shouts. He's crouched on one side of the cabinet, a bloody handkerchief up to his nose. The other agent is crouched nearby, covering him. "You weren't supposed to see any of this. How many messes am I going to have to clean up tonight?"

I use the confusion and dart to the next desk. Blaster shots pepper the filing-cabinet drawer with holes. I open the desk and dig through a bunch of small packets of potato chips and candy bars until I find a little key.

Maybe luck *is* with me.

I toss the cuffs to the floor and take a fleeting look at my wrist, which is rubbed raw and deep red. I'm about to slam the desk door shut when I see another key—a car key with a tag on it that says 013.

I pocket it, just in case—if I can get to the parking lot, number thirteen might be my way out of here. I'm going to have to escape this little town somehow, and if this place is crawling with Mogs, I definitely won't be able to get away on foot.

On the other side of the station, the cops have realized that the black-eyed, tattooed Mogs are shooting the blasters that likely killed their fellow officer, and they shout all kinds of questions at the bastards. The police train their guns on them. I use that to my advantage: I fire a bullet that shoots straight through the chest of one of the Mogs. He lets out a groan, and then he's just a pile of dust on the floor.

The officers shout in confusion. Purdy orders the other agent to take me down, and I fire a shot in their direction. The mostly full coffeepot on top of the filing cabinet shatters, spilling glass and scalding liquid onto the other agent's head. He cries out in pain as I throw the drawer that had been attached to me seconds before. It smashes out a window on the side of the office—no bars on the outside.

"Dammit," Purdy shouts. "Take care of them. I'll get the woman."

The remaining Mog crosses over to the cops in a few quick bounds and swings a thick fist. The sheriff falls in a heap. I make for the window, shooting behind me in Purdy's direction until the gun clicks. I miss him.

Still, I caused him to take cover, which buys me a few extra seconds. I jump through the broken-out window. Glass slices my body, grazing me at several points, but it's nothing serious. At least, not compared to what will happen if I get dragged away by Mogs.

Outside, the air is cool, and I sprint towards the little parking lot at the back of the station where I see a handful of police cars. I pull the key labeled 013 out of my pocket, ready to make my escape.

But there is no car 013.

Dammit.

I'm about to make a desperate run for it when I spot two police motorcycles parked against the side of the building. Big, hulking bikes. One of them has #13 painted on the side.

That's my way out of here.

It takes me a few seconds to even figure out where the key goes. Then I just push anything that will move until I finally hit a switch on the right handle that turns the damned thing on. The engine revs when I twist one of the controls—it's not unlike some vehicles I've seen on Lorien—and the whole blasted machine nearly shoots out from between my legs, ramming into the wall beside it.

"Whoa," I murmur, trying to get my balance again.

A shot sounds behind me, and the clear-plastic shield on the front of the bike shatters—Purdy's out of the station now, with a new gun pointed in my direction. I immediately regret leaving my blaster behind. It looks like he's having trouble focusing. A filing cabinet to the nose will do that to you, I guess. Still, I'm not taking any chances. I twist the handle again and drive forward, too fast at first. The bike wobbles, and it feels like I'm going to fall off. But I keep going, slowly accelerating until I can tell the momentum is holding me in place. I don't even try to figure out how to turn on the headlight as I make my way back to my motel room, remembering the path we took to get to the station in the first place.

The few minutes it takes me to cross town feel like hours, and I'm sure at every turn I'm going to be met by a line of Mogs. But the streets are quiet, giving me a chance to wonder just how deeply the Mogs have infiltrated the United States—or all countries, for that matter. How much have they brainwashed this planet?

Is Earth even salvageable?

My thoughts go back to the police officers. There's no way Purdy will let them live. Not after they've seen the Mogs. I grind my teeth until my jaws ache. If I hadn't come here, they'd still be alive.

Or maybe not. They were investigating the base, after all. They'd caught wind that something was wrong there. It was probably only a matter of time before the Mogs and the FBI made some kind of move. I just sped things up. Soon Dulce will probably be nothing more than a ghost town.

I must look wild by the time I get to the motel, because when I walk into the office to tell the clerk I lost my key, she jumps. But she hands over a spare. Then it's only a couple of minutes before I've packed my laptop and stashed belongings into a spare bag and am out on the road again, leaving Dulce and these Mog bastards behind me. I can't stay—they'll be looking for me now, and there's no place to hide in this tiny desert town. I have to get as far away as I can, before the reinforcements that Purdy has surely called in arrive.

I jet through the darkness, the night wind whipping against my face, and as I race through the streets, I can't help but laugh at the fact that, against all odds, I have somehow managed to escape. My coat flaps behind me in the wind, and without warning, my thoughts go to my brother, Zane. I wonder if this is what he felt like when he was flying.

It's only after a few miles that the shock starts to wear off and I realize that Janus's ship—no, it's not his anymore—that *my* ship is being held by what is likely a veritable army of Mogadorians and government agents.

How am I ever supposed to recover it?

CHAPTER
SIX

IT'S NOT DIFFICULT TO GET BACK TO MY BASE once I'm out of Dulce.

I ditch the police bike in the first city I come to, figuring I look a little too out of place on it not to arouse suspicion. I catch a bus, the first one that's heading east. The desert slowly fades into green pastures.

In Texas I get a new ride. I opt for a motorbike of my own this time. I'll pick up another SUV later, but for now I want to feel the wind on my body, to hear it rushing past the black helmet I buy, drowning out all thoughts of what I'm supposed to do now that I know the Garde can't be reunited at this time and that my ship is being guarded by forces I'll probably never be able to take on single-handedly. Not in a fight, at least. I can't help but dwell on the fact that the Mog presence on Earth is much, much deeper and more expansive than I ever imagined.

Or is it? Maybe Dulce is an anomaly. It might be the only place where the Mogs and the government are working hand in hand. Those could be the only Mogs on this planet, for all I know. The scant amount of intel I had on Janus and the ship meant that it should have been somewhere in the northeastern part of the country. And yet the Mogs or the FBI—whoever found it—took it across the country. Why transport it all the way to New Mexico, unless that was the only place to hide it?

More questions. Each time one is answered, five more come up.

There has to be something else I can do. I can't just sit around this planet for the next few years waiting for the last of the Garde to develop their Legacies, counting on them to reemerge as unstoppable war machines.

I'm near the Texas-Arkansas border when I realize my goals haven't changed all that much. Sure, the ship is a setback, but my other concerns—figuring out what the hell the Mogs are doing on this planet—are still relevant. Only now the focus has shifted. Instead of being concerned with what they're doing here, I should be trying to figure out *how* they're operating. Maybe Dulce *is* just the beginning of their campaign on this planet. If so, there may still be time to stop them. If the Mogadorians are only beginning to infiltrate the government, maybe there's still time to save humanity.

All I have to do is figure out how deep the corruption runs and then expose it. In a way it's the same thing I was attempting to do on Lorien. Only now it's not my people I'm trying to push into action but another planet entirely. One that has no idea that there are not only intelligent beings throughout the universe, but that they've already infiltrated Earth.

But how do I convince a world full of people who might not be exactly open to the idea that they're not alone in this galaxy?

When I get back to Yellowhammer, with its useless gate and rolling hills, I go straight to the back office. I type up a letter explaining to the human race who the Mogadorians are and that the Earth's governments may have been infiltrated by these bloodthirsty monsters. I give a firsthand account of what I saw at Dulce. When I'm done, my fingers hover over the keyboard. I can get the word out. I can manipulate code and make it so that this article is on the front page of every popular website on the internet. No one would be able to ignore it. I could link it to all the evidence I've gathered on the Mogs and Loric on Earth so far so that the human race could help me protect my people.

But I hesitate. I think again about what I'm doing. Even if I leave out any mention of the Loric, upload-ing this information is a hostile act against the Mogs. Exposing them will surely have consequences.

What if in trying to warn Earth about what's going on I push the Mogs to act themselves? To invade, or conquer. Or the Garde to come out of hiding, long before they're ready to do so.

What if I inadvertently start an interplanetary war?

I stare at my screen for what feels like a long time. Eventually I save the document I've written but keep it to myself.

I realize that maybe I've been thinking on too large a scale. Before I try to get the entire human race on my side, I can start with just a few. Seek out those who already think that there might be life on Mars or Jupiter or hiding in Orion's Belt. I know they're out there. I've read their messages in forums and chat rooms and on message boards. I've inspected their blog posts, trying to figure out if they're insane or if maybe the close encounters they've described were with the Loric, or the Mogs. Malcolm is proof that they exist, that they're passionate and that they can be helpful—though, having seen him and his son together, I don't think I'd want to push him into endangering his family anymore.

I can gather a small troop of spies and informants. People I can send to do investigations while I stay out of sight. It'll be tricky weeding out the best candidates, but worthwhile. I'll find those without families. People without ties or attachments. People like me. Slowly but surely, I can introduce them to what I'm really doing—who our real enemy is.

They're my starting point. Just like Pittacus started with Malcolm. There are believers all across this planet. I just need to reach out to them.

In between fortifying the security of the ranch and its surrounding area, I set up a website. It looks normal enough—like a dozen other conspiracy theory web pages or sites dedicated to proving the existence of aliens—only this one is built on my code, set to harvest the data of anyone who visits it. With that kind of information, I can win over anyone. And who knows: if the Mogs stumble across it, maybe I'll be able to track them as well.

I call it "Aliens Anonymous."

When it's time to create my own identity on the site, I pause, staring at the cursor blinking on-screen. I need not just a username, but a new persona. Someone I can establish as a trustworthy figure so that I can gather allies. A person I can be for a long time.

I think of the Garde and what I'm trying to do. After a few seconds I tap out a single word:

GUARD.

CHAPTER
SEVEN

SLOWLY, YELLOWHAMMER RANCH STARTS TO change. It begins with the installation of cameras throughout the property, along with several traps and hidden automated weapons. Once the perimeter feels secure, I focus on the inside of the house. I seal up the windows to the office, fortifying the walls, turning it into a safe room. I replace the normal door with a blast door that will only open when my fingerprint is scanned, and hide that behind a quilt I pull off one of the extra beds and hang on the wall. If anyone was to search the house, they'd likely have no idea there was a room in the back unless they really started calculating measurements. If I was ever attacked, the room would protect me. At least for a little while, long enough for me to reload my weapons and perform a few last-second computer operations. The only weak spot when I'm done with my renovations is the floor. That's where

I plant the small, remote-activated explosive device I put together from parts purchased on the darker sections of the internet.

The bomb is an emergency fail-safe, though it's perhaps odd to think of it in those terms. It's not protection for me, really, but for the Garde. If something were to happen—if it looked like I'd lost the ranch—just a few clicks in a program and I could ensure that all my work and information went up in flames. I'd rather it be destroyed than fall into Mog hands.

Even though I know better than to try to reunite the other Loric, I do my best to serve as their guardian. I continue to delete any news stories that sound even the least bit connected to them, saving copies for myself so that I can in some way keep a sense of where some of the Garde might be.

For the most part, I don't find much. I hope that means that the Garde are settled safely, in hiding. Establishing new identities. Getting stronger.

Although I'm diligent, I can't help but think that I'm missing things. I'm only one person, and this planet is so much bigger than Lorien. Still, I do my best. The users of "Aliens Anonymous" are sometimes helpful, my team of informants growing. They've pointed me to a few events or news pieces that look as though Mogs may be involved. It's difficult to weed through them all, though. Many of the users who flock to the website are lunatics or trolls, a term I've learned and often witnessed in action since starting "Aliens Anonymous."

But there are some who are true believers, who give me useful information and follow my suggestions when I say that they should investigate their theories further and report back to me. I keep myself at a distance from them, putting their data to use but trying not to dwell on the particulars of their lives too much. They work with me, but I am alone. A few of them lose interest. One or two disappear completely. I tell myself that they too have just grown bored.

I track my enemy's movements as well, trying to think like a Mogadorian. I learn about the sighting of weird spacecrafts in West Virginia, the descriptions similar to some of the Mogadorian ships I've seen, and of tattooed gangs seen in various parts of the world. It has been more difficult to suss out information about their involvement with the US government than I had expected. The FBI and other agencies have firewalls unlike anything I've ever seen—much too advanced for this planet. It's my assumption that, along with whatever promises the Mogs are making to the United States, they're also offering them technology. It reminds me of the Grid on Lorien, but even more advanced. Impenetrable. I refrain from pushing too much for fear that this technology could track me in ways I never imagined. What I need is an in, like when the Grid failed on

Lorien and I was able to get my own hardware attached to the system.

I don't know how I'm going to get that, though, because the last thing I want to do is go storming some Mog base again.

The ship is never far from my mind. I draw out blueprints and write down everything I can remember about the computer systems and construction of ships from my time at the LDA. I try to estimate what state it might be in after the long trek from Lorien to Earth. I doubt its power crystals could handle another intergalactic flight, and so I try to figure out how I might adapt the ship's power core to run on the fuel systems available on this planet. My research delves further into engineering than my actual training ever took me at the LDA and is mostly hypothetical. Still, I start to build a few preliminary adapters and secondary power sources. I want to be prepared.

I keep tabs on Dulce as much as I can. It seems like my fears have been realized. The sheriff and officers I left behind are found dead, and the blame gets put on drug cartels moving through the area. Soon after that the town slowly dissipates and dries up. A private investor buys most of the land. I track the funds back to a few dummy accounts. It's obvious that the Mogs or the FBI are responsible. I manage to hack into a satellite feed that gives me a visual of the base during the day—after a decryption program is run over the images—but it's neither detailed nor very helpful. Still, I keep the feed running on one of my many monitors at all times. If they move my ship, I want to know about it. I catch a few Mog transporters moving on video. I save these clips and add them to my growing info bomb: a digital packet of information I've gathered about the Mogs, about their history on Lorien and even my own writing about what happened to my home planet and my experience in Dulce. Earth is not ready for this information. The *Garde* are not ready for this to be revealed. But one day soon they will be.

Time passes. I gather intel. I like to think I'm helping, but I'm not sure.

Two years blink by and I decide to leave Yellowhammer Ranch. I get too comfortable in the wooden farmhouse, too familiar with the rolling hills. The place suddenly starts to feel claustrophobic. I don't abandon it completely—it could still come in handy—but I gather most of my equipment and all of my data and leave for a new secluded location in the Oregon woods. It's there that I finally get a glimpse into Agent Purdy's personal files thanks to his incompetent assistant, who likes to work on unprotected wireless networks in coffee shops. I manage to get into Purdy's email account and read through a few messages detailing an operation code-named MogPro. It's mentioned in passing, never defined, but I understand that it has something to do with Mog infiltration of the government. I take some screen grabs and save a few files, but after a couple of minutes in his email account, my computer completely freaks out. It crashes, not in a way I've ever seen before. I fear I've been discovered.

I leave Oregon minutes later, never looking back.

I move often after that, setting up safe houses around the country. The deeper I dig, the less safe I feel staying in one place for too long. But moving has its downsides. I'm in the midst of relocating when a blog post slips through the cracks:

Nine, now eight. Are the rest of you out there?

By the time I see it and wipe it away, it's too late. I trace the poster's IP address to a physical address in London. After that it only takes a few minutes to discover that a twelve-year-old girl was found murdered there shortly after the post went up.

One of the Garde, no doubt. If her math was correct, that means she was Number Two. If she's dead, that means so is One, and likely their Cêpans.

Our numbers continue to decrease.

And our allies keep disappearing. I keep track of Malcolm Goode, but not long after I met with him, he disappears, leaving his truck and glasses behind in a

grocery store parking lot in Paradise. I go back to the
message board I used to find him in the first place and
try to track down the others he corresponded with.
Their years-old communications lead me to other dead
ends or, more often, missing persons.

The authorities don't seem to have any leads on
where Malcolm might be—they posit that he might
even have left on his own—but I have no doubt that
the Mogadorians or the FBI tracked him down. When I
read this news, something inside my gut twists, and all
I can see is the face of the little boy standing outside of
Malcolm's office, staring up at me. At least the rest of
the Goodes seem to be safe. I shudder to think that the
Mogs might be using them to try to get information out
of Malcolm. I consider going back to Paradise and taking them to one of my safe houses. But would they go?
If not, would I take them against their will? Should I
even risk exposing myself at all by going back to Ohio?

No. That's not my place or role in all this. I coordi-
nate from behind the scenes. I warned Malcolm they
would find him. I did everything I could. He should
have left.

When I'm not moving or researching, I gather weapons, ammunition, medical supplies, cash—any and all
resources that might come in handy. I plant caches of
them in my safe houses, which I no longer view as my
own but as places that the Garde may one day use.

When they're ready. When they're strong.

One day soon they'll make a move, and I'll be watching, waiting to finally expose the Mogadorians on Earth and help the last of my people destroy them.

CHAPTER
EIGHT

BY THE TIME THE MOGS MAKE THEIR BIG PLAY
in Paradise, years have passed and I've settled into a
new base: an old orchard and pecan-processing plant
in Georgia.

It's so obvious to me when I read the reports—both
public and those I find in the Paradise Police Department's files—that this is a Mog incident. Something
big. The Mogs wouldn't just attack a high school without a reason. Especially not one that happened to be
located in the small town where Malcolm Goode lived.

I think back to what Malcolm had told me about one
of the Cêpans saying he'd return to Paradise when his
Garde was of age. When I find the YouTube clip of a
boy who goes by the name John Smith basically flying
out of a burning house, my assumptions are confirmed.
At least one of the Garde faced off against the Mogs in
Ohio.

I write up a big story on "Aliens Anonymous," positing that the incident at Paradise High School is somehow related to alien activity. I don't mention the Mogs or Loric by name. The trick to running this blog is playing dumb and never really showing off what I know. I'm baiting the hook, trying to find someone who has more information. The website has grown to have a dedicated user base over the years, and typically it doesn't take too long for someone to bite.

I don't get the full story until a user named JOLLY-ROGER182 contacts me through the site. He tells me what happened at the high school and about the "evil ETs" that he and some of his friends fought off. Within no time, I deduce that his real name is Mark James based on the information he gives out (a love of football, his ex-girlfriend's name), which I cross-reference against information I find in the Paradise Police Department's files on the burning down of the James's residence. He thinks he's being really sly, but his internet activity is an open book to me until I teach him how to block his IP address and send encrypted messages.

It's not until I discover that he's met Number Four and Number Six that I get really interested. Not only am I finally messaging with someone who has had direct contact with some of my people, but from Mark's stories it sounds as though the Garde are finally coming together. I can't help but feel a rush of adrenaline knowing that after all these years the work and planning I've been doing might finally be useful, that we can expose the Mogs and the FBI soon.

At first Mark is just another informant. I dumb down my speech and feign excitement when he first brings up the words "Mog" and "Loric," as if I've never heard them before. He seems harmless enough, and I assume his interest will eventually die down—until he mentions that his ex-girlfriend, Sarah Hart, is dating Number Four. When I read this, I almost can't believe my eyes. Here's my possible direct link to the Garde. I try to get any information that I can about Four's whereabouts, but it seems that neither Mark nor Sarah knows where he and Six went when they left Paradise. It feels like something big is about to happen. The Garde and Mogs are coming out into the open. War is finally upon us.

There's something else too. The FBI start following Mark and Sarah around. An agent gives Mark a contact number, which he then passes on to me. I call it, using a satellite phone and a voice changer just to ensure my anonymity. I get someone I recognize on the other end of the line.

Special Agent Purdy.

My blood starts to boil. I wish I could reach through the phone and smash in his nose again. Instead, I hang up and destroy the phone. Purdy seemed to have a fair amount of authority in Dulce, and I don't want to risk him tracking me down using methods that I don't know about. I can't be too careful.

And then everything escalates very quickly. Sarah disappears. Mark freaks out. His concern and passion are unbridled, worn on his sleeve. He tries to find her any way he can, his desperation to uncover the truth about what's been going on rivaling even my own. I find myself talking to him more and more—with far more frequency than with my other contacts. Maybe it's because this has become personal for him too. I admire his passion.

During his investigations, he discovers print copies of a now-defunct newsletter called *They Walk Among Us*, a publication I'd been feeding information and funds to for years, working to expose the Mogs little by little. He suggests we change the website name to "They Walk Among Us" to attract the newsletter's readers. I agree. It's a good idea.

Unfortunately, Mark's not always the smartest kid. His overzealousness is problematic. He pulls a stunt where he sneaks into the police department looking for clues and sees a Mog for himself—the FBI-and-Mog partnership in action. Mark likely should have ended up in their custody or dead, but with some kind of luck he managed to escape.

With Purdy's laptop.

Mark messages me after he swipes it.

Mark: They've got Sarah in Dulce. At that secret base from TWAU!!

Mark: I'm going after her. I gotta. I'm leaving Paradise right now. We're gonna bust this thing wide open.

I almost laugh. Of course that's where she is.

I start to type back to him, warning him that Dulce is a no-go. That it's too dangerous. But as I'm looking at my satellite feed from the base, I notice something strange. There's a very subtle glitch in the bottom corner of the screen. I keep watching and realize that I've been looking at a loop of the same twenty seconds of footage over and over again from the satellite feed.

Shit. I curse myself. I don't appear to have been hacked, but there's no telling how long I've had the fake feed running on my monitor. Why? Was this just an ordinary precaution? Or is there something more to it?

It takes me a few minutes to find a way around the repeating video, and finally the current state of Dulce comes into view. There's smoke rising from the base, and it looks like several buildings have collapsed.

Something has gone down very, very recently in Dulce. And I need to know what.

An idea forms in my head. Mark James is going to Dulce. It's not like I'll be able to talk him out of it. Not when Sarah is involved. I can help him along the way. Give him supplies. Guide him. In return he'll tell me what the base is like now. What happened there.

Besides, if he gets taken into custody, he'll need someone on the outside to try and save him.

And so I respond:

Be careful. The place is probably crawling with Mogs and FBI agents. Don't do anything stupid.

It only takes a few seconds for him to reply.

Mark: Wouldn't dream of it.

It takes all of a few hours for Mark to get locked out of Purdy's computer, and I curse myself for not immediately insisting that he send the damned thing straight to me. It's probably the same sort of firewall that fried one of my computers in Oregon. We're possibly kicked out of the machine for good—or at least until I can figure my way around Mog securities—so my focus turns to making sure Mark gets to the Dulce base alive so he can tell me what the hell has happened there. To ensure that this happens, I put together a little care package and meet him in person at a closed-down gas station on the Colorado–New Mexico border. I manage to get there only a few minutes before he does after driving through the night on my bike, going much, much faster than is either legal or safe. He wouldn't be talked into waiting a few days, insisting on going straight to Dulce. Not that I blame him—it doesn't seem like all that long ago that I was in his position.

I give him a box packed with supplies—even one of Raylan's concussion/EMP grenades that I've been carrying around with me from base to base all these years—and have him sign a fake confirmation slip. I play the part of the courier.

He doesn't think twice about the fact that I can't be GUARD once he sees me. I'd been ready to play dumb, but I guess after referring to me as "dude" about a hundred times over the last few weeks, he never really gave any thought to the fact that his online partner might be female. I don't correct him. If for some reason he ends up detained at Dulce and I can't get him out, it'll be in my best interest if he can't identify me.

He looks different in person than in the photos I tracked down of him online. Strung out, with dark circles under his eyes. The events of Paradise and Sarah's disappearance weigh on his face.

I find myself oddly concerned about him.

"You should get off the road and get some sleep," I say. "You look like shit."

I don't hang around to converse. Instead, I check into a hotel on the Colorado side of the border and wait for him to report back. Part of me feels like I should have given him more warning, but I tell myself again that he'll be fine. This isn't like Zophie, when I left her alone, thinking that Janus could still be alive. Mark is well aware of the dangers he's facing.

The sun is rising when I finally get a message from him. I'd just about given up hope that he was still a free man.

> **Mark: Dulce's a bust. FBI is abandoning it. Sarah's gone. I think John and others got her out.**

> **Me: You got in and out and no one saw you? I'm impressed.**

> **Mark: Nah. Ran in2 agent Walker from Paradise. She let me go. I think she's turned against the Mogs.**

If the Dulce base is being abandoned, now is the time for me to claim my ship. Assuming they didn't move it while the video loop was in place. The thought fills me with warmth, my blood pumping through my veins.

Plus, if the FBI agents at the base have turned on the Mogs, it means at least some of the humans are beginning to see that working alongside those monsters is a death sentence for the human race. They're not just blindly following them.

Maybe there's hope for this species after all, I think. And in doing so, I realize, perhaps for the first time, what respect I have for Mark. Someone who has been fighting for his friends and his planet this whole time. Trying to save his people from whatever horrible endgame the Mogs are trying to enact.

And here I've been, withholding information from him. Using him for my own means. As a pawn.

When it comes down to it, I'm no better than one of the Elders.

Maybe I can make up for that. I wonder what he's going to do now that Sarah's not where he thought she would be.

Me: Where are you going now?

Mark: No damn clue. Can't go home. Bad FBI are still looking for me.

Perhaps it's the rush of adrenaline pumping through me or that lingering pang of guilt for not being completely honest with him—for whatever reason, I feel like I owe it to Mark to help him. I can guide Mark from afar.

I message him back, instructing him to drive toward Alabama. I know just the place he can hide out for a while and continue his work: Yellowhammer Ranch. Only, it's been a while since I've been on the property, so I tell him to take his time—that I'll have a space set up for him just as soon as I get a few personal things in order. The last thing I need is Mark James wandering onto the grounds of Yellowhammer only to get blown up by a defensive trap I forgot to defuse.

CHAPTER
NINE

I HEAD FOR DULCE. FOR MY SHIP.

I pass half a dozen black SUVs all speeding through the desert about five miles away from the perimeter of Dulce Base. I consider this fortuitous timing—if these are the FBI agents Mark mentioned, then they have indeed abandoned the place.

Still, I have my reservations about this operation. It's a bright morning, for one thing, meaning I can't rely on the cover of night, and the memory of what happened the last time I tried to infiltrate this base is fresh in my mind. But I won't get another opportunity like this. Who knows how long it will be before the Mogs or the rest of the FBI realize that no one at this base is responding?

Besides, this time I've come prepared.

I pause at a section of the fence surrounding the base that's been destroyed and take out some of the gear from my backpack—thermal-imagine binoculars that can sense heat signatures through six inches of steel. Nothing pops up on them. At least nothing that reads as a human or Mog. There are a few fires and lights I can make out, but nothing that suggests anyone is patrolling the base.

Regardless, I proceed with caution and park my bike near a pit that's been created by the roof of the first underground floor of the base collapsing in on itself. I take a look around and note some burned-out Humvees and a knocked-down watchtower. Mark thinks the Garde broke Sarah out, and if that's the truth, they certainly have grown strong.

I hop down into the base and pull out a small electronic tablet of my own design, part computer and part tracker—a device that can hone in on the frequencies of a Loric ship when within a certain range. I wasn't sure it would work until now, but it pings, telling me that yes, Janus's ship is still down here somewhere. Waiting for me.

I breathe a sigh of relief.

The agents must have left the place in a hurry, because every office I pass is disheveled, files strewn about. Several big computer terminals looks damaged, as if in leaving, the FBI didn't want anyone else getting its information. That's a concern I can understand. I'll have to come back up and see what data I can harvest once I've found what I've actually come for.

I make my way down several floors. Eventually I get to a hallway that's dark, lights all knocked out. It's the only place I've been in the base where every door is shut. I make my way through the corridor slowly, on the tips of my toes, trying hard not to make a sound. I pass a door with a slit of a window in it, which I peer through carefully.

A man stares back at me.

He shouts, slamming his fists against the door. He's got on a white button-down shirt spotted with blood. Suddenly, there's banging from all the doors in the hallway, and I realize that I must have wandered into some sort of brig or detention area. The sound is deafening, echoing off the hard surfaces of the corridor and destroying all hopes of a stealthy exploration through the remainder of the base.

And so I start to run.

I pass a few laboratories and office spaces before finally flinging open a door that leads to it in all its silvery, beaten-up glory. The ship.

The vessel is big, the size of a house, but with the ability to glide and turn effortlessly through the air. The gleaming metal of its hull shines, even after all these years, made of a material native to Lorien. Its curves are all perfectly rounded, sleek and aerodynamic.

It takes my breath away.

There are all kinds of wires connected to the portion of the hull housing the crystals that supply power to the ship. I find a computer terminal on the opposite side of the room and tap on it, bringing the station to life—now that I'm here, it's easy to break through their passwords. I try to find some sort of journal or report system, downloading everything I can to my own tablet along the way. From what I can tell, the researchers here have been trying to figure out how to duplicate the crystals' energy to incorporate it into their own war machines. Their records show that they've managed to charge the spent crystals at least a little bit, but that's all, and the charge only lasts for a short period of time. I doubt I could get out of Earth's atmosphere on it.

That's fine for now. At the moment I just want to get out of *here.*

With a little more searching, I find controls that appear to operate some sort of dock. I flip them on, and sixty feet above me the ceiling begins to part. Sand, dirt and debris fall in. I narrowly avoid a pile of bricks and what looks like a Humvee tire that come crashing down.

For a second I pause, shaking my head, thinking of how terrible it would be for me to die just as I've finally found this ship that I've been after for so long.

The hangar doors above me open fully. I take a few steps toward my prize and pause. I can still hear the whirring noise I'd thought was the door mechanism, getting louder.

It's then that I see the edge of the Mogadorian ship just over the lip of the hangar. In seconds half a dozen pale, sneering faces are looking down at me, all pointing weapons in my direction.

I duck behind the computer station just as blaster fire starts to fill the air. Sparks rain down around me, burning my skin as the terminal is destroyed. I curse under my breath—hopefully these controls shorting out don't overload the wires attached to the ship.

I'm too much of a target where I am. The quickest way to stay alive would be to try and cross the room and head back inside the base. At least there I'd have plenty of options for cover. But I have to assume that the Mogs are already starting to filter down through the hallways and stairwells of the facility, and without any idea of how many alien bastards have just landed on the ground level, the base could quickly turn into a death trap. Somewhere I could get boxed in too easily.

Besides, now that I've found this ship, I don't intend to let it out of my sight.

So I reach into my backpack and pull out one of the many toys I've acquired and learned to use since the last time I came face-to-face with a Mogadorian: a powerful, compact submachine gun. Earth weapons might be crude and inefficient, but practicing out in the barns and woods around my many safe houses, I've witnessed exactly how devastating they can be.

If I can make it inside the ship and power it up, I may be able to get out of here alive. If not . . . Well, that's not really an option. I think of Janus and Zophie, and how when I first arrived on this planet I thought for sure that the three of us would one day be riding in this ship together. Now the best I can do is reclaim it for them. For Lorien.

I brace myself as much as I can against the floor, peek over the top of the sparking computer terminal and fire away. A few of the Mogadorians who are descending a zigzag metal staircase from the surface are ripped apart, turning into wafts of dust that filter down into the hangar. The others take quick cover, and I use this moment of surprise to make a break for it, tossing my bag ahead of me and basically throwing myself under the ship in the center of the room, using it for cover. Blaster fire blackens the cement floor, barely missing me. But I make it, somehow.

I'm able to access a manual override switch to the boarding hatch. A metal ramp rolls out from the back of the craft. One of the Mogs from above jumps down, sliding over the ship and onto the ground. There's a snap when he lands, and when he stands, one of his arms hangs limply at his side. That doesn't stop him from staggering forward, firing at me. Several of his fellow troops follow his lead, and I barely manage to climb onto the ramp, firing blindly behind me the entire time. I run, trying to avoid their blasters, but a few shots hit my backpack. I've reinforced the thing with Kevlar, mostly to protect my laptop and gadgets inside, but it stops the shots from burning through my body. Still, the force sends me sprawling onto the ramp. I roll over and return fire, scooting as fast as I can towards a touch-screen panel on the wall just inside the ship. I dust one of the Mogs following me as I manage to tap on the screen and get the ramp to start closing in just a couple of seconds—the few years of training I had at the Lorien Defense Academy all coming back to me in a rush.

The other Mog on the ramp stumbles forward as it folds up. He gets thrown past me, deeper into the ship. The interior of the vessel can be programmed with all sorts of holographic partitions and "walls," but right now it's just one big, empty room. There's no place for him to hide, and he's a pile of ash before he ever manages to pick himself up off the ground.

I run to the front cabin. My hands fly over buttons and screens. In front of me, a Mog has climbed onto the nose of the ship and is hammering away at the tinted cockpit window with the butt of his blaster. He'll have a hell of a time trying to break through the reinforced glass—I try not to pay any attention to him.

"Come on, come on, come on," I chant to myself as the instruments start to flicker, going online. And then they come to life, as if goaded on by my will. The crystals still have some life in them.

I can feel the engines powering up, the reassuring hum and slight vibration that permeate the entire ship. I engage auto-launch protocols, which should at least get me up into the sky, where I can chart a course or take over the controls myself. The Mog on the windshield struggles to find his balance as the ship starts to shake and lift off the ground. He howls as he falls backwards, tumbling to the cement below.

It's working, I think. *I'm getting out of here.*

My eyes widen as I get to the ground level. Sitting in front of me is the small Mogadorian ship I'd spotted from below, but also a large one that must be used to move troops around the planet—*lots* of troops. Mogs mill about around it, all their eyes on my silver craft. They freeze for only an instant before they start to fire. What looks like a cannon on the bigger ship turns towards me. Who knows what kind of firepower a vessel like that might have?

I flit through the on-screen menus in front of me until I find what appears to be a log of the ship's weaponry. Most vessels on Lorien were unarmed, but I guess the Elders equipped this one with every possible armament it could carry. Weapons I've never even heard of before. I wonder, again, how far their planning went and how long they knew that the Mogs were coming for us. I don't have long to reflect, though, because I've still got guns trained on me. And so I touch an icon that appears to be some sort of grenade projectile and target the enemy ship.

A small sphere of energy shoots from just below the cockpit. It sticks to the side of the rising Mogadorian vessel. Nothing happens.

Shit.

I can see the Mog cannon powering up, energy gathering around it. I tap on the weapons screen again.

"Don't tell me you're a dud, you son of a—"

The sphere explodes in a wave of energy that knocks back my own ship. The autopilot levels me off, and then I take over the controls and hit the accelerator, flying high into the sky, far, far above New Mexico, shouting at the top of my lungs as I dart through the air. I check my radar, but there's no one following me. I swing the vessel around, surveying the damage from hundreds of feet above in the clear sky. The Mog ships don't exist anymore. There's nothing *left* to follow me—only blazing hunks of twisted metal

Energy courses through me, filling my head with fuzzy warmth.

"We did it," I say before I realize the words are even coming out of my mouth. "We have the ship."

I'm not sure who I'm talking to, who the "we" is—if I'm addressing Zophie, or the other Garde spread across the planet, or even Mark, my unwitting partner in this Dulce operation.

On the way back I stop over at Yellowhammer Ranch, setting the ship down in the backyard by the dilapidated barn. The place looks untouched since the last time I saw it—if not a bit overgrown. I find one of the keys hidden in a sliding panel on the side of the house and go inside, pulling off some of the drop cloths that are still on the furniture. I reprogram the door to the secret office to open to Mark's fingerprint, which I have on file thanks to the fingerprint ID system in the laptop I sent him charging into Dulce with.

Inside the office I take stock of the weapons organized on shelves against one wall, and then boot up the security system, checking to make sure all my cameras are still in operation. A few electronic trip wires and traps are still live around the ranch, but I disable them so that Mark isn't met with an automated weapon upon his arrival. I can always teach him to reset them later, when he's settled in.

I keep the bomb beneath the office primed, ready to be set off in the event that the safe house falls into enemy hands. Just in case.

This will make a nice home for Mark. At least for the

time being. Until I can figure out what to do with him, or until he finally manages to get in contact with Sarah and the rest of the Garde.

I wonder if I should just wait here for him, to reveal myself to him in person. I have the ship, after all. Things are going well.

But I recognize this feeling. The thought that things are finally going my way and that everything's falling into place. Every time I've allowed myself to be comforted by such hope, things have gone terribly wrong. People have died. My world shattered, needing to be rebuilt.

I just need a little more time. To patch up the ship and figure out my next move. And he needs to recoup too. I'm not ready to lead my protégé into battle. Not yet.

In the morning I'll take the motorbike stored in the old barn into town and bring back a few fresh supplies for Mark: food, water, extra ammunition. A small gesture of thanks for being my first set of eyes on Dulce Base. For now, though, I scrawl a note in thick black marker on the back of a folder and set it beside a shotgun for him to find later.

I hope you're ready for war.
-G

CHAPTER
TEN

THE SHIP BARELY MAKES IT BACK TO MY ORCHARD base in Georgia. I fly beneath radar and try to stay in cloud cover as much as possible along the way. By this point, the acceleration is hardly faster than that of a car or motorcycle—the battery is almost dead. The crystals are fading.

I manage to get the ship parked in the big old pecan-processing plant in the back. I guess it's technically now a hangar.

Most of my energy and resources are immediately focused on figuring out how to get—and keep—the ship up and running for good. I start installing various adapters and fuel lines I've created over the years, hoping that all my work hasn't been for nothing. I go over the research I've swiped from the Dulce computers to see what the scientists have been doing to try and repower the drives. I manage to connect the crystal housings to an electrical output just like they'd done in Dulce. If nothing else, that should buy me a few days' worth of power.

The only reason the ship doesn't have my full attention is because one of my sensors picks up some strange activity on Mark James's old burner cell phone. I've been monitoring his communications since I got involved with him on the website, just to keep tabs on him. It's something I've done with everyone I've worked with from the blog—though Mark is definitely the person I've gotten closest to. It looks as though someone has sent him messages from "GUARD" telling him to meet up with them. Communications that definitely didn't come from me.

Somewhere, Mark slipped up. The enemy has found him.

I try to warn Mark, but I'm too late. Fortunately, he manages to escape from a team of FBI agents still loyal to the Mogs, but at the cost of his gear, his truck and, from what I can tell, a bit of his mental stability. And he was shot in his arm as he fled the ambush, though he swears it's just a flesh wound. He's stressed out, lost and feeling hopeless. When I talk to him on the chat client I built for "They Walk Among Us," he sounds depressed. I'm suddenly worried that he might give up, even after all he's been through. And I can't have that. Not now that I've gotten so used to him always being in touch. I realize that he's the only person I talk to on a regular basis. He's the closest thing I've had to a friend since Zophie died. So I do my best to try and remedy these things with a new vehicle and directions to Yellowhammer Ranch. That all seems to perk him up a bit.

At Yellowhammer, Mark connects Purdy's stolen laptop to some computer equipment I left behind, allowing me to copy the entire contents of its hard drive to cloud storage. I isolate Purdy's files and begin a full-fledged attack on their firewalls and security—cut off from the rest of the Mogadorian and FBI networks, I have no fear of being caught as I break into every hidden corner of his hard drive. What I discover is a wealth of information about MogPro and the specifics of the Mogadorian involvement with the US government. As I work, Mark finally manages to get in contact with Sarah. As Mark thought, she'd been traveling with the Garde. She's an invaluable source of information, and the link to my people here on Earth that I've been searching for.

Things seems to be going smoothly.

Which is why I shouldn't be surprised when everything falls apart.

I'm installing a new power line in the ship that will use the primitive fuel sources on this planet when I get a message from Mark saying that he's screwed up and thinks the Mogs might have a lead on Yellowhammer. He asks if he should abandon it completely or go back for his notes and files. I tell him it's his call.

He heads back to the ranch with Sarah to pack up. I'm left to wait for word from him. I pull up the cameras at Yellowhammer just in time to see him and Sarah rush inside and start packing.

Then everything goes black. I can't reestablish a connection. All I've got are monitors full of static.

My heart falls into my stomach.

Every second that passes makes me more impatient, more worried that I should have told him to leave everything and run from Alabama. As I wait, I pull up a program on one of my monitors: the controls to the bomb planted underneath Yellowhammer Ranch. At what point should I assume the worst and detonate the fail-safe, keeping the Mogadorians from getting any of Mark's notes? What if I set off the bomb too early and end up killing Mark and Sarah in the process? In that moment, alone in my safe house, all I want in the universe is to see Mark's name appear on my cell phone. He's been my eyes and ears for the past few months. We've been in constant contact.

I can't lose him.

Nor can I believe that JOLLYROGER182, the "Aliens Anonymous" user who referred to Mogs as "janky-looking assholes from another planet" in his first message to GUARD, has become a valuable asset not only to the Loric cause, but to me personally.

The clock ticks. I stare at the button that will destroy Yellowhammer. I wonder if I have it in me to press it after all this time. Would I risk sacrificing Mark and Sarah to keep information from falling into Mog hands?

Relief bursts through my skull when my phone dings. It's a text from Mark, saying they were attacked but are all right.

I call him back on one of my burners that has a voice modulator built in. My voice comes out electronic, distorted on his end of the line.

"How far are you and Sarah from the house?" I ask when he answers.

"I don't know. Maybe a mile? I can still see it in—"

I click the button. There's static on the line as Mark's microphone picks up the sound of Yellowhammer Ranch exploding.

"That should take care of any Mogs remaining on the property and thoroughly wipe our tracks," I say.

Mark doesn't sound too thrilled about the fact that he'd been sitting on top of a bomb all this time, but I'm too focused on typing to pay much attention to his concern. Instead, I tap into his truck's built-in GPS and input the coordinates to the Georgia safe house.

It's time to move forward in the fight against the Mogs. To join my fellow Loric.

The first step is to finally reveal myself to Mark and Sarah.

When Mark and Sarah show up, they look stunned—likely due to a combination of seeing me, the ship and the automated weapons that target them when they trip my security system. The incredulous silence doesn't last, though, as they begin to ask a million questions. I assess the situation and prioritize; Mark is feverish, and the bullet wound in his arm is completely infected. The first thing I do is give him a shot of the antibiotics I've got stashed away with other medical supplies. He's fine with that. The next part, less so.

"Motherfffff—" He holds out the "f" as I splash the injury with rubbing alcohol.

"Is he okay?" Sarah asks. She stands a few feet away from me, and I can see the concern in her eyes, not just for Mark's condition, but for the fact that someone she doesn't know is treating it.

"He'll be fine," I say. "The antibiotics will do most of the work. He should be back to normal in a few days."

"But I've got a big game tomorrow, Coach," Mark says flatly.

"I'm confused," Sarah says. She turns to Mark. "You didn't know she was a woman? Or *Loric*?"

"I just thought that since GUARD was so good with computers . . . ," Mark starts.

She narrows her eyes a little.

"What?" Mark asks. "Okay, yes, I just assumed she

was a dude. My bad. I guess 'GUARD' is technically gender neutral."

"You're from Lorien." Sarah says this more than asks.

I nod.

"And being older . . . you must have been there when the planet was attacked."

I nod again, slower this time. Sarah's face seems to soften.

"I was on a different ship than the chosen Garde," I say. "There were only a few of us."

"Ella . . . ," she murmurs, and the name stops my heart.

"What do you know about her?" I ask, taking two long steps until I'm towering over Sarah. "Have you met her? Is she with Number Four?"

She shakes her head.

"The Mogs took her," she says slowly.

I swallow hard. "And Crayton? Did they take him too?"

"Crayton," Sarah whispers. It takes a few seconds for her to place the name. "No. I'm sorry. . . . He was killed a while ago. In Spain, right before Ella joined the others."

The shock of all this must register on my face, because suddenly Sarah isn't looking at me like she's afraid I'm going pull a blaster on her. Instead, she's got a hand on my back and a chair under me before I even realize that I'm sitting down.

"Of course," she says. "I should've realized you didn't know. You were on the other ship with them. Oh God, I'm sorry."

My hands shake. I wonder how Crayton died—protecting Ella, no doubt. Where could she be now? What might they be doing to her? My hands shake as I try to figure out what to do next.

The Chimæra they call Bernie Kosar rubs against my legs in the form of a dog, staring up at me with a long tongue hanging out. His tail drums against the floor.

"I think he likes you," Sarah says.

I crouch down, looking into his dark eyes.

"I knew many of your kind once," I say, thinking back to those days that seem so long ago, when Zophie and Crayton and tiny baby Ella and I were all cooped up in our ship with a dozen Chimærae. "I hope to see more of you again one day."

He lets out a little whine and licks a salty tear from the side of my face.

"Uh, if it's any consolation," Mark says, "it sounds like Ella turned out to be a total badass? Like, apparently she was at Dulce and caused some damage."

She was at Dulce. When? How close was I to her?

I wipe my cheek with my sleeve and look over at Mark. He's shifting on his feet, his forehead wrinkled with concern. I think he's trying to make me feel better.

"Yeah, so, anyway," he continues, nodding to the back of the hangar. "Maybe you could show us the inside of this thing? I've never been in a spaceship before."

I smile a little. "Keep your eyes open, Jolly Roger, and maybe you'll fly it one day."

CHAPTER
ELEVEN

"HOLY SHIT," MARK SAYS AS WE STEP UP THE
metal ramp and into the ship. "I mean . . . holy *shit*."

"Wait until you see her at top speed," I say. "If I can
get her to run on Earth fuels."

"Fingers crossed," Sarah murmurs. Her eyes are
wide as she looks around.

"Superstition won't get this beauty up and running. I
was just putting the finishing touches on the new fuel
line when you two arrived. Let's see if I was successful."

"You mean we're going to take off right now?" Mark
asks.

"No. I'm just going to start up the engines, with any
luck."

He looks a little nervous.

I tap on the instrument panels when we get to the
cockpit. They slowly flicker on. The ship hums to life
around us.

"That seems like a good sign," Sarah says.

"Here comes the real test," I say.

I touch a few more of the controls. The ship slowly begins to lift off the ground. Beside me Mark clutches the back of one of the mounted chairs in front of the controls and whispers a dozen curses.

We're a few feet off the floor and hovering inside the hangar when the entire craft starts to shake, then suddenly drops a few inches, causing my two human companions to cry out in alarm. But the ship recovers. It levels itself off until all systems look normal.

"By Lorien," I murmur. "I think it's going to work. The ship's running off the fuel line I've installed, plus we have a few days of backup from the charged crystals."

"That's . . . good?" Sarah asks.

"It's very good," I say.

I set the ship back down and power off. Mark looks a little shaky on his feet. There's a sheen of sweat on his forehead.

"I think I should probably sit down," he says.

Sarah touches his forehead. "His fever's breaking."

I take them back down and into what used to be the foreman's office when the hangar was still a processing plant. Now it's filled with computer equipment and monitors.

We start to trade information. We learn about each other.

I give Mark and Sarah an abbreviated rundown of my history, leaving out the parts about me using Mark or tracking all of his communications—though, by the look on his face, I'm guessing he's figured that out by now. Sarah gets me up to date on the latest with the Garde, who they are and what Legacies they've manifested. She tells me everything she knows about the Mogs. It's easier to get information now that I don't have to use Mark as the middleman between us or avoid talking about my identity. I learn that not only has Malcolm Goode been found, but his son, Sam, has joined the fight. I can't help but smile at this, to know that Malcolm has been reunited with that little boy from outside his office. I can't say that they're safe in the middle of all this, but at least they're together.

I ask a lot of questions about the girl Ella has become and find out that she is a strong, sensitive young Garde. Just the kind of person I imagine Crayton would have wanted her to be. Sarah has spent a significant amount of time with her, and I can tell that she's worried about Ella as she speaks. That she cares for her.

"Everything happened so fast in Chicago," Sarah says, her eyes looking off into the middle distance. "Ella was having some kind of vision and then suddenly the Mogs were there. We were overpowered."

"Mogadorian scum," I mutter.

"We'll get her back." Mark grins a little. "And we'll

waste a bunch of those pale freaks along the way. Ashes to ashes. Dust to—"

"Really, Mark?" Sarah asks.

"What?" His eyebrows draw together for a second. Then he relaxes a little. "You're right. I should have saved that for after we'd killed What's-His-Ra or something."

Sarah doesn't say anything, just smirks a little and rolls her eyes.

She turns to one of the monitors at her side, one that's tuned to a twenty-four-hour news station. Her eyes get wide, and several small sounds come from her mouth, but no actual words form.

"Oh, come on," Mark says quietly, concerned. "It wasn't *that* bad. Sarah?"

"Oh God," she manages.

Several of my computers start beeping, telling me that something important has happened. That news is breaking.

"Sarah, what is it?" Mark is by her side in a few swift steps. And then he too is unable to form words.

It's only when I join them that I realize what's wrong.

A giant Mogadorian warship is hovering over New York City.

"It's happening," I murmur. "The invasion has begun."

It's not just New York; the ships are everywhere, over cities across the planet. We watch the news in shocked silence until Sarah's satellite phone rings, and we all move at once. As Sarah speaks to Number Four, I spring into action, opening my laptop. Reporters are starting to talk about some sort of conference at the UN—something that's been alluded to in MogPro documents I'd uncovered on Purdy's computer but never really understood. This invasion is so much different from Lorien's: there is no fire or missiles. At least, not yet.

"I think they're going to pretend to be diplomatic about this," I say.

"That would explain why they've cozied up to the government so much," Mark agrees. He pulls a laptop out of his bag—the one I gave him back before he tried to get into Dulce—and starts typing.

"Get me everything damning you have about the US and the Mogs that you haven't sent me. If the Mogs are going public, so are we. It's time to tell this planet everything we know. I want this info on the front page of every website, every—"

"Way ahead of you," he says with a grin. "I'm sending you a zip file that includes the worst of the worst of MogPro *and* a collection of the most relevant posts I did for 'They Walk Among Us.' Some I haven't even proofed or uploaded yet."

The files show up on my screen. They're the perfect complement to the info bomb I've been putting together myself over the last few years.

"This is great, Mark." I nod to him.

He shrugs. "I'm not letting these dickwads try to pull a fast one on the human race."

"It sounds like the others are on the same wavelength," Sarah says, hanging up from her call. "Sam just sent us some video. Footage of John using his powers to heal someone and some clips of Mogs shooting. I was thinking we could make a video or something to explain what's happening?"

"That's good," Mark says. "We could link all this MogPro info from it. GUARD—I mean, *Lexa*—could you, I don't know. . . . push a video to the front page of YouTube or something?"

"Easily," I say. "You two focus on getting that ready. I'm going to take care of a few last-minute adjustments to this ship and make sure she's ready for travel. And fully stocked—I've accumulated an arsenal of weapons here."

Mark bangs his fist against the desk he's set his laptop on.

"Dammit," he says. "I was going to use that video of John going all Superman and jumping out of my burning house, but I can't find it."

"Of course not," I say, tapping on my computer. "I scrubbed that video from the internet as soon as it came to my attention. I also managed to crash the cell phone it came from. Here, I just sent you a copy I saved for my records, along with some other images and footage I've collected over the years."

As I start to walk away, I hear Sarah whisper to Mark.

"She's good."

"You don't know the half of it," he says back.

I start a final inspection on the new fuel line for the ship, trying to cram days of work into a few hours. I pause only when Sarah starts shouting, and I watch on television as fighting breaks out at the United Nations. Number Four is there, looking powerful and unwavering as he faces Setrákus Ra, the leader of the Mogadorians. Sarah is pale as she watches but doesn't say anything. When the TV feed cuts out, she just nods.

"I'm ready to record the voice-over."

They get back to work. So do I. Hours pass, and when I finally take a break for water and an energy bar I find Mark and Sarah still huddled around Mark's laptop.

"Hey!" Mark says. "Come look at this!"

He and Sarah scoot apart as they bring up a video to full screen and hit play.

"This is our planet, but we are not alone in the galaxy." Sarah's voice comes through the speakers, cool and measured, as the video zooms out on a picture of the Earth. The footage switches to the YouTube clip of Number Four and then to him hovering his glowing hands over someone I hardly recognize as the secretary of defense. John appears to be healing him. Sarah continues.

"There are aliens among us. *Good* aliens. Refugees from the planet Lorien. This is John Smith, one of the Loric Garde—a boy blessed with incredible powers. He fights for Earth now. It's his home."

The video switches to clips of Mogadorians with blasters herding humans around on what look like the streets of New York.

"The ships above our cities now are not friendly. They are the Mogadorians—the bad aliens who destroyed John Smith's home world. They have come here to enslave us and to take Earth for their own. They have even found allies in our own government."

Various documents and bits of text pop up on the screen—I recognize them as MogPro files. The footage suddenly switches to a graphic showing the locations of the Mog warships. It looks like a screen grab Mark took from one of the news stations.

Sarah concludes: "We are not alone. They walk among us. We must join forces with the Loric and fight the Mogadorians."

The video ends.

"So, if they click anywhere on the video, it takes them to the website and to all the files we've put together," Mark says. "And there'll be a link in the description, obviously. Do you think it's okay?"

"It's the best we can do on short notice," Sarah says. She bites her lip as she stares at the screen.

"It's great," I say. "Upload it to 'They Walk Among Us,' in case the video gets pulled."

When it's uploaded, I manipulate a few lines of code and algorithms so that the video is at the top of every internet search and all over the front page of YouTube. The number of views skyrocket over the course of a few minutes, faster than the counters can keep up with. Even with everything that's happening across the planet, the video spreads. Mark says it's "gone viral." In a world suddenly full of questions, we, for once, are able to offer some answers.

Before long it's being shown on news stations across the globe.

I may have had doubts about many things on this planet, but the way information spreads here has proven to be more impressive than I could ever have imagined.

Mark continues tapping on his computer while Sarah tries futilely to get Number Four on her satellite phone. She never takes her eyes off the news. Night falls. I go back to working on the ship. Ideally I'd have some time to take it out for a few tests before storming into battle, but I don't have that luxury now—not with warships parked over cities across the globe. Still, I take the time to triple-check my work and run every diagnostic test I can think of. The last thing we need is a systems failure in the middle of a fight with the Mogs.

It's light outside when I'm finally satisfied with my work and come back out into the hangar. Mark is slumped over the desk, mouth open as he sleeps, snoring softly.

Sarah gives me a weak smile.

"He passed out while refreshing the view counts. I figured he could use the rest." She stares at the phone in her hands, and it's obvious she still hasn't been able to get in contact with Number Four.

"From what I've seen of him, Number—John is quite the impressive Garde. I'm sure he's still fighting."

Sarah nods a little. "Yeah. Of course he is."

She gets quiet, and it feels as though the energy has been sucked out of the room. After being alone for so long, I am perhaps not the best at small talk. And so I grab a couple of bottles of water from a mini fridge and slam one down next to Mark's head. He jumps, springing to life.

"What? Where?" His eyes dart around and his breathing quickens until he remembers where he is. "Oh, right. What'd I miss?"

Sarah's phone starts ringing before either of us can answer.

"It's him," she half shouts as she jumps to her feet. "He'll know what's going on in New York."

"Right on cue," Mark says through a yawn. "Our ET savior."

Sarah answers on the third ring. Her face is bright—hopeful despite everything going wrong across the planet.

"John?" she asks, breathless, and the few seconds before the voice on the other end of the line responds are an eternity.

"All right." Mark rolls his chair over to me. He stretches his arms over his head and cracks his neck. "What now?"

"I've waited years for this fight to arrive." I point to the ship. "I say we join the rest of the Garde and show the Mogadorians what this old girl can do. There's no use hiding in the shadows anymore."

"Hell, yeah. Let's kick some Mog ass."

"It's time we take the fight to them." I turn to Mark. I can't help but smile a little. "I want to see if Ella remembers me when we free her."

DISCOVER HOW MARK JAMES FIRST
MET GUARD BACK IN PARADISE!

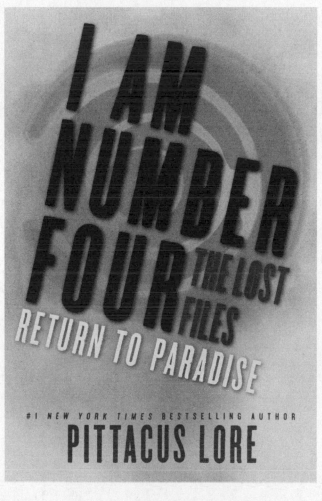

CHAPTER ONE

I HAVE TO KEEP REMINDING MYSELF WHO I AM the first week at the new school. Not, like, I lost my memory or something. I *know* who I am in a literal sense. But I have to keep forcing myself to remember what being me means. So all week I keep a single thought repeating through my head:

You are Mark James.

It's what I think on Monday when some douche bag trips me while I try to find an empty seat among a precalc classroom full of strangers.

You are Mark James, the guy everyone at your old school looked up to. These idiots will learn.

And Wednesday when someone loots my locker during weight training and forces me to walk around in sweaty gym clothes for the last two periods.

You are Mark James, all-conference quarterback. They're just jealous.

And at lunch on Thursday when I sit on the tailgate of my truck and someone in a loud old Camaro zips past, hurling an oversize Styrofoam cup of orange soda at me while yelling what I think is "ass pirate."

You are Mark James, and you are the best fucking athlete the Paradise High Pirates ever saw.

If someone had asked me a year ago what my future held, I'd probably have said something like "Mark James, Ohio State star quarterback." Maybe if I'd had a beer or two I'd go so far as to say, "Mark James, first-round NFL draft pick."

What I wouldn't have said—what I couldn't have even imagined thinking—was anything remotely close to "Mark James, survivor of an alien attack."

For my entire life, the future seemed set for me. As soon as I threw my first pass, I knew what I wanted to do. Paradise High QB, college football star, NFL hopeful. But now the future is this stupid, dark thing I can't predict, and I feel like my whole life has been heading towards something that doesn't even matter. Might not even exist if we end up conquered by a bunch of superpowered aliens. I mean, my all-conference trophy was used to *murder* an alien. A Mogadorian. A bunch of pale, janky-looking assholes from another planet came to Earth hunting for a very human-looking alien named John Smith—*ha*—and his invisible friend. Then they destroyed my school.

My kingdom. Almost killing me in the process.

Some people did die. I guess I should count myself lucky, but I don't *feel* lucky. I feel like someone who's just found out that vampires exist or that reality is actually an elaborate video game. Everyone else keeps going on as usual, but the world has changed for me.

There are only a few people who know what really happened at Paradise High. Everyone thinks the school's in shambles because weirdo-drifter/new student John Smith went crazy and jumped through the principal's window one day, then came back that night and caused massive amounts of damage that took out half the building. Then he fled town. Word is that he's some kind of teenage terrorist or member of a sleeper cell or a psychopath—it depends on who is telling the story.

But one exploding school can't stand in the way of education, so now everyone from Paradise is being shipped to the next town over where there's an actual building for us to go to. It just so happens that the next school over is Helena High, our biggest rival, who I beat in the best football game of my life, capping off an undefeated season by completely annihilating their defense. So, yeah, I guess I can see why I'm not the most loved guy in school. I just never thought I'd spend my last semester of high school washing orange soda out of my hair. Maybe if I was still the same old Mark James I'd think it was kind of fun even. I'd be dreaming up ways to get back at the other students, ways for me and my football buddies to prank them and get the last laugh. But filling someone's locker full of manure isn't as high on my list of priorities now that I know beings from another world are walking among us and that a complete alien invasion is possible at any time. I *wish* manure were still higher on my to-do list.

A bunch of my teammates have told me I've gotten quiet and seem different since it happened, but I can't help it. It's kind of pointless to talk about cars and partying when I was literally almost squashed by some kind of extraterrestrial monster. How am I supposed to go back to being fun-loving, beer-chugging Mark James after all that? Now I'm "Paranoid That Aliens Are Going to Hunt Me Down" Mark James.

I can deal with the new school. Hell, I probably deserve it for the shit I put people like John through back in Paradise. It's only a semester, and then I'll have graduated. Maybe they'll even be able to fix up the school auditorium in time for me to walk the stage in Paradise. What sucks is that I can't tell everyone what's going on. They'd throw me in a mental institution. Or worse, those bad aliens—the Mogs—would be after me to try and shut me up.

At least I have Sarah to talk to. She was there. She fought with me, almost died beside me. As long I have Sarah, I don't feel like I'm going to go crazy.

CHAPTER
TWO

THERE ARE BIG SCHOOL BUSES SHUTTLING KIDS
back and forth between Helena and Paradise, but I was
able to talk the principal into letting me drive myself.
I told him I wanted to stay late and work out—that I
didn't want what happened in Paradise to keep me
from being an unstoppable college football machine.
He said that was fine: I'm guessing partly because he
hopes anything I do in the future will make Paradise
High look good, and partly because everyone in town
still feels kind of bad for me because I threw a party
and some kids accidentally burned down my house.

I don't *think* that had anything to do with aliens. At
least, I've made sure to tell everyone who insinuates
that John blew up my house that it was really a couple
of stoners down in the basement who were lighting
stuff on fire for fun. That usually shuts people up—
especially adults who like to pretend that stuff like

that never happens in good old Paradise. Besides, John saved Sarah and both of my dogs. There's a YouTube video to prove it. No one should be giving him shit for that night. He gets a free pass on that one.

I meet Sarah in the parking lot after the last bell on the Friday of our first week in Helena. She waits for me at my truck. It's kind of gray outside, and she's got on a plaid sweater that makes her eyes look like they're practically glowing blue. She looks gorgeous.

She always does.

Sarah Hart was—*is*—the love of my life. Even after she dropped cheerleading and came back to school as some kind of emo hipster who suddenly didn't want to be dating the star QB. Even after she dumped me and started sorta dating an alien.

I smile at her as I approach, all teeth. It's a reflex. I can't help it. She smiles too but not as wide as I'd like.

Even with the "You are Mark James" mantra in my head all day, sometimes I don't feel like me at all. Instead of being the cool, put-together guy I've always been, I start worrying about intergalactic war and if Mogs are watching me have breakfast. But even when I start to wonder if I should be building a bomb shelter out in the middle of the woods or something, part of me wants to stay planted in the world I knew before there was definite proof of aliens on Earth, where I'm just a dude who's trying to win back his ex-girlfriend.

If this whole ordeal has had any bright side, it's that I see a lot more of Sarah than I did before. I like to think that me saving John's life impressed her, maybe even showed her that there's more to me than she thought. Someday when this is all said and done, Sarah is going to come to her senses and realize that even if John is a good alien, he's still freaking E.T. And I'll be waiting, even if it means fighting off space invaders to keep her safe and show her I'm better than he is.

The waiting totally blows.

"You're begging to get jumped, aren't you?" she says as I get closer.

At first I'm confused, but then I realize she's nodding at my chest, where my name is embroidered in gold over the heart on my Paradise High varsity letter jacket.

"What, this?" I ask, flexing a little and puffing out my chest. "I'm just repping our school. Trying to bring a little bit of Paradise to hell. That way we all feel like we're at home."

She rolls her eyes.

"You're provoking them."

"They're the least of my problems these days."

"Whatever," she says. "Your truck still smells like orange soda."

Once we're in my truck, Sarah leans her head against the passenger window and exhales a long breath, as if she's been holding it in all day. She looks tired. Beautiful but tired.

"I got a new name in bio today," she says, her eyes closed.

"Oh yeah?"

"'Sarah Bleeding Heart.' I was trying to explain that John wasn't a terrorist who was going to try to blow up the White House. Like, literally, someone said that they heard he was going to blow up the White House."

"Now who's the one asking for it?"

She opens her eyes just enough to glare at me.

"I feel like all I do now is defend him, but everyone else refuses to listen. And every time I try to say something about how they don't know the whole story, I lose a friend. Did you know that Emily thinks he kidnapped Sam? And I can't even tell her that it's not true. All I can say is that John wouldn't do that, and then she looks at me like I'm part of some big plot to destroy America or something. Or worse, some lovesick loser who's in denial."

"Well, you've still got me," I say reassuringly. "And I try to defend John whenever I can. Though I don't think I've been very good at it. All the guys on the team think he was able to kick our asses after the hayride because he was trained as a special agent from Russia or something."

"Thanks, Mark," Sarah says. "I know I can count on you. It's just . . ."

She opens her eyes and looks out the window as we speed past a few empty fields, never finishing her sentence.

"Just what?" I ask, even though I know what's coming. I can feel the blood in my veins start to pump a little faster.

"Nothing."

"*What*, Sarah?" I ask.

"I just wish John was here." She gives me a sad smile. "To defend himself."

Of course, what she really means is that she wishes John was here because she misses him. That it's killing her not to know where he is or what he's doing. For a moment, I feel like my old self again as my hands tighten around the steering wheel. I want to find John Smith and punch him square in the jaw, then keep hitting him until my knuckles bleed. I want to go straight into a rant about how if he really loved her, he wouldn't have left her here to get picked on and laughed at. He would have manned up. Even if he did leave to find other aliens like him to save our planet. If I were in his shoes, I'd have figured out a way to keep Sarah *and* the world safe. And happy.

I can't believe these are the types of conversations I have with myself on a daily basis now.

Being super pissed at John just makes me sound like the Mark that Sarah broke up with. So instead of talking shit about him, I swallow my anger and change the subject.

"I've been thinking a lot about what's happened lately. How the FBI and stuff have been handling it. My dad says that it's kind of weird how they're keeping the local law enforcement in the dark. I mean, he's the sheriff and they aren't telling him anything about what's going on."

"Yeah, but isn't that so they can keep a lid on the investigation?" Sarah asks. "That's the FBI's *job*, right?"

"My dad doesn't think so. He should at least be kept in the loop, even if he can't tell the rest of his officers about what's happening. Plus, I know they found some bodies at the school and there was a lot of damage, but John got moved straight to the FBI's most-wanted list. That seems a little extreme, right? Especially considering there's no *actual* evidence that John was the one behind all this."

"So, what? Do you think this is some kind of government conspiracy?" She sits up straighter in the passenger seat, leaning towards me.

"I just think maybe they know more about what's going on with John's people than they let on. I'm *guessing* some of the people in black suits are smart enough to realize that it wasn't just some angry teenager who dug gigantic claw marks in the football field."

"Jesus, Mark, you're starting to sound like Sam," she

says. Then she shrugs a little. "But I guess he was right about some of that stuff we all thought was crazy. That would make sense. I mean, if stuff like this is happening across the country, *someone* is keeping track of it all, right? The FBI swooped in here really fast. Maybe they're working with John's . . . species?"

I can't believe Sarah has fallen for someone who could be classified as another species.

"Or else they're working with the monsters with all the glowing swords," I say. "Which would mean we've just allowed the opposing team to set up shop in town."

Sarah lets her head fall against the window again.

"Where are you, John?" she whispers, her breath fogging up the glass in front of her. "Where are you?"

We're quiet for the rest of the drive home.

All I can think of is the promise I made to John when everything was going down at the school—that I would keep Sarah safe. Of course I'll do that. I'd be doing it even if he hadn't asked me to. But it makes my insides twist up to know that he's the one she's thinking of while *I'm* the one whose actually looking out for her.

LEARN THE TRUE STORY OF
FIVE'S SECRET PAST!

#1 NEW YORK TIMES BESTSELLING AUTHOR
PITTACUS LORE

I AM
NUMBER
FOUR THE LOST
FILES

FIVE'S LEGACY

CHAPTER
ONE

"THE MOGS ARE HERE!"

My eyes shoot open as I jerk upright, hoping that sentence was just something from a bad dream.

But it's not.

"They're here," Rey whispers again as he crosses over the floor of our little shack to where I'm sleeping on top of a pallet of blankets.

I'm off the floor in seconds. Rey's solar-powered lantern swings in front of my face, and it blinds me. I flinch away and then he turns it off, leaving me in complete darkness. As he pushes me towards the back of our home, all I can make out is a sliver of silver light peeking through the window.

"Out the back." His voice is full of urgency and fear. "I'll hold them off. Go, go, go."

I start grabbing at the air where he'd stood moments before but find nothing. I can't see anything: My eyes still burn from the lantern.

"Rey—"

"No." He cuts me off from somewhere in the dark. "If you don't go now, we're *both* dead."

There's a clattering near the front of the shack, followed by the sound of something—or someone—slamming against the front door. Rey lets out a pained cry but the inside of the shack is still nothing but an abyss of black in my eyes. I know there's a metal bar over the door that's not going to hold up against much more than a little force. It's for show more than anything else. If someone *really* wanted into our shack, they could just blow through the flimsy wooden walls. And if it's the Mogs . . .

There's no time to think, only to react. It's *me* they're after. I've got to get to safety.

I rip away the piece of cloth that serves as a makeshift curtain and throw myself through the little window. I land with a plop in a three-inch puddle of mud, slop, and things I don't even want to imagine—I'm in the hog pen.

A single thought runs through my mind. *I'm going to die a thirteen-year-old boy covered in pig shit on an island in the middle of nowhere.*

Life is so unfair.

The hogs squeal—I've disturbed their sleep—and it snaps me back into the moment. Old training regimens and lectures from years before take over my brain and I'm moving again, checking my flanks to make sure there are no Mogs that have already made their way to the back of the hut. I start to think about what their plan of action might be. If the Mogs actually *knew* I was on the island, I'd be surrounded already. No, it must be a single scout that stumbled upon us by accident. Maybe he had time to report us to the others, maybe not. Whatever the case, I have to get out of the line of fire. Rey will take out the scout. He'll be fine. At least that's what I tell myself, choosing to ignore how frail Rey's looked lately.

He *has* to be okay. He always is.

I head for the jungle behind our shack. My bare feet sink into the sand, as if the island itself is trying to slow me down. I'm dressed only in dark athletic shorts, and branches and shrubs around me scratch at my bare chest and stomach as I enter the cover of the trees. I've done this sort of thing before, once, in Canada. Then, coats and a few bags weighed me down. But we'd had a little more warning. Now, in the sticky-hot night of the Caribbean, I'm weighed down only by my lack of stamina.

As I hurl myself through the dense vegetation, I think of all the mornings I was supposed to spend jogging along the beach or hiking through the forest that I *actually* spent playing solitaire or simply lazing

around. Doing what I really wanted to do, like drawing little cartoons in the sand. Coming up with short
stories told by stick figures. Rey always said I shouldn't
actually write anything down—that any journal or
notes I wrote could be found and used as proof of who
I am. But writing and drawing in the sand was temporary. When the tide came in, my stories were gone.
Even just doing that caused me to work up a sweat in
this damned climate, and I'd return to Rey, pretending
to be exhausted. He'd comment on the timing of my
imaginary run and then treat me to a rich lunch as a
reward. Rey is a taskmaster when it comes to doling
out things to do, but his lungs are bad and he always
trusted that I was doing the training he told me to do.
He had no reason not to—no reason to think I wouldn't
take our situation seriously.

It wasn't just the avoidance of having to work my ass
off in the heat that kept me from training. It was the
monotony of it all that I hated. Run, lift, stretch, aim,
repeat—day in and day out. Plus, we're living out in the
middle of nowhere. Our island isn't even on any maps.
I never thought the Mogs would ever find us.

Now, I'm afraid that's coming back to haunt me. I
wheeze as I run. I'm totally unprepared for this attack.
Those mornings lazing around the beach are going to
get me killed.

It doesn't take long before there's a stitch in my side

so sore that I think it's possible I've burst some kind of internal organ. I'm out of breath, and the humid air feels like it's trying to smother me. My hands grasp onto low-hanging branches as I half-pull my way through thick green foliage, the bottoms of my feet scraping against fallen limbs and razor-sharp shells. Within a few minutes the canopy above me is so dense that only pinpricks of the moonlight shine through. The jungle has given way to a full-blown rain forest.

I'm alone in the dark in a rain forest with alien monsters chasing after me.

I pause, panting and holding my side. Our island is small, but I'm only maybe a fifth of the way across it. On the other side of the island a small, hidden kayak is waiting for me, along with a pack of rations and first aid gear. The last-chance escape vessel, something that'll let me slip into the dark of the night and disappear on the ocean. But that seems so far away now, with my lungs screaming at me and my bare feet bleeding. I lean against a tree, trying to catch my breath. Something skitters across the forest floor a few feet away from me and I jump, but it's only one of the little green lizards that overrun the island. Still, my heart pounds. My head is dizzy.

The Mogadorians are here. I'm going to die.

I can't imagine what Rey is doing back at the shack. How many Mogs are here? How many can he take on?

I hope I'm right, and it's just a single scout. I realize I haven't heard any gunshots. Is that a good sign, or does it mean the bastards got to him before he was able to fire off a single round?

Keep going, I tell myself, and then start out again. My calves are burning and my lungs feel like they're about to split open every time I inhale. I stumble, hitting the ground hard and knocking what little breath I had out of me.

Somewhere behind me, I can hear movement in the trees.

I glance around. Without a clear view of the sky, I can't even tell which direction I'm going anymore. I'm totally screwed. I have to do something.

I abandon the plan to cross the island. I'm in no shape to do so. For a moment I think of burrowing down into the brush—maybe finding something to hide in until I can slip through the forest—but then I think of all the fist-sized spiders and ants and snakes that could be waiting there for me, and imagine a Mogadorian scout stepping on me by accident.

So I head up instead. Gathering every ounce of strength I have, I use a few sturdy vines to pull myself hand over hand up to a low branch on a nearby tree. All I can think of are the many different types of beasts Rey's told me the Mogs can command, any one of which would like nothing more than to tear me apart.

Why don't *we* have giant hell-beasts to fight for us?

My arms are shaking by the time I squat on the limb, the wood creaking under my weight as I stare into the blackness, hoping over and over again that nothing will emerge from it. That I can just wait this out.

That it will all just go *away*.

There's no telling how much time passes. If I'd been more put together or hadn't been so taken by surprise, I might have remembered to grab my watch on the way out the window. It's weird—time always seemed like it didn't mean anything on the island, and now it means everything. How many minutes before more of them arrive? How many seconds before they find me? I try to keep from trembling, and my stomach from turning over—between the running, my fear, and the damp smell of pig that clings to me in a thick coat of sludge, I'm teetering on the edge of vomiting. Maybe the stinking layer of crap will help keep me camouflaged, at least.

It's not a very reassuring silver lining.

Finally, a silhouette starts to take shape in the darkness. I draw in closer to the tree. The figure is human sized. Maybe even a little hunched over, leaning on a cane as he steps into the dim moonlight. He's wearing a blue linen shirt, khaki cargo pants, and sneakers that might have been white at some point. His beard is white, streaked with black, his wild hair almost silver.

I recognize him immediately, of course. Rey.

He's got something held against him, wrapped in a piece of cloth. I start to call down to him, but he's already staring holes into me, his lips quivering, as if he's fighting every urge to yell. He simply stands there, the silence hanging in the thick air between us. Finally, I break it.

"Well? Did you get him?"

Rey doesn't respond immediately, just looks away, staring down at the ground.

"What'd you forget?" His voice has a slight rattle to it.

"What?" I ask, my breath short.

He throws his parcel down on the ground. Part of the cloth falls back, and I can make out a familiar corner.

"The Chest?" I ask. My *Loric* Chest. The most sacred thing I own. The treasure I'm not actually allowed to look into. The container that supposedly holds my inheritance and the tools to rebuild my home planet, and I can't even peek inside until Rey thinks I'm ready to—whatever *that* means.

"The Chest." Rey nods.

I scramble down the tree, half falling to the earth.

"We should get going, right?" I ask. My words are spilling out now, my tongue stumbling over the letters as I try to say a million things at once. "You don't have any weapons? Or our food? Where are we going now? Shouldn't we be—"

"Your Chest is the second most important thing you have to protect after your own life. It was stupid to leave it. Next time, it's your priority to keep it safe."

"What are you—"

"You made it half a mile into the forest," he says, ignoring me. His voice is getting louder now, filled with barely restrained anger. "I didn't want to believe it, but I guess this is proof. You haven't been doing your training. You've been lying to me about it. Every day."

"Rey . . ."

"I already knew that, though." He sounds sad now. "I could tell just by looking at you."

My mind is racing, trying to figure out why we're still standing here. Why he's worried about my training when there could be a whole fleet of Mogs on their way after us. Unless . . .

"There aren't any Mogs here," I say quietly.

Rey just shakes his head and stares at the ground.

This was a test. No, worse than that: This was Rey's way of trapping me and catching me in a lie. And even though, yes, I technically have been less than honest about my training regimen, I can't believe Rey would scare me like this.

"Are you kidding me?" Unlike Rey, I don't have the power to keep my anger from clouding my voice. "I was running for my life. I thought I was going to *die*."

"Death is the least of your worries for now," he says, pointing at my ankle. Underneath the layer of mud and crap is an ugly red mark that appeared a few days ago. A mark that's starting to scab over, and will soon turn into a scar. The mark that—thanks to some other-worldly charm—shows me that another one of my fellow Garde has been murdered. Two is dead. Three and Four are all that stand between death and me.

I am Number Five.

I suddenly feel stupid for thinking I was about to be killed. Of course I wasn't. Numbers Three and Four have to die before I can. I *should* have been worried about being captured and tortured for information. Not that Rey ever tells me anything.

And I realize what this is about. Ever since the scar appeared, it's like something within Rey snapped. He's been getting sicker the last few years, and I'm not anywhere as strong as he thinks I should be. I haven't developed any of the magic powers I'm supposed to have. Neither of us can put up a good fight. That's why we're here on this stupid island, hiding.

Rey's eyes have been on the ground, but he finally raises them to mine, looking at me for a long moment. Then he nods at the Chest.

"Carry it back," he says. Then he's shuffling off into the darkness, leaving me in the sparse moonlight, staring at the duffel bag that contains my Chest.

We weren't under attack. It was only a test.

I'm not going to die on the island. At least, not tonight.

I pick up my Chest, hugging it close to me, letting the corners dig into my stomach.

I stare into the blackness that Rey has disappeared into, and in that moment there's only one emotion filling me. Not fear or relief or even shame for being found out. It's the feeling that the only person I have in this world has betrayed me.

CHAPTER
TWO

THE SUN RISES AS I WASH OFF IN THE OCEAN and think of Canada, the first place I remember living here on Earth.

I really liked Canada.

In Canada we ate butter tarts and French fries covered in gravy and rubbery globs of cheese, all served out of carts on the sides of the roads. Even when it was summer there it wasn't all that hot. I learned a little bit of French. Rey didn't like the cold, but I did. He was Albert in Canada, a name he'd picked after seeing Alberta on a map, thinking it would make him sound like more of a local. "Old Al" he called himself sometimes when talking to servers or cashiers. I always thought it was funny when he dumbed his personality down and pretended to be my grandfather at times like that, using words like "whippersnapper" that he'd picked up from the TV. No one questioned the kindly old man and his grandson.

I was Cody then. I liked being Cody. I was a person, not just Five. At night, Rey would tell me about Lorien and the Mogadorians and the other Garde—my kindred spirits scattered across the world—and how one day we'd bring about the glorious return of our home planet. Back then, everything seemed like a fairy tale. All the aliens and powers and other worlds were nothing but stories to get me to do my chores. Didn't clean up after yourself? Lorien didn't stand a chance. Forget to brush your teeth? The Mogs would get you for sure.

Then they actually came.

We'd been living up near Montreal for six months—maybe a whole year—when Rey found out they were coming for us. I'm still not sure how. All I know is that suddenly I was running through the woods behind our little cottage while a few Mogadorians tracked me. I was six years old, scared out of my mind. Eventually I'd hidden in a tree. I thought I was a goner until Rey appeared, taking out the Mogs with a broken-off shovel and a shotgun he'd bought on the black market. He's always been good with tools.

"Albert . . ." I'd said from the tree. We always called each other by our false names, never knowing who was listening. "Are they gone?"

"Albert's dead," Rey had said. I knew what he meant, even though I was so young. I'd felt it in my gut. It meant we weren't safe. It meant we couldn't stay there, in that place I liked so much.

So we went on the move, and we didn't stop for a long time.

Rey was Aaron after that, followed by Andy, Jeffrey, and then James. I was Zach, Carson, and then Bolt, which was the last name I got to pick before Rey started choosing them. Maybe I'm forgetting a few in there—it all seems so long ago. I know that I was Carson when Rey's cough first appeared, along with the dark hollows under his eyes. We were camping in the Appalachians. He thought it was the cold that was making him sick, so we started moving south, making our way through the United States and towards a warmer climate. Eventually—after a few sketchy boat rides Rey arranged for us—we set up camp in Martinique, where we stayed for a while. But Rey's cough just got worse. He kept telling me he was feeling better, but at some point I stopped believing him.

I was always the better liar.

As a kid, I thought of lies as little stories or games. Sometimes people we came across would ask questions—Where were my parents? Where was I born?—and I'd just start talking, making up these elaborate histories for Rey and me. Having secrets means you do a lot of lying. Not because you're evil or a bad person or anything like that, but out of necessity.

Really, Rey *trained* me to lie about all those morning runs and hikes. I make a mental note to tell him this later.

Sometimes I wonder if Rey is crazy. Like, what if he's just a really messed-up old guy who stole me from a loving, normal home and all of this alien stuff is simply made up? Maybe he gave me drugs or brainwashed me into having fake memories of some place that couldn't possibly exist. All my life I've heard about Lorien, but the only proof I have that any of it is true is a few weird-looking guys who came after me in Canada.

Well, that plus two scars that appeared like magic on my ankle and a Chest that's supposed to house all kinds of treasures. A Chest that doesn't open no matter how much you prod at it—I know, because I've tried about a million times to find out what's inside over the years.

The treasure of Lorien. Sure. A lot of good it's doing out here in the middle of nowhere.

I don't mind the beach, really. I mean, I get why people go there on vacation. When we first got to the Caribbean, we stuck to the bigger, more populated resorts, just living on the fringes. We'd watch the tourists roll in every year, their brand-new beach clothes a parade of bright colors as they sipped drinks out of giant coconuts and pineapples that weren't even native to the islands (not that they'd have known). But when

One died—when that first scar formed on my ankle—
Rey flipped out. I was nine years old and it was like
the final string keeping him in check snapped, and he
went into full-on survival mode. No more people. We'd
have to live life completely off the grid. And so he'd
cashed in whatever possessions we had, bought a few
supplies and a small sailboat, and headed out to find
the most deserted, godforsaken place he could. Gone
were the restaurants and air-conditioning. No more
TV, video games, or hot showers. Just a beach and a
shack. I don't know what kind of deal Rey must have
struck to find this island, but I'll give him one thing—it
must be hidden away pretty well. A few times a year
people mistakenly wash ashore here, but Rey always
gets rid of them fast.

And that's where I am now. Washing up in the ocean.
A dark cloud forms around my body as I scrub the pig
shit off in the clear water at the shoreline. That's what
the future holds for the great Number Five, one of the
seven most important people left on the planet.

It's not fair.

CONTINUE FIVE'S STORY AND DISCOVER
WHY HE JOINS THE MOGADORIAN ARMY!

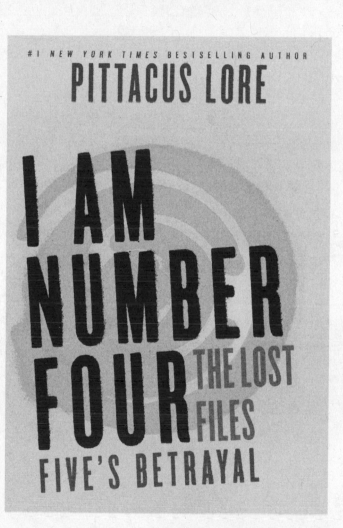

#1 *NEW YORK TIMES* BESTSELLING AUTHOR
PITTACUS LORE

I AM NUMBER FOUR THE LOST FILES
FIVE'S BETRAYAL

CHAPTER
ONE

THERE WAS ONCE A PLACE THAT WAS BEAUTIFUL and lush and full of life and natural resources. Some people lived there for a long time, but then others came along who wanted or needed the land and everything on it. So they took it.

There is nothing special about this story. Open any history book on Earth—and probably every other planet—and you'll see a version of it play out continuously, on loop, over and over again. Sometimes the land is taken in the name of spreading a better way of life. Or for the sake of the native people. Occasionally the takers seize it based on some intangible reason—some divine right or destiny. But all of these reasons are lies. At the center of every conflict is power, and who will wield it. That's what wars are fought over, and why cities, countries and planets are conquered. And though most people—especially humans—like to pretend that gaining power is just an added bonus on top of whatever a conflict is *supposedly* about, power is the only thing that anyone is really after.

That's one great thing about the Mogadorians: they don't really bother with pretense. They believe in power. Even worship it. They see its potential to grow and serve their cause. So when you're someone like me who has extraordinary abilities, you become one of two things to the Mogs: a valuable asset, or an enemy who will eventually be destroyed.

Personally, I like being alive.

The Mogs don't pretend that they took my home planet of Lorien—which I barely remember—for any reason other than because they needed its resources. It's the same reason they're on Earth now. A planet as big as Earth will serve the Mogs well for decades— maybe even centuries—before they have to go looking for another home. And the humans . . . well, it's not like there's anything really special about *them*. They're pretty weak for the most part and are only barely managing to keep the planet alive as it is. One day soon there will be a full-scale invasion, and all their petty problems won't mean anything, because suddenly there will be some incredibly powerful extraterrestrials lording over them. Showing them how to live. Giving their lives purpose.

And I'll be one of their new rulers. Because the Mogs

have seen the potential in me. They've promised me a spot as a commanding officer in the Mog ranks, with North America as my kingdom. My personal playground. And all I have to do is fight alongside them and help them capture the other Garde remaining on Earth. Then I can help the Garde see that there's no way the Loric are ever going to defeat the Mogs. I'm assuming they were spoon-fed the same stories Rey, my Cêpan, told me when I was growing up: that the Mogs were our enemies.

But that's not true. Or at least it doesn't *have* to be true. Not if we join them.

After sitting around training and waiting for almost my entire life, it feels good to finally have an actual mission. To have a purpose. To not just be hiding and waiting for something to happen to me. It makes me actually *want* to train and study and get better, because what I'm working towards now isn't some fairy tale Rey fed me over dinner on the island, but a future I can see.

I've learned a lot about the reasons why wars are fought and won in the last few weeks since I've been living in a Mog compound somewhere in the middle of West Virginia. In fact, most of my "research" hours are spent in an interrogation room that's been converted into a study for me, where I learn about famous battles and conflicts or read the Great Book, which is the story of the Mogadorians and how their intellect and abilities outgrew their planet and forced them to seek other worlds to rule and guide. About how the Loric refused to share their resources or listen to reason when it came to adopting the Mogs as rulers. It's a book written by Setrákus Ra, the unstoppable leader of the Mogs, and, well, let's just say if I'd read it earlier, I would have had a much clearer viewpoint of the fight between the Mogs and the Loric than I did when I was hiding in a lean-to shack on a deserted island. I've begun to wonder if all my memories of being so young and happy on Lorien are just because I was too dumb and little to know what was really going on. I mean, any civilization that puts their last hope in a bunch of toddlers on spaceships has got to be a little bit out of whack, right?

Ethan's helped me see these things. He's helped me realize that I have a choice in this war, even though the Elders didn't want me to have one. It was strange at first to find out that my best friend was working for the Mogs—and that I'd technically been under Mog care for the better part of a year without knowing it—but I can't blame Ethan for keeping things a secret from me at first. I'd been so brainwashed by my Cêpan's stories of the Garde triumphing over the armies of the Mogs and returning Lorien to its former glory that I probably wouldn't have seen reason if he'd been up front with me at the beginning. Ethan is what some of the Mog commanders here have called a rare example of a human who has the intelligence to side with the winning team.

Still, it's so strange to be here underground. I'm technically an honored guest of Setrákus Ra, but I haven't proved myself yet. All they have is my word that I'm now loyal to them, but words don't carry a lot of weight with the Mogs. They believe in action, and results. And so I study and train and wait for the day when I get the chance to show them I am capable and ready to lead in their name. I follow orders. Because even though someday in the future I'll become invaluable to the Mogs, right now I'm just a former enemy living under their roof.

I'm buried in a book about the founding of America— particularly the expansion of European empires across the country—when Ethan comes into my study, flashing the toothy grin he always has plastered on his face.

"Good afternoon, Five," he says.

"Hey," I say, closing the book in front of me. Ethan's arrival means study time must be over. As much as I'm looking forward to being in charge of Canada and the United States, reading about the endless cycles of wars they've been caught up in can be monotonous. At least once the Mogs take over, war will be a thing of the past. There'll be no armies capable of standing up to them.

"How did you find today's reading?"

"There was some pretty dirty biological warfare going on back when Columbus and other explorers were first coming over. Smallpox blankets? It's kind of insane."

Ethan's grin doesn't flinch.

"The beginning of every great empire is stained with a little blood," he says. "Wouldn't you say it was worth it?"

I don't answer immediately. Ethan's eyes shift almost imperceptibly, but I catch them. He's glanced at the one-way mirror at the other end of my desk. It's easy to see what he's getting at. Others are watching. Here in the Mog compound, someone is *always* watching.

I tense up a little. I'm still not used to being under constant surveillance. But it's necessary, as Ethan's explained, so that the Mogs know they can trust me. It makes me only want to say things that will impress whoever's watching, or show off how smart I am. I'm getting better at keeping my brain focused on that.

"Definitely," I say.

Ethan nods, looking pleased. "Of course it's worth it. Keep reading that book tomorrow, and write down a few positive things about the conquerors' tactics."

"Whatever our Beloved Leader requires of me." I say this almost as a reflex. The first few days I was here, I heard it so many times that I just kind of adopted it. I probably say it ten times a day now without even realizing it half the time.

"Did you read the assigned passages from the Great Book?" Ethan asks.

"Of course. Those are the best parts of the study sessions." This is completely true. The other books are boring and make me suddenly understand why teenagers like me were always complaining about homework on TV shows I saw before coming to the Mog compound. But the Great Book is, well, great. Not only is it written much simpler than the other books, it also answers a lot of questions I've had throughout my life. Like why the Mogs went after Earth even though they had Lorien, and why they started hunting down the Loric once they got here, even though there were so few of us. The book explains that the Loric were weak but sneaky, and the Mogadorian belief that leaving even one enemy alive gives them the power to recruit others and multiply, gain power and one day rise against you.

Also, it's really bloody and violent, which makes it much more fun to read. I can see it play out in my head like one of the action movies I used to love to go see when I was still in Miami.

"And what did you learn about today?" Ethan asks.

"About how Setrákus Ra bravely fought our Elders. How they tried to trick him and poison him, but our Beloved Leader was courageous and bested them, anyway."

"*Our* Elders?" Ethan asks, slight concern on his face.

I correct myself. "I mean the *Loric* Elders. It makes me even more excited to meet our Beloved Leader."

I have not had the pleasure of meeting Setrákus Ra in person yet. Apparently someone higher up thought it wasn't a good idea to give a superpowered guy like me an audience with the future ruler of the solar system until I've proved myself.

Ethan grins and pulls something out of his pocket. He tosses it on the table, and it bounces heavily a few times and then rolls. I stop it with my telekinetic Legacy and lift it in the air: a steel ball bearing almost as big as a Ping-Pong ball.

"What's this?" I ask.

"Consider it a gift. Use your power on it. See how it feels."

I float the ball over to the palm of my hand. With a little focus, my body suddenly takes on a metallic sheen. I drum my fingers on the table in front of me, and the sound of metal meeting metal fills the air. Ethan calls this Externa, the ability to take on the properties of whatever I touch. It's the newest of my abilities and the one that probably needs the most work.

I shrug as I crack a metallic knuckle.

"It feels like I'm made of steel. But I could have just touched the table and gotten the same kind of effect."

"But the table's not going to be with you all the time.

From now on, this ball bearing should be. I don't want you to find yourself in the middle of a fight with nothing but sand or paper to turn into."

"Thanks." I smile. It's definitely not the flashiest or most expensive thing Ethan and the Mogs have given me, but I can see how it might end up being useful. I shove the ball bearing into my pocket, where it settles beside a red rubber ball I've carried with me for a long time—a trinket from a kid's vending machine.

Ethan tosses me a rolled-up sheet of paper. I push some books out of the way and spread it out in front of me. It's a map of the Western Hemisphere.

"What's this for?" I ask.

"I just wanted to make sure we had all the information correct on it. For record keeping and stuff like that."

The map includes a thick red line that zigzags across the United States and down into the Caribbean. There are dates printed along the markings.

"This is a map of all the places I lived growing up," I say.

"Correct. Just give it a once-over when you have a chance. I guessed on a lot of the dates based on stories you'd told me."

"But what good is any of this information?"

Ethan shrugs. "Just in case the Garde somehow caught your trail or tried to track you down, we'd know where they might be searching. We'll want to put a few scouts in those locations, just in case."

I nod, looking over the map. It's weird to think of myself as being young and powerless with Rey in all these places. Ethan comes up behind me and looks over my shoulder.

"Where was it that you said your guardian started to get so ill?" he asks.

I point to a place where the line dips into Pennsylvania.

"Around here somewhere. I'm not sure where exactly. We were camping in the mountains."

Ethan scowls.

"There are some of the finest hospitals in the country in that area. You know, if your Cêpan hadn't forced you to stay hidden on the island for as long as you did, he probably would have lived," Ethan says. "It's a shame he was so shortsighted that he couldn't see the inevitable future of Mogadorian progress."

"He thought the warmer air would help him."

"What he probably needed was a shot of antibiotics." Ethan shakes his head and crosses his arms. "I'm just glad you were able to get off the island before you ended up going crazy and talking to the pigs. I still can't believe someone as powerful and smart as you was expected to raise those slop-covered animals."

I laugh a little. Over the last few weeks I've told Ethan

basically everything I can remember about my life. All about the tiny little shack and the pigs I raised and how I trained myself to use my telekinesis on my own. He and the other Mogs seemed really impressed by that part. Like I managed to become something great even when every card in the deck was stacked against me.

When I look at Miami on the map, my mind flashes with memories of the time I spent there before Ethan took me in. When I was just a punk-ass street rat wasting my powers on petty stuff like picking pockets, totally oblivious to how much authority I should have been wielding. There was a girl. Emma. My partner in crime who turned on me when she saw what I was capable of. Who was afraid of what I could do instead of respecting my abilities. I frown at the memory, and my stomach drops a little because it's been a while since I've thought of her. There had been a time when she was my only friend in the world, but she was just using me too, wasn't she? I was the one with the real talent. She was just riding on my coattails.

There's a knock on the door, and then a Mog enters. One of the vatborn messengers and servants in the compound. I straighten up in my chair. This is a reflex. Even though I've been here a few weeks, I'm still getting used to seeing Mogs every day. More than that, I never know what they're going to ask me to do when they show up in the interrogation room that's been turned into my study or track me down in my bedroom. For all I know, they could be telling me that I've failed some test of theirs I didn't even know I was taking.

"You weren't responding to your radio," the Mog says to Ethan, clearly a little ticked off.

Ethan points to the little earpiece that's hanging out of his collar.

"Of course not," he says. "All of your superiors know that I never wear my earpiece when I'm with our guest." He motions to me. "It would be rude."

"Commander Deltoch requests your presence in the detention wing," the Mog says.

"I'll be there at once." Ethan nods.

"You *and* the Loric."

I tense up. What do they want from me in the detention wing?

"Is that how you would address an honored guest in this base?" Ethan asks. "How about 'sir'?"

The Mog seems a little apprehensive but nods his head to me.

"Sir," he says.

"Dismiss him," Ethan says to me.

"What?" I ask.

"You're going to have to get used to giving orders at some point."

I look at the Mog, who's got a full-on grimace now. I suddenly feel awkward. I hate it when Ethan does this. He's always trying to make everyone on the base treat me like their king or something. And while I'll be leading them one day in the future, I'm still unproven potential, and the last thing I want is anyone stirring up animosity against me.

"Five," Ethan says.

"You're dismissed," I say.

The Mog hesitates a moment. I assume his orders were to escort us to the other side of the building. I can almost see him trying to figure out who outranks whom in his head before Ethan clears his throat and, in a flash, the servant is gone.

"Conflicting orders, I'd imagine," Ethan says as if he could read my brain.

"Do you think I'll get him in trouble?"

Ethan's face goes serious.

"You can't worry about that. Don't forget who you are. When the Mogs take Earth, you'll be one of their officers. A leader. You may be new here, but you are the powerful Number Five. Show them mercy now, and they won't respect you when you're in charge."

"I need a chart to keep the ranks all straight in my head."

"Just always act like you're at the top of the food chain. Now come along," Ethan says, motioning towards the door. "Let's see what Commander Deltoch is up to with the prisoners this afternoon."

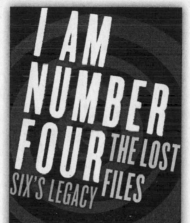
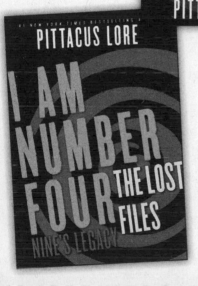
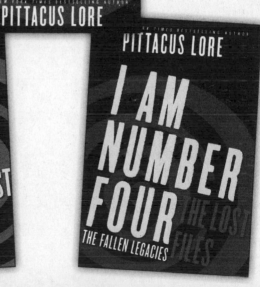

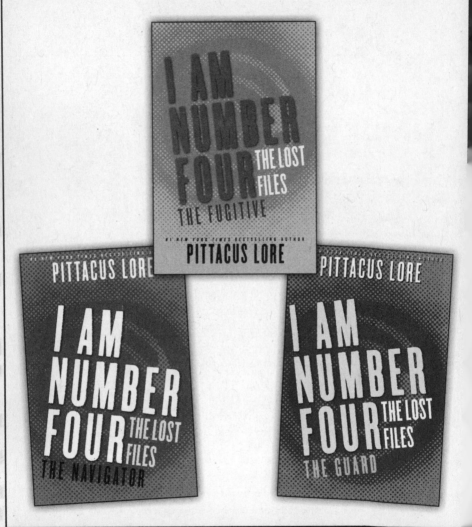